Blitz Writing

Also published by Handheld Press

Blitz Writing

Night Shift

&

It Was Different At The Time

by Inez Holden

edited by Kristin Bluemel

Handheld Classic 8

Night Shift was first published in 1941 by John Lane The Bodley Head. *It Was Different At The Time* was first published in 1943 by John Lane The Bodley Head.

This edition published in 2019 by Handheld Press Ltd.
72 Warminster Road, Bath BA2 6RU, United Kingdom.
www.handheldpress.co.uk

ISBN 978-1-912766-06-2

2 3 4 5 6 7 8 9 0

Series design by Nadja Guggi and typeset in Adobe Caslon Pro and Open Sans.

Printed and bound in Great Britain by Short Run Press, Exeter.

Contents

Kristin Bluemel is Professor of English and Wayne D McMurray and Helen Bennett Endowed Chair in the Humanities at Monmouth University in New Jersey. She has published widely on interwar and wartime writers and artists including Mulk Raj Anand, James Joyce, George Orwell, Agnes Miller Parker, Dorothy Richardson, Stevie Smith, Flora Thompson and Virginia Woolf. Her most recent book is a co-edited volume called *Rural Modernity in Britain: A Critical Intervention* (Edinburgh University Press 2018)

Introduction

BY KRISTIN BLUEMEL

Inez Holden was a London novelist and short story writer, at least as famous during her life for her flamboyant lifestyle, fantastic conversation, and celebrated friends — including HG Wells, George Orwell, Evelyn Waugh, Anthony Powell, Arthur Koestler, Stevie Smith, Mulk Raj Anand, and William Empson — as she was for her literary accomplishments. Working and writing without the supports of education, family, or wealth, Holden published seven novels, two story collections, and one wartime diary during some of the most tumultuous decades of the twentieth-century. Throughout this period she also maintained an extraordinary private diary, the surviving volumes of which begin in the midst of the London Blitz and continue well after the end of the war until August 1960. Here she records in astute and often humorous detail her encounters with prominent London personalities, including her brief affair with Orwell, as well as her impressions of hundreds of anonymous, memorable, ordinary Londoners.[1] With the publication of Inez Holden's *Blitz Writing: Night Shift* and *It Was Different At The Time,* contemporary readers are invited to read Holden on her own terms, as a writer worth knowing because of her unique voice and perspective on Second World War London. Holden's Blitz writings teach us about compassion amid crisis, of community amid difference, of the power of the written word to inspire hope amid violence and despair.

Night Shift is a novel about working-class characters conscripted into a London factory called Braille's that produces camera parts for reconnaissance planes. *It Was Different At The Time* is a wartime diary covering the years 1938–1941 with entries that Holden collated from her private diaries of that period. The entries record Holden's work in hospitals, in a government training centre, as a fire watcher, as an occasional broadcaster for the BBC, and as a guest at 'Hogsnorton', a farcical name for the BBC Centre in Worcestershire. Both novel and published diary also record in spare, clear prose the sensations, destruction, and human costs of the London bombings, of Londoners' resistance to the assault on their city, of the 'incendiaries, dive-bombers, and guns' that contributed to 'a hideous melodrama let loose over London' (154). This style — restrained, realistic, accessible — tempts us to believe in the possibility of apprehending in Holden's work an unmediated wartime reality, a pure translation of Home Front experience as told by a keen, distanced observer. *Night Shift* and *It Was Different At The Time* may strike readers as two chapters from the same book, two moments in the same moving picture of life during the Blitz. Yet novel and published diary have distinct narrators and purposes and each short book offers up a unique interpretation of Blitz experience and survival. *Blitz Writing* brings these two interpretations into conversation with each other, urging readers to move from a recognition of Holden's cinematic realism and documentation of London living to understanding Holden as an artist.

During her lifetime, Holden achieved publication but not fame, her novels and short stories and journalistic work failing to attain the popularity or influence achieved by many of her writer friends. This edition of *Night Shift* and *It Was Different At The Time* asserts that Holden is due for discovery and recovery, that her work will find new readers who will appreciate her writing for its own sake. These readers will see in the seemingly transparent style of her writing the glass of her art, appreciating her vibrant personality — her wit, intelligence, and humour — and the ways her social positioning as a woman and a worker enriches our historical imagination of life during the Blitz. Many readers will be drawn to *Blitz Writing* out of an interest in Britain's wartime past, but this is not the only or best reason to pick up this book. Holden's individual, enduring voice is the greatest attraction in *Blitz Writing* and her representation of the extraordinary people who so bravely, so humanly navigate wartime's material and social hazards is its greatest contribution to the literature of the Second World War.

Life into Art

Holden's father was Wilfred Millington Holden of Wellesbourne, Warwickshire, whose family is listed in *Burke's Landed Gentry* (1952) as the Holdens of Bromson; her mother was Beatrice Mary Byng Paget, born to the Pagets of Darley House, Derbyshire. There are virtually no archival sources confirming details of Holden's childhood and youth. Instead, we have the vivid memories of friends and relatives which, though subject to the vagaries of all such personal accounts, lie at the heart of any biography. Holden's cousin, friend and original literary executrix, the writer Celia Goodman, recorded in a 1994 memoir in the *London Magazine* that Holden's mother was an Edwardian beauty who had owned fifteen hunters and was known as the second-best horsewoman in Britain (Goodman 1994, 29).[2] In her twenties Holden herself was considered to be a bohemian society beauty, and the three novels she wrote during those years, *Sweet Charlatan* (1929), *Born Old, Died Young* (1932) and *Friend of the Family* (1933) record the frivolous, absurd lives of privileged characters who could have stepped out of the pages of Evelyn Waugh's *Vile Bodies*. Yet Holden's life was marked by transformations of consciousness and circumstance, and neither her bohemian life in the 1930s nor her gentry origins could define or predict her political, social, or literary alliances. In the 1920s Holden was a party girl who consorted with and was sketched by Augustus John. By 1941 she was an experienced author, earning for *Night Shift* jacket quotations from HG Wells and JB Priestley, the latter describing the novel 'as the most truthful and most exciting account of war-time industrial Britain'.

Holden's full name was Beatrice Inez Lisette Holden, and this unusually large number of names suggests parental attention. However, Goodman tells us that Holden's parents did not bother to register their daughter's birth and Holden told her friends that she was unsure if she had been born in 1903 or 1904. She described her parents as not merely ill-suited but as united in mutual antagonism. One of her foundational memories was her father firing a gun at her mother and missing.

When she was fifteen, she went to Paris and then London, living on her wits and her exceptional good looks (Goodman 1994, 29–30). Goodman's daughter Ariane Bankes finds in Holden's childhood trauma the sources of her adult eccentricity: 'Inez was utterly original, utterly *sui generis* [...] She simply did not subscribe to the conventions of society, and her crossing of boundaries is entirely explicable in terms of her early rejection by her family and her subsequent rejection of all that her family stood for — class values and all'.[3]

Holden's first novels were published when she was in her twenties. Her second novel, *Born Old, Died Young* (1932), features an adventuress heroine named Virginia Jenkinson who ignores the practical matters of her own wellbeing, suggesting something of the attitude Holden herself might have had at the time. The author Anthony Powell, who saw Holden frequently in London during the war years, certainly believed that Virginia Jenkinson was Holden's fictionalised self-portrait, claiming in his autobiography *Messengers of the Day* that Holden in her twenties lived 'fairly dangerously in a rich world of a distinctly older generation' (Powell 1978, 24). Holden would have resisted terms like party girl, adventuress, society beauty, bohemian, Bright Young Person, that others have used to describe her social position in the 1920s and 1930s. Although she wrote about debutantes, film stars, chorus girls, bohemians, and millionaires, her journalism of the 1930 makes it clear that she considered herself an outsider rather than a member of London's high life. In 1932 an editor at the *Evening News* introduced Holden to readers in an article 'Farewell to the Bright Young People', as a writer who 'knows London's fashionable Bohemia well', but Holden herself ends the piece with the sentence, 'Personally I don't mind who gets labelled a Bright Young Person so long as it isn't me!' (Holden, 30 August 1932). Holden's article 'The Adventuress Of To-Day' paints a sympathetic portrait of the modern adventuress who resembles in some ways other portraits of Holden: 'The modern adventuress [...] cannot work or scheme or even save money. She is the sort of person who "simply can't do anything about anything". To some people she seems appealingly helpless, and to others, just appallingly hopeless; finally, they are either moved, or irritated, into helping her. And that is how she lives' (Holden, 20 July 1932).

Holden's first novel, *Sweet Charlatan* (1929), was also her first to feature Bright Young Things, and is frivolous enough to feature a witch character named Rose Leaf, whose roles as hostess and murderess seem to demonically attract the young hero, Cedric Dorn. The only sympathetic character in the book's cast of absurdities is Cedric's young wife, the bohemian waif, Autumn. Autumn leaves Cedric to Rose Leaf, but we are able to imagine some positive fate for her given the following revelation:

> Once she [Autumn] had been enslaved by the frail affectations of Cedric, the belated Beardsley gesture, the sweet superficiality [...] all this silly brilliance had ceased to hypnotise, and Autumn herself had returned to almost schoolgirlish simplicity of speech and thought and was even now considering the importance of doing what one liked. (Holden 1929, 181–82)

Here is Holden at her satiric socialite best. Yet the subdued earnestness of Autumn's escape from superficiality and the affirmation of her desires suggests that Holden might have maintained a latent sympathy for her that arose from her own changing goals and identity. Autumn's repudiation of the 'epigrammatic outlook' of a Beardsley or Cedric in favour of simplicity of speech points towards Holden's movement in this same direction. The best examples of Holden's affirmation of simplicity of speech, suitable for the dark, pared-down years of the Depression, are the stories that she published in a collection titled *Death in High Society* (1934), some of which were later reprinted in her 1945 collection *To The Boating*. Holden had translated these stories, which had previously appeared in magazines like *Harper's Bazaar*, *Nash's* and *The Evening Standard*, into Basic English, an experimental language of 850 words developed by CK Ogden. Ogden believed that anyone with a phonograph, anywhere in the world, could learn Basic on his or her own in thirty hours. Basic English came to be associated with Orwell's totalitarian Newspeak in *Nineteen Eighty-Four*, but it was inspired by egalitarian impulses and pacifist ideals. As Ogden explains in the foreword to *Death in High Society*, Basic English 'is an all-round language for everyday use, which may be turned into a language for the expert by the addition of short special lists'. He introduces Holden as his expert on the short story, assuring readers that Holden's stories 'are representative of an important part of the reading material on which the value of Basic for general purposes has to be tested' (Ogden 1934, 8–9).

Holden's stories in Basic provide other hints about her path from a writer of socialite farces to working-class documentary fictions. While rich and foolish characters still dominate her Basic stories, working-class characters begin to earn our interest. For example, the title story, 'Death in High Society', begins with the departure of two nameless cleaning women from the London home of Esmée Earnshaw, who watches them secretly and vindictively from the comfort of her long, grey limousine. We witness Esmée leave her car and sneak into her own house in order to check up on the thoroughness of her cleaners before she gets trapped mid-floor in the lift that she had installed in order to 'get more work done in less time' (Holden 1945, 118). The story ends three weeks later with a satisfying, macabre retribution that gives the cleaning ladies the last word. 'Well,' says the first, 'here we are again dear. Where is she now, eh?' The second replies, 'Keep your nose out of other cats' milk' while she makes her way with 'slow, stiff feet [...] in the direction of the lift' (Holden 1945, 119).

Sharing Esmée's class status, Holden's chronic state of being in debt or without any cash taught her to identify with poor working people and to give generously to others whenever she could. For example, when the Orwells were bombed out of their home on 28 June 1944, Holden gave them the use of her flat near Portman Square. In or out of luck and cash, her friends affirm that she maintained a sense of style and drama uniquely her own. Goodman writes that Holden 'simply found life endlessly amusing and interesting and was able to make it seem equally so to others. She was a keen and fascinated observer of human nature at all levels, but she was never malicious and she had a depth of compassion that prevented her from judging harshly any but the most odious characteristics' (Goodman 1994, 34). Others were not always so generous to Holden. It was one of the small tragedies of her life that HG Wells, whom she admired personally more than perhaps any other writer, ejected her from his mews flat in 1941, blaming her for a disastrous dinner party with Orwell where the two men argued about Orwell's recently published criticism of Wells in a *Horizon* article (Bowker 2003, 288).

We can imagine some of the forms Holden's generosity would take if we turn to the work of her friend of the 1930s and 1940s, the poet and novelist Stevie Smith. Smith used Inez Holden as the basis for her fictional character Lopez, who emerges in the first pages of Smith's 1949 novel *The Holiday*. Lopez is the hostess of a wonderfully successful party that nurtures a 'quick love-feeling' among its guests amid a feast of rationed 'spam, ham, tongue, liver-sausage, salad-cream, cherries, strawberries (out of tins), whiskey and beer' (Smith 1980, 13). Smith develops her Lopez character in later pages of *The Holiday*, tempting us to imagine her friendship with Holden in the same terms that Smith's heroine, Celia, uses to describe her relationship with Lopez. Celia tells us that she keeps close to [Lopez] for company. Here is this admirable girl, I think, who has this admirable courage and this admirable high heart, for she is not a sad girl, she is not walking round in fury and despair. She writes and entertains the Government and the Section people, and the editors, and all the time it is nothing but a wonderful adventure for her to have, it is in the spirit of the Scarlet Pimpernel, or Sideways Through Patagonia, it is like that. (Smith 1980, 55–56)

Before publishing *The Holiday*, Smith used Holden as a model for another Lopez character in her short story, 'The Story of a Story' (1946). In this story, Lopez is described as 'a very clever quick girl, she had a brilliant quick eye for people, conversations, and situations' (Smith 1981, 52). Lopez is an incorrigible gossip and this quality too seems to have been Holden's. Powell used her as the model for his flamboyant character Roberta Payne in *What's Become of Waring* (Taylor 2003, 284). Decades later Powell described her as 'a torrential talker, an accomplished mimic, her gossip of a high fantastical category; excellent company when not obsessed by some 'story' being run by the papers, of which she was a compulsive reader' (Powell 1978, 24). Bankes confirms Powell's impressions of Holden's character. While she concedes that 'It is of course very difficult to convey the personality of someone as unique as Inez,' she fondly remembers that 'her maverick qualities were what set her apart, and made her the remarkable figure that she was'.[4]

In 'The Story of a Story', Smith conveys some of what might have been Holden's remarkable character. Smith's protagonist, a writer named Helen, has drafted a short story based on the personal troubles of friends named Bella and Roland. Lopez rang up 'all the friends, and the friends of the friends, the people who knew Lopez and who knew Helen, and who knew Bella and Roland' to tell them about the story, turning social exploitation into social exposure

(Smith 1981, 16). Lopez's collusion with Helen's desire to make life serve the interests of art reminds us how difficult it can be to keep novelists as friends. Smith and Holden were both ambitious and accomplished writers, both mimics, both gossips, but their Blitz alliance did not survive the 1950s. Smith's biographer Frances Spalding attributes this falling out to Holden's jealousy over Smith's greater literary success (Spalding 1988, 151).We can imagine from 'The Story of a Story' that Holden would have her own story, the other side of 'The Story of a Story', to tell about Lopez and Helen. It is amusing to guess at correspondences of personality between Holden and the fictional characters reportedly based on her, but art is not life. We are left with shadows of Holden in the writings of others, while her substance remains in her own words, the novels, stories, and diary entries that she left us about the interwar and war years.

The Poor People's War

Skilled at the satiric portrayal of wealthy, upper-class families like her own, Holden herself was never assured of income and can accurately be described as working poor. Bankes explains that despite Holden's lack of formal education, 'she was intelligent and witty enough to be an intellectual, and to move in intellectual-bohemian circles. As it also happens, she sympathised more with the working class than any other class — but she didn't belong to any class, by choice. She was an outsider'.[5] Spalding notes in her biography of Smith that Holden had grown increasingly bitter about gross social inequalities resulting from differences of wealth (104). In reaction to these feelings, the leftward drift of literary culture, and perhaps, her increasing intimacy with George Orwell, Holden developed a political consciousness and by the mid- to late-thirties identified herself as an anti-Communist socialist. While it is hard to know what turns anyone into a writer, let alone what turns any writer into a socialist writer, in Holden's case we have not only the evidence of her published work, but also the unpublished evidence of her diary.

Holden's diary suggests that the Blitz itself was a source of her increasing commitment to socialism as a vehicle for improving the lives of plain and poor people. Angus Calder, in his landmark social history of the Second World War, *The People's War*, theorises that Britain came closer to social revolution during this war than at any time since the seventeenth century's Civil Wars. Aiming to recreate the feel of everyday life for ordinary people within the contexts of grand battles and personages, Calder borrows the words of writers to turn art back into an account of wartime life, citing Richard Hillary, Elizabeth Bowen, Graham Greene, J B Priestley, Vera Brittain, John Strachey, Barbara Nixon, John Lehmann, and Inez Holden (Calder 1969, 200). He also includes the astonishing statistics of loss that put London in 'a grim litany of names – Guernica, Dresden, Hiroshima, Hanoi – which have become symbols, obscuring rather than representing the facts of life and death' (261).

Among those statistics, it's worth repeating the most essential: that 'Blitz' is the shortened version of 'Blitzkrieg', German for 'lightning war'; that the Blitz was the German bombing campaign against British cities undertaken in preparation for a planned German invasion; that the Blitz is generally assumed to have begun on 7 September 1940 and to have ended on 11 May 1941; and most chilling of all, that 15,775 Londoners died in the Blitz and 1,400,000 became homeless (Bell 2009, 158). Calder tells us that on the first day of the Blitz, German bombs

> poured chiefly on Stepney, with its inimitable mixture of races [...] on the tailors of Whitechapel; the factories, warehouses and gasworks of Poplar; the woodworking firms of Shoreditch; the docks of West Ham and Bermondsey. They poured on the sweated clothes trade, on the casual labour of the docks, on petty businesses Jewish and Gentile. (Calder 1969, 189)

As this brief excerpt from Calder's history suggests, workplaces and poor people bore the brunt of the Blitz. It is this working poor people's war to which Holden belongs.

Between September and mid-November 1940, 'an average of 160 bombers dropped an average of 200 tons of high explosives and 182 canisters of incendiaries nightly' on London (194). Yet amid all the destruction, workers reported for their shifts and managers to their desks. In factories such as the one Holden represents in *Night Shift*, there was little absenteeism due to raids. Calder notes that while 'the central London population had dropped by a quarter by the end of November,' there were approximately 'half a million munitions workers alone living within a fifteen-mile radius of London' (202). Holden's Blitz writings gives literary shape to Calder's claim that 'people adapted themselves to the fear which returned night after night' (200), her fictional workers impatient with 'easy heroical talk and pat-off patriotism' (74). Instead, they value the 'hope of better money' and draw on 'a great capital of comradeship' for strength (68). Holden's acute ear for sound humanises such everyday examples of courage in the conversations of women workers, Jewish shift managers, Home Guard members, engineers, air raid wardens, and nurses, all of whom contribute to her portrait of civic endurance. The anonymous narrator of *Night Shift* muses, 'It was strange the way the talk could go on [...] we worked all the time we were there, and yet conversation crept in — cut-up scraps of conversation between the times of fixing up a machine, counting pieces of work and waiting for a new drill or tap to be fixed' (13).

Holden *listened* to the Blitz; sound itself becomes a theme connecting the chapters of *Night Shift*. We hear the workshop machine background noise of 'thump-hum-drum' and the 'sudden violent hissing of the steam jets' and the 'clattering sound of someone dropping or tripping over some castings' underneath the outside noises, 'the air-raid orchestra of airplane hum, the anti-aircraft shell bursts, ambulance and fire bells' (4). The novel ends with a devastating event sandwiched between two small sounds of a penny whistle and birdsong. The narrator's thoughts about the political and social meaning represented by these sounds conclude the novel: 'Between these two sounds there showed a chink of light through which I could see the start of a more hopeful life, a future in which the courage of people could also be used for their greater happiness and well-being' (85). Historians like Calder agree that this quiet vision of a more just, more egalitarian Britain emerging from the noise of total war was the motivation guiding many workers back to their dangerous posts day after day, night after night, as they fought their war in the factories of London.

Night Shift

By the time *Night Shift* was published in 1941, Holden had abandoned her reputation as a bohemian adventuress and party girl for the politicised identity of socialist writer. The novel's narrative style contributes to this impression as it adopts the seemingly objective, truth-telling stance associated with 1930s documentary fiction, its female narrator described on the dustjacket as 'having no very definite personality, acting rather as the lens of a moving camera'. Sympathetic to its working-class characters, this narrator also pays attention to a pampered, bourgeois character named Feather who is, to the bemusement of her colleagues, working on the night shift at the camera parts factory. The narrator tells us that Feather is 'the sort of girl who would have been "ladying it" at a First Aid Post attached to some auxiliary service' and wonders if 'something had happened to shake up her journey in the slow coach of security' (5). If Holden has displaced her gentrified class origins from the first-person narrator to Feather, the last chapter of the book might suggest new ideas about the social identity of the novel's author. There is no record of how Holden met HG Wells, but she was his tenant in a mews flat behind his house near Regents Park in 1940 while she was writing *Night Shift*. He saw Feather as a disguised version of Holden, writing in a note, 'Your book is first rate[.] Bravo Feather[.] I admit you can write[.] HG'. Holden admired and trusted Wells as both a writer and mentor and she took the time to carefully transcribe into her diary entry of 18 December 1942 these words of praise. Wells's words 'First rate' appear in promotional materials for Holden's novel.

Night Shift has much in common with other published documentary accounts of wartime factory life.[6] During the early 1940s, when paper shortages made print publication increasingly difficult, Holden, like many other writers, was trying to get her documentary accounts of everyday life in wartime London onto BBC radio programmes. The BBC files on Holden and Holden's diary show that she was repeatedly encouraged or even requested to compose pieces for Overseas Service programmes or occasionally the Home Service, only to be told later that her work couldn't be used. She wrote in her diary on 9 June 1941, 'I am short of money and do not know quite what to do about a job, the BBC never does come off' (quoted in Bluemel 2004, 22). Two months later, in August 1941, she wrote:

> Again the BBC drama has cropped up. It is now recurring, the same sort of problem as an un-requited un-ending passion. I went for the appointments board. I set out with new stockings, a well-brushed dress, a hat and shoes [...] The three middle aged men sat at an immense table, the grey haired staff administrator rather like a bank manager [...] There was a lot of getting up to their feet bowing and shaking hands. It went well. But all the same I got a note after six days which regretted that they were not choosing me to join the staff pool. So the possible war job, near at hand with good salary and work which I could have done went away in thin smoke. (22)

After drawing this portrait of hopes raised and dashed for a BBC job that would have brought money, stability and prestige, Holden bravely writes, 'as it is not as fundamental as a love affair I could not mind much' (23).

Holden did get some pieces accepted and produced by the

BBC, in part through bookings advanced by George Orwell who worked from 1941–1943 as Overseas Eastern Services Director. But Holden's troubles with BBC men are as noticeable as her successes. Pursuing her interest in documentary, in autumn 1940 Holden made a successful pitch to the BBC for a talk on an Out-patients' Department Casualty station in Camden Town. After she had written up the talk, she received a dismissive letter dated 5 November 1940 from Ormond Wilson of the BBC Overseas Department, who explained, 'We have had your material in one form or another several times by now, and it really comes to this — that only a completely fresh angle on the Blitzkrieg can now be used' (BBCWA). Wilson tempered his rejection with compliments, and Holden tried again, only to experience the same frustrating rejections just at the point when she expected to be paid. She complained to Wilson on 7 January 1941 that each time she had written or given a talk for his programme she had been told that it is 'exactly what you are needing etc, etc but on fifty percent of the occasions, for some reason, only half of the talks get produced — and paid for' (BBCWA).

Holden did not know about the extent of the censorship that occasionally kept her work off the air. Although the BBC had always been politically neutral, radio was brought under the control of the Ministry of Information (MOI) during the Second World War and was censored more heavily than any other media (West 1985, 13, 21). As a result, every word that was broadcast on the BBC was supposed to be censored for policy and security (21). The more 'sensitive' pieces were sent from BBC censors to censors at the Ministry of Information.

The most trouble Holden got into during her time writing for the BBC involved a documentary talk she wrote in 1942 about conscripted workers in a Royal Ordnance factory. 'Work and Bed — You Might As Well Be Dead' draws on her observations of workers' lives that she recorded in her private diary and that she later used as material for her wartime novel *There's No Story There* (1944). The title of the piece is the motif that workers repeated to each other, expressing their feelings of resignation, amusement, and depression aroused by the dangerous routines of factory work. Holden begins her piece by recording in objective tones the workers' activities and emotions, but then takes a more activist position, recommending that the government forget about improving factory lives with 'pep talks' by outsiders and encourage instead such things as University Extension lectures and works clubs. This script came to the attention of officials at various ministries, including an enraged Sir Frederick Leggett of the Ministry of Labour. Leggett objected that the talk had been submitted too late for the Ministry to take action on it and that it was 'a deliberate attempt on the part of the BBC to depress young women going into industry'. GR Barnes of the Home Talks Department responded to Leggett's criticism by telephone. Barnes's note about this conversation reads:

> I gave [Leggett] the BBC's point of view in the matter saying that all our evidence showed that workers did not want to hear sunshine of how well Government Departments were doing, but wished to have their questions answered and that that was the BBC's intention provided those answers were accurate and did not embarrass the work of the Government Department concerned. (27 May 1942, BBCWA).

Barnes's record of his spirited defence of the BBC's handling of Holden's piece shows how Holden's efforts to bring her documentary voice and vision to a broader public entangled her in the web of masculine professional hierarchies that defined wartime civilian life. Holden's diary entry of 30 May 1942 provides a glimpse of her private reaction to the 'terrific affair', demonstrating both her desire to keep the authorities happy and her unwillingness as an artist to broadcast the story once it had been altered to 'read in a way that was directly opposed to what I believed to be true about factories and what I had written elsewhere' (quoted in Bluemel

2004, 24).

Two years later, in 1944, the political philosopher Constance Reaveley published an article in the *Spectator* called 'The Machine and the Mind' that treated as new and revolutionary the idea that middle-class intellectuals, even an academic like herself, should go into the factories. Describing her work on a capstan and the demands and satisfactions of working on a grinding-machine, she comments:

> I watched the life of the factory. I thought a good deal went on that ought to be more widely known about and understood. I thought I would write to the Bishop and urge that young men in training for Holy Orders should work for six months or so in a factory (or mine or shop) to get an insight for themselves into the way people live and work. (Reaveley 1994, 148)

Reaveley is also eager to write to the head of a woman's college, suggesting that 'a girl who wanted to write, and would work in a factory for a few months, could produce stories for factory girls about factory girls, which would give them a lot more interest than anything there is on the market for them at present' (149). But Reaveley did not write to bishops or heads of women's colleges. Holden, without the incentives or prospects of university students or dons, did what Reaveley had only speculated about, publishing 'stories for factory girls about factory girls'.

Red Modernism

A Blitz context has made *Night Shift* the best known of Holden's factory stories. It invites readers to think back to peacetime documentaries of the 1930s, to the heyday of what we might call Red Modernism, and to books like Jack Common's account of working-class life, *Seven Shifts* (1938). Holden shared Common's belief in the value of workers' lives and the ability of documentary writing to bring readers over to the side of the workers, to unionisation, to protest, to socialism. Fortunately, Holden's wartime documentation of factory life focuses on exactly what is omitted from Common's collection: descriptions of women workers. Common was aware that his book was weakened by its lack of women's voices, admitting that *Seven Shifts* suffers from 'one serious omission: it does not include any contribution from the women's side of the world of work'. He promises 'to make good [the lack] in a subsequent volume, which the women will have to themselves' (np). Jenny Hartley's ground-breaking collection of women's writing of the Second World War, *Hearts Undefeated* (1994), suggests that Jack Common's failure and Holden's success might be due to the unique circumstances of home front life. Hartley tells us that the energies of the Red Decade were not enough for women to contribute to the literature of labour, to tell their stories of new positions in public and private life. Rather, it took the mass social upheavals of the Blitz, of the transformation of homes into the home front, for women to realise that their ordinary lives were the materials of an extraordinary history. Novelist Kate O'Brien spoke for many women in a 1941 *Fortnightly* article that insists, 'You would need to be half-dead not to feel observant and curious *now* about the general scene — and all our note-taking, the good with the bad, will be useful some day, to those whose job it will be to "compose" this time, in terms of history or of art' (quoted in Hartley 1994, 5).

According to Hartley, O'Brien's consciousness of herself as a witness to a curious 'general scene' was shared by innumerable women who 'until this century [...] were rarely involved in war and rarely wrote about it' (5). The new genre of women's war writing, begun in the First World War, expanded in the Second with more women reporting a consciousness of their place in a public drama of epic proportions. Hartley brings together excerpts from over a hundred published, public pieces of women's war writing, much of it focused on the Blitz. She points out that hundreds of additional examples of women's unpublished writings from the war remain in the archives of the Imperial War Museum, evidence that well-known authors of Second World War literature like Elizabeth Bowen, George Orwell, Patrick Hamilton, and Graham Greene were joined by hundreds of unknown writers, all of whom recorded for future 'composers' their perceptions of a unique historical moment. Of course, everyone who wrote about the Blitz while suffering through it had no knowledge of when it would end or whether Britain would emerge victorious in war. These peculiar conditions seemed to suspend Britain's historical narrative, marking an 'exceptional parenthesis' in the country's national consciousness (8). Hartley echoes the words of historians like Calder when she asserts, 'For the first time in this country the whole population was involved in the war, the women and children as well as the men. Bombs are no respecters of age or sex' (5). The revolution in social roles that the Blitz and total war brought about endured long after many other ideals of 'The People's War' had faded from public life and memory.

It Was Different At The Time

Reading Holden's published Blitz diary, *It Was Different At The Time*, against her unpublished diaries shows us how the pressures of public audience transformed what might be seen as the more complete, more spontaneous writing of the private diary, even as the latter was intended to serve as a 'Journal to be used as Material'. These words appear at the top of the first page of the first Blitz diary entry of 16–17 April 1941. This self-conscious labelling of private writing as a mine of material for publication means that the diaries never really were private. They were always semi-private, semi-public documents, composed initially with the hope of reaching a broad audience in some later, transformed state. By the time *It Was Different At The Time* reached this broad audience, it had undergone deletions and edits that might be seen by historians as a dilution of Holden's private record of the Blitz. Yet it is here, in the gaps between private and published diary, that we can come to understand Holden's artistry, her contribution to Second World War literature. Composing and recomposing her life, she gives us in *It Was Different At The Time* a pared down, organised, controlled version of the Blitz. In *It Was Different At The Time* we have evidence of Holden's mature writing, her response at the level of image and art to the impact of the bombs that seem to have blown away excess emotion and expression from her prose. We also have signs of what she learned from and how she responded to other writers who taught her during the war years to experiment with the possibilities of voice and perspective and politics.

The most important writer to influence *It Was Different At The Time* was George Orwell, who had initially agreed to work with Holden as a co-author of this Blitz diary.[7] Orwell's biographers attribute the failure of this joint project to the very different styles of the two writers and to Orwell's involvement with his journalism and BBC work. *It Was Different At The Time* (1943) was published after *Night Shift*, but its first entry is April 1938, a couple of years before the bombings and the conscription of young unmarried women that provides the setting for the conversations in *Night Shift*, and a full three years before the first surviving entry in Holden's unpublished wartime diary. Comparing the latter chapters of *It Was Different* to the pages of Holden's unpublished diary, we can retrace her steps as she lifted out paragraphs and moved around, edited, pruned, and adjusted sentences originally written at the time of the experiences described. Some of the most powerful Blitz scenes in her private diary serve double duty, appearing in heavily edited and fictionalised form in *Night Shift*, and then in edited, non-fictional form in *It Was Different At The Time*. Holden's return to the events and images of 16–17 April 1941 suggests that the following scene was at the heart of her Blitz memory, the most traumatising, most inspiring, and one of the most beautiful:

One week during this month there were two nights of intensive bombardment which came to be known as the 'Wednesday' and the 'Saturday.' [16 and 19 April 1941] On the Wednesday I remember walking down [HG Wells'] mews in the moonlight, a large fire to the right in the direction of Paddington giving a red light behind the trees, and shining through the leaves, which made them look like copper beeches in the country in the early summer. (171)[8]

We can gain a more detailed version of this Wednesday raid from *Night Shift*, as it forms the basis of Holden's final catastrophic chapter about bombing during the sixth deadly night shift. In the novel the historic Wednesday is disguised as a fictional Saturday but it is clear that the two nights are actually based on the same experience, because Holden tells us in *It Was Different At The Time*, 'I was working on a night shift in an engineering shop at this time, and this, my night off, had not been restful. I was too tired to sleep, and went out in the early morning to look at the burning goods station. A small group of rather tired people stood in the road watching' (172). This scene was also one of the most human moments of the Blitz that Holden recorded in her private diary, as her awed description of what she there calls mass murder includes a gentle, loving description of her landlord HG Wells as a half naive, half divine prophet in sandals walking across the garden.

The images and impressions of Home Front life served as memoir, draft, and emotional support as Holden, like everyone else in London during the Blitz, tried to make sense of what she referred to as 'the outward horror' of the bombs and ruin that also brought inward pain and trauma. Some of the passages are so lyrical we can understand why Orwell characterised Holden's style as 'feminine impressionistic writing' (recorded in Holden's unpublished diary, nd), flowing between commas and dashes though focused on the sights and sounds of war and work. In other passages, we see Holden adopting the techniques of Mass Observation, the influential social research organisation begun in 1937 that had 500 voluntary members keeping diaries throughout the war as well as paid investigators recording people's everyday behaviours. Holden's narrator functions like these Mass Observation investigators, documenting conversations among ordinary Londoners in an air raid shelter, a First Aid Post, on the streets after an air raid, or among children playing games.[9] Everywhere we see signs of her interest in all kinds of human speech and behaviour, people of every origin and affiliation serving as material for her art. We also see her desire to preserve in a victorious, postwar Britain the new social relations made possible by the erosion of traditional hierarchies of class and sex. Turning her thoughts to other people, to the condition of mind of Londoners now freed from the worst of the Blitz bombings, she writes:

> Public opinion is in a strange state, there's a kind of lull as if people were waiting for the future to make itself known and when this happens they will know how to act, the whole war with the slaughter the bombing and the outward horror is still like a gigantic marking of time in a morass of mud — we have to win the war and we have to have the revolution. (quoted in Bluemel 2004, 22)

This is the quality of living through the 'exceptional parenthesis' that Hartley describes. Yet even without such intersections with or confirmations of public history, Holden's diary is a valuable record of the experiences of an independent, unattached woman working her way through war, writing her way into the radical literature of the 1940s. The names (or symbols of names) of famous Left writers that jump out at us from the diary are not there for effect but represent an experience, impression, or interaction that might become the basis of a story destined for *Harper's* or the more highbrow *Horizon*. These famous, public personalities are not any more important to the flow of the private diary than the dozens of unknown characters — friends, workers, landladies, supervisors, eccentric artists like Holden herself — who wander in and out of the diary's pages. Holden even writes about her own emotional affairs as though looking from the outside in, referring to them as stories that concern some unfortunate third party and not herself. Telling stories as habit, as profession, as self-defence, Holden entertained workers, writers, lovers and lords with her wit and sophisticated sense of the absurd. Despite a career that produced no best-sellers and earned no literary awards, she composed a life out of the colourful scraps of material that others left behind and wove from them stories of the everyday art of survival in a city that was falling down and in a country defying destruction.

Notes

1 The surviving volumes of this diary are held by Holden's literary executrix, Ariane Bankes. I am deeply grateful to her for sharing with me Inez Holden's diaries and granting permission to quote from them in *The Radical Eccentrics*.

2 Celia Kirwan Goodman (1916–2002) was the twin sister of Mamaine Koestler, wife of Arthur Koestler. George Orwell proposed to Celia Goodman in 1945, when he was already suffering from the tuberculosis that would kill him in 1950. Both Celia and Inez were loyal friends to Orwell, visiting him in the Gloucestershire sanatorium and then the London hospital where he died.

3 Personal correspondence, 5 October 2003.

4 Personal correspondence, 5 October 2003.

5 Personal correspondence, 5 October 2003.

6 See for example Mass-Observation's *War Factory* (1943) and Amabel Williams-Ellis's *Women in War Factories* (1943).

7 See Orwell's dry 'War-time Diary' chapters in volume 2 of his *The Collected Essays, Journalism & Letters*. See Crick for an account of the origins and dissolution of the Holden-Orwell war diary project (264).

8 Amy Bell notes that 'the Wednesday' and 'the Saturday' raids were heavier than any previous raids and that German bombers dropped over a thousand tons of high-explosive and incendiary bombs on London during each raid. The combined death toll was 2,380 people, more than a tenth of all Londoners killed in the Blitz (Bell 2009, 158).

9 See the 2009 reprint of Madge and Harrison's 1939 *Britain by Mass Observation* and Beaven and Griffiths's 1998 study of M-O's relation to working-class communities.

Works Cited

BBCWA (British Broadcasting Corporation Written Archives).

Beaven, Brad and John Griffiths, *Mass-Observation and Civilian Morale: Working-Class Communities during the Blitz 1940–41*, Mass-Observation Occasional Papers Series, 8 (Mass-Observation Archive, University of Sussex, 1998).

Bell, Amy, 'Landscapes of Fear: Wartime London, 1939–1945', *Journal of British Studies*, 48.1 (2009), 153–75.

Bluemel, Kristin, *The Radical Eccentrics: Intermodernism in Literary London* (Palgrave Macmillan 2004).

Bowker, Gordon, *George Orwell: A Biography* (Palgrave Macmillan 2003).

Calder, Angus, *The People's War* (Ace Books 1969).

Common, Jack, *Seven Shifts* (Secker & Warburg 1938).

Crick, Bernard, *George Orwell: A Life* (Little Brown and Company 1980).

Goodman, Celia, 'Inez Holden: A Memoir', *London Magazine*, Dec/Jan 1994, 29–34.

Hartley, Jenny (ed.), *Hearts Undefeated: Women's Writing of the Second World War* (Virago 1994).

Holden, Inez, 'The Adventuress of To-Day', *Daily Mail*, 20 July 1932.

—, 'Death in High Society', in Inez Holden, *Death in High Society* (Kegan Paul, 1934), 11–23.

—, 'Farewell to the Bright Young People', *Evening News*, 30 August 1932.

—. *Sweet Charlatan* (Duckworth, 1929).

—, *To the Boating and Other Stories* (John Lane, 1945).

Madge, Charles, and Tom Harrisson, *Britain by Mass Observation* (1939; Faber and Faber 2009).

Mass-Observation, *War Factory: A Report* (Gollancz 1943)

Ogden, C K, 'To the Reader', in Inez Holden, *Death in High Society* (Kegan Paul, 1934), 7–10.

Orwell, George, *Orwell: My Country Right or Left, 1940–1943*, ed. by Sonia Orwell and Ian Angus, vol 2, *The Collected Essays, Journalism, and Letters* (David R Godine, 2000), 339–409.

Powell, Anthony, *Messengers of the Day*, vol 2 of *To Keep the Ball Rolling: The Memoirs of Anthony Powell*. 3 vols (Heinemann 1978).

Reaveley, Constance, 'The Machine and the Mind', in *Hearts Undefeated: Women's Writing of the Second World War*, ed. Jenny Hartley (Virago 1994), 148–49.

Smith, Stevie, *The Holiday* (1949; Virago 1980).

—, 'The Story of a Story', in *A Very Pleasant Evening with Stevie Smith: Selected Short Prose*, (New Directions 1981), 14–23.

Spalding, Frances, *Stevie Smith: A Biography* (Norton 1988).

Taylor, D J, *Orwell* (Chatto and Windus 2003).

West, W J, 'Introduction', in *George Orwell: The War Broadcasts* (Penguin 1985).

Williams-Ellis, Amabel, *Women in War Factories* (Gollancz 1943).

Works by Inez Holden

Holden wrote dozens of pieces of journalism and short fiction for fashion and middlebrow magazines like *Harper's Bazaar*, *Punch*, *The Cornhill Magazine*, and *The Strand Magazine*, as well as short fiction published in the wartime magazine, *Horizon*. All of this work is uncollected, as are Holden's postwar film scripts written for J Arthur Rank.

Novels

Sweet Charlatan (Duckworth 1929)

Born Old, Died Young (Duckworth 1932)

Friend of the Family (Arthur Baker 1933)

Night Shift (John Lane 1941)

There's No Story There (John Lane 1944)

The Owner (Bodley Head 1952)

The Adults (Bodley Head 1956)

Story collections

Death in High Society (Kegan Paul 1934)

To the Boating and Other Stories (John Lane 1945)

Non-fiction

It Was Different At The Time (John Lane 1943)

Further Reading

Bourke, Joanna, *The Second World War: A People's History* (Oxford University Press 2001).

Brittain, Vera, *England's Hour: An Autobiography 1939–1941* (1941; Continuum 2005).

Calder, Angus, *The Myth of the Blitz* (1991; Pimlico 1997).

Clarke, Ben, *Orwell in Context: Communities, Myths, Values* (Palgrave Macmillan 2007).

Ellis, Steve, *British Writers and the Approach of World War II* (Cambridge University Press 2015).

Feigel, Lara, *The Love-Charms of Bombs: Restless Lives in the Second World War* (Bloomsbury 2013).

Fussell, Paul, *Understanding and Behaviour in the Second World War* (Oxford University Press 1989).

Hartley, Jenny, *Millions Like Us: British Women's Fiction of the Second World War* (Virago 1997).

Hewison, Robert, *Under Siege: Literary Life in London 1939–45* (Methuen 1988).

Hodgson, Vere, *Few Eggs and No Oranges, A Diary Showing How Unimportant People in London and Birmingham Lived through the War Years 1940–1945* (1976; Persephone Books 1999).

Joannou, Maroula, ed., *The History of British Women's Writing, 1920–1945*, vol 8 (Palgrave Macmillan 2013).

Miller, Kristine A, *British Literature of the Blitz: Fighting the People's War* (Palgrave Macmillan 2009).

Mitchison, Naomi, *Among You Taking Notes: The Wartime Diary of Naomi Mitchison*, ed. by Dorothy Sheridan (1985; Phoenix 2000).

Munton, Alan, *English Fiction of the Second World War* (Faber and Faber 1989).

Panter-Downes, Mollie, *London War Notes* (1971; Persephone Books 2015).

Sheridan, Dorothy, *Wartime Women: An Anthology of Women's Wartime Writing for Mass-Observation 1937–1945* (Heinemann 1990).

Suh, Judy, 'Women, Work, and Leisure in British Wartime Documentary Realism', *Literature/Film Quarterly* 40.1 (2012), 54–76.

Wasson, Sarah, *Urban Gothic of the Second World War: Dark London* (Palgrave Macmillan 2010).

Night Shift

by Inez Holden

The text for this edition of *Night Shift* was scanned from the first edition, and was silently corrected for typographical errors and punctuation consistency.

Monday

'Follow me.'

The man walked down the workshop at a great pitching pace; his white coat was almost as long as the aprons Italian waiters wore in peace-time restaurants.

This engineer was second-in-charge of the night shift; he always barked out his 'Follow me' when he had a new job ready for one of the workers, and each time he did this it was treated as a family joke. Several of the factory hands smiled, and the one who was sitting next to me said, 'Hark at old Sid'.

I looked up and saw him go by with a bit of a roll on like a sailor on shore leave.

The distance between Sid and the girl following him was widening. She had stooping shoulders and her high heels handicapped her. Because she was too thin the Government overall looked awkward as if, in putting it on, she had wrapped herself up into a parcel and then lost interest on the way to the post office. Her hair was twisted at the top of her head into a kind of cockatoo's coif; she had a gentle expression of great sweetness, and as she passed by us she shut one eye in a very slow, laborious way.

'Nan's always winking,' said Mabs on my right.

Mrs Chance, sitting on Mabs's right, answered, 'A wink's kind of old fashioned, isn't it? Not the sort of thing you expect to see nowadays.'

'Follow me,' shouted Sid. I wondered how his voice was able to get through the workshop sounds. The thump-hum-drum of the machinery was only the foundation of noise. From time to time there was, also, the sudden violent hissing of the steam jets which were used for cleaning out the bits of work, and the clattering sound of someone dropping or tripping over some castings they tried to count or pile up. This last noise was the worst of all; it ran along the workers' nerves like monkeys jumping on telephone wires; whenever it happened someone muttered 'Clumsy', or 'Why can't people look what they're doing?' These noises were inside the workshop. From outside there came to us the air-raid orchestra of airplane hum, anti-aircraft shell bursts, ambulance and fire bells. Sometimes bomb concussion caused the floor to give a sudden shiver. Whenever this happened, one of the workers would look up to catch the eye of another; they became aware of an uneasiness shared between them; it was the same hooded anxiety I had seen signalled beneath the brows of strangers sitting in a tube train which halted uncomfortably long between stations.

When Sid reached the lathe at the far end of the room near the blacked-out window he did not trouble to see if Nan had caught up with him; all his attention was given over to the machine itself. He looked closely downwards at this lathe as a child might stare at flowers or insects. He switched it on, listened like a musician, and, after switching it off, slowed it up by holding on to the machine belts.

Sid took the micrometer out of his waistcoat pocket; it was kept in a steel spectacle case, and he had towards it the same reverent, careless attitude of a doctor towards a stethoscope.

After Sid had set up the work he looked round for Nan. She had already stumped up to his side and was watching in silence. 'I got this measured up with the "mike". See. Now all you got to do is this.' He took out one of the silver screws from the metal box beside him. 'This has got to be cut and whatever you do don't let it go no ferther than that.' He threw the finished silver screw into an empty metal box. 'Now, do you think you've got it?'

'Yus, I think so.'

She tried the operation; Sid watched. He had lit a cigarette;

through the smoke his vision seemed to be narrowed down to the cutting knife of the lathe. Sometimes Sid would say, 'Wot's a working man without a fag?' and once one of the workers took the trouble to answer him, 'That's right, Sid.' When I saw Sid staring with such intensity at a piece of machinery through a cloud of 'fag-haze' I thought again of this inconsequent answer.

'You'll get into it,' he told Nan. 'Put your work wot's finished in this box; don't forget to keep 'em separate from the other lot and count 'em when you've done.' Sid started walking back down the workshop at a great pace. He did not seem to look where he was going but steered his way with the intuition of a dancer in a crowded ballroom. I wondered if he was guided by the workshop sounds; had he become suddenly deaf, would he, in that instant, have gone bumping into workers and reeling against machinery.

'I say, Sid, I've broken this tap.'

He wheeled about like a reined-round polo pony. 'Wot, another one!'

'Well, it's very difficult, Sid; I mean it really is difficult.' The girl had very straight hair which fitted round her head like a cap. Her hair was fair. Sonny, the eighteen-year-old worker from the Government training institution, had started calling her Feather. This was because although it was the rule for workers to bring their own cups to the factory, for the tea that was brought to them at four o'clock in the morning, the fair girl had forgotten to do this five nights running. It was on the fifth evening that Sonny had said to her, 'Oh! you are a Feather, really.' So they fell into calling her Feather.

I did not know why this girl was in the factory. She was not of the working class, and I thought she was the sort of girl who would have been 'ladying it' at a First Aid Post attached to some auxiliary service. Perhaps something had happened to shake up her journey in the slow coach of security. Anyhow, her hair was still sleek and well brushed like the soft coat of a luxurious pet animal. Feather seldom spoke about herself, but made up for this by whining about her work. 'Sid, these taps are always breaking.'

'It's because you don't do it right.' Sid sat down on the chair opposite the drilling machine. This chair looked like a piano stool and Sid a student reading a difficult piece of music.

It was at this moment that one of the white-coated inspectors came by, the one with smoothed down gold hair whom Feather called 'Flash Jim'. He was tall and elegant, his face was pointed into a prow of exasperation. He had come on to Braille's factory from à Court's. All the aircraft inspectors and engineers who had left à Court's to come to Braille's had this same sort of elegance, so that Feather had taken to calling them 'Mr à Court's young gentlemen'.

Dick Strauss, the Jewish foreman from the day shift, was battle-dressed as a Home Guard corporal. He was one of the most hard-working engineers at Braille's, but he was not yet on duty, and somehow the khaki uniform gave him a lounging look. Alfred, the first foreman of the night shift, was listening to something Strauss was telling him about plans for the reorganisation of a part of the work, but the two engineers, talking together, seemed as unhurried as race-meeting men leaning on paddock rails watching horses walk round and round.

'I asked him a question,' Jim said, nodding his head towards Alfred. 'But would he answer me? not he; the bloody fellow, of course he'd got to have his little chat first.'

While Sid was setting up work he was always intent on it, so that it seemed as if no words could come to him from outside. All the same, he did hear what Flash Jim was saying, but resentfulness could not disturb him because he was himself as free from jealousy as he was from sense of competition or class consciousness; he had never been hit by these things. He looked in the direction of the leisurely talk. 'Wot, that bloke over there, do you mean?' he said, and returned to silence and fierce attention on his work. Jim walked away soothed as if a long-seething quarrel had been suddenly smoothed over.

When Alfred had finished the conversation with Strauss he came over to the place where we were working to see how things were going. He had given up his job as chief inspector on the day shift in order to get the night shift in good working order. 'But when I get you all up to a high degree of efficiency,' he said, 'I can go back to the day shift and leave Sid to carry on here.' Alfred could not understand why some of the women in the workshop needed to be told the same things several times over; he thought, 'if they can't cotton on to engineering at once then they should be sacked, because that's the only way to assemble a good staff.' Alfred was a non-union man who had worked at Braille's ever since the age of sixteen. He was getting rather fat for thirty-three now, but the standard of life at which he was compelled to exist was still too thin for him.

Alfred wondered why Feather was here; he knew she had come to the factory without an unemployment card, so it was clear to him that she had never done any work of this kind before. He would have liked Feather to tell him about her life before the war, but she had not done so, and a direct question relating to the personal life of an individual was considered bad manners in the factory. All the same, Feather's way of speech, her fluctuating energy and fatigue, her gracious manners and the expensive careless look of her hair gave him the daydreams of posh life, an image of well-lit restaurants with food at five times its true value, clothes of good material, carpets so soft that you might be walking on kittens, and an endless expensive noise of bands, clattering knives and forks and useless conversation. He did not believe that anyone with any private income or influence would willingly work in a factory, and so he felt sorry for Feather. Without knowing the reason for his pity, he placed her in his thoughts somewhere between the high life and the rough deal.

This foreman in full charge of the night shift wore a good class of spectacles, and now he gave forth a look of smouldering suspicion and bullying mistrust; it was an expression which lent itself very readily to the lenses of Alfred's glasses.

'What's happening here, Sid?' he asked. 'Another tap broken. You know these taps are costing the firm more than the work's worth.'

Feather gave Alfred a dappled look through a strand of fair hair which had fallen over her eyes. 'Sid is fixing it up for me,' she said. 'Sid is always kind.'

Alfred had no words ready for these silly airs and graces, but gentle-hearted Sid was quick to answer, 'Oh well, I'm patient enough I know, but only till I start, mind you.' This kindness of nature was something stronger than Sid's conventional will. He did not want to seem 'cissy-like' because he was a tough fellow all right. 'When I start I don't arf kick up a row, I don't,' he said.

'Look here,' Alfred explained to Feather. 'You don't need to use force. Just bring this down gently and let it get back of its own accord. Like this, see.' The tap broke again. 'Like that, see,' he repeated, his hatred smouldering through the lenses of his glasses again. Sid smiled. Feather laughed on a high trill. A new tap got fixed and she settled to the work again. Alfred and Sid walked away in opposite directions like two assailants stepping out for a duel.

Mrs Chance, who had come to work at the machine next to Feather, said, 'How about when Alfred broke the tap, sister? I bet he wasn't half annoyed. It does you good when something like that happens; makes you feel it can't be all your fault when one of them white-coated fellers goes and does the same thing.'

Behind us there was the notice board and the clock with the clocking-in machine. The girl called Mabs sat on the other side of Mrs Chance and near me; she dabbed the machine oil on her work with the thick paint brush and sang, 'Oh, I wish I was a rich man's daughter'. When she was not singing she talked in an apathetic tone. 'This is the best place to work,' she said. 'It's near the clock. It's alf-past eleven now, so in anourananarf we can go down.' This 'going down', which came into the conversation during the early part of the evening, meant the journey down the stairs and through the underground passage which led outside to a shed where we had a break in the work for one hour and some food.

'The second half of the evening always goes quicker,' Mrs Chance said. 'Course I don't mind none of the work, because I know I'm not staying. You see, I've got this trouble with my hands.' She shut and opened her strong-looking fingers. 'It's bin like that ever since I had an accident, see; I got my legs run over by a bus. The doctor says I shouldn't work with my hands at all. After a time they turn black, they do. The doctor says it's a sort of inner bleeding. Still, all the work you do nowadays is with your hands, isn't it? so I got to get on with it.'

Mabs lost interest when she was not talking about herself. Her own life was a burden to her. She was like a pedlar, trudging along with a great weight of goods, whose only happiness is in being able to unpack the parcel and set out the store. Mabs liked to talk about the items of her own life and bark up the value of the various incidents. She went on with her singing. 'What say, let's be buddies; what say, let's be friends.'

Feather said, 'Do they know about your hands here, Mrs Chance?'

'Oh yes. It's surprising how quick that sort of thing gets round. Alfred came up to me about an hour ago and asked if I was doing all right, and another of the fellers, that there Jim, come round a little while back. He said, "How are your hands holding out, Mrs Chance?" so I think they're going to put me on some inspecting work on the day shift. I don't know that work, but I'll have to learn, shan't I?'

'I wonder if me and Joe could get on to the day shift,' said Mabs. 'Night work isn't so bad in one way. I mean you do get the days to yourself, but I suppose night work tells on your health.' She spoke as if night work was a snooper in sneaker slippers which could creep up on us all by stealth.

Mabs looked across the room towards the machine on which her husband Joe was working. It was difficult to know what her wandering pale green eyes really saw, because she did not keep them fixed on to one point: She was like a zoo animal looking at humans from out of a cage; can it be known if it is looking at anything or only just looking? 'Do you think it will tell on our health?' she asked again; but because she did not put the insistence of someone needing an answer into her voice, she got none.

'My husband didn't want me to come here on nights,' Mrs Chance said. 'He wanted me to be at home, but he's working up at a big ambulance station Tottenham way himself, so I don't see why he should grumble. Still, he'll be better pleased when I'm on the day shift. After all, we haven't got the home we had. We used to have a big house, down Kilburn way it was; we let out some of the rooms and we had a good living, but it got bombed. The ceiling fell in on the piano. You never saw such a mess. We're still there, but of course we can't let the rooms now, so I came here. As a matter of fact, I'm letting my stepdaughter down coming into a factory at all.'

'Why?' said Feather, 'You mean you can't be with her?'

'Oh no, she's sixteen now, but I've brought her up nice. She's high school.'

'Oh,' said Feather.

'Oh yes, definitely high school,' repeated Mrs Chance.

If Mabs did not look out of her green eyes she looked in with them; they flickered now for a moment. The shadow of the class within the class had fallen between the two workers — the good living, the high school, the piano in the Kilburn house — but Mabs only went on singing, 'Oh, roll on one o'clock, roll on supper-time.'

The night shift was a new thing in the factory. Messrs Braille were working twenty-four hours now, they had switched over from the peacetime cinematograph work to the war-time making of camera parts for reconnaissance and bombing airplanes. They were Government subsidised, but the reorganisation was a revolution for the firm. They had to take on new workers, skilled engineers, some from à Court's and other firms, also semi-skilled engineers and men, boys and women from the Government training centres. But the night shift still had under fifty workers, so these only used the centre workshop; the pay was a little better than that of the day shift, because it was night work.

It was not easy to reach the factory by nine o'clock as some of the buses stopped early; this meant a ten-minutes' walk to Braille's from the cross-roads and the bus halt, and sometimes at this hour an air raid had already started. At half-past six in the morning we clocked off and went home. It was cold then and often it rained. The inspectors and foremen usually left a few minutes later than us, but before we were able to get on to the right or the best bus they passed us on their motor bicycles, seeming like strange creatures from another world; those who wore the yellow mackintosh suits looked like turtles, the goggles of others gave them the appearance of monstrous insects; two or three were round-helmeted as if for speedway riding, and these last looked like Gothic ghosts come back to the world in a mechanised form.

Inside the factory we had not yet reached supper-time.

Nan looked at us from the other end of the workshop. She mouthed a question. We held up our hands — both hands for ten, two fingers more to make twelve, then a knife-cut sign with the side of the hand for half-past.

'It's funny how slow an-arf-our can go,' said Mabs. 'You'd think it was thirty days 'stead of thirty minutes, you would really.' She looked across at Joe and said out her same affectionate sentence: 'I'm fed with you, Joe,' and then to Feather, 'I don't think no harm will come to Joe with them two.' She meant the two trousered girls who were working on milling machines near Joe. They came from Folkestone, but they had been working on the land before taking the Government training course. Their mannishness had a sort of sad innocence about it as if they had given up softness because they thought it would be of no use in a tough world. Green-pants was older than Grey-pants; she had an upturned nose and a face drained of gentleness; she was like a rag that has been wrung out. Grey-pants had less character, but she, too, had adopted the same boyishness as a defence against life. The strange thing about these two girls was their lack of genuine toughness; they complained much more than any of the other women workers, and it was on this Monday evening that I had heard Green-pants saying, 'We've had some jobs in our time, been in service and all, but this is the worst job we've struck yet.'

'Funny thing,' Mabs told Feather, 'one of them girls in pants told me to-day as she was saving a bit out of her wages each week to buy a moonstone ring; she don't look the sort to trouble about rings and suchlike, do she?' Mabs looked towards Joe again. 'You don't have no more good times after you're married, you don't,' she said.

It was strange the way the talk could go on. We worked on nine-and-a-half hour shifts for six nights a week; it was true we had one hour each night off for a meal, but it was difficult to get any food; then it meant a long wait at the food counter, fetching plates backwards and forwards from the cooking stove to the benches where we sat to eat. No one spoke much during the onehour break. Many of the workers were tired when they reached the factory; we worked all the time we were there, and yet conversation crept in — cut-up scraps of conversation between the times of fixing up a machine, counting pieces of work and waiting for a new drill or tap to be fixed in the machine. But even in prisons, where there are more difficulties, the chatter gets through; words are sent out from the side of the mouth in chapel between snatches of hymns. As I listened to the words around me, it was clear to me 'there'll always be a conversation'.

'Soon be time for us to go down,' said Mrs Chance. 'I suppose the raid's very heavy now. You can't hear much with all this machinery on the go, can you.' As the second foreman in charge white-coated his way past us, Mrs Chance called out, 'Sidney!' It was always considered a good joke to call the second foreman in charge of the night shift by his full name; we only spoke out both syllables of his name when we were going to say something funny or else something serious which we had to turn into a joke. The air raids was one of these compulsory jokes. 'Sidney, what's old Adolf doing at the moment?'

'Oh, he's quietened down a bit now.'

At one minute to one most of the workers had gathered round the notice board to clock out for the night meal. They stood for a moment like a group waiting to be photographed. Just before the minute hand jerked up to the appointed hour they all reached out towards the rack holding their hour cards on which their names and numbers were written. One by one they dropped the cards into the clocking-in mouth, knocked in the knob, like a blow to the front teeth, and taking out the cards put them back in the rack.

Sid called out to Nan, who was still at the far end of the room, 'Can you put out those two lights before you come down', and the foremen, inspectors, charge hands and workers swung round the staircase and descended into that catacomb passage of pieces of metal waiting to be sent up for inspection.

We walked along, on either side of us there was the wire netting; it gave the impression of a cinema set concentration camp. The light was dim and in this underground passage the round metal cases looked like heaped-up skulls. The workers went out of the door at the end, and up two or three steps into the dark cold night. Alfred called out, 'No torches. Don't forget he's over.' Exasperated Jim said, 'Perfectly ridiculous; how can he see what he's doing on a night like this? Wasting his petrol; that's all he's doing, wasting his petrol.' The shed where we were to have our meal was lit up. The workers got as near as they could to the counter; some of the foremen went behind the counter.

'Well, I suppose we must do what we can to help you, Ma.' Ma wore her cretonne overall; she had a kindly better-than-human look, like an animal dressed up as a member of a family in a children's picture book. Ma might have been Tom the rabbit's aunt or some such picture character of comfortably caged-in childhood.

Every evening there was the same trouble about the food. It was a short play performed once nightly with alternating villains; sometimes the swine of the show was the man who ran the canteen. 'No use my coming here when there's nothing for me to cook,' said Ma. On other nights the main brute was the day shift. 'Oh, it's all right for the day shift; they get plenty to eat because there's plenty of them, but there's nothing for the night shift. Oh no, it doesn't matter about the night shift. They don't need no food, they don't.'

Ma said, 'I can cook the stuff for you all right if it's here, but it isn't. What do you want, dear, bubble and squeak? All right, but it costs money now. Eightpence halfpenny.'

Some of the workers came clattering into the shed like zebras going down to the water to drink. These did get something to eat; others did not hurry so much and brought small attaché cases of sandwiches. Two young engineers from the day shift came in wearing their Home Guard uniform; one of them leant his rifle up against the counter and went behind to help pour out the cups of tea. Last of all, Feather found her way to the canteen.

'Hullo, dear, you're always last,' said Ma. 'There's not much left now. You want to get down first one night.'

Feather walked to the end of the counter where the Home Guard boy was pouring out the cups of tea. 'How much is it?' she asked.

'You don't pay for the first one,' he said. 'If you have a second cup of tea, it's three 'a'pence.'

Sid walked by. 'I see you broke another tap,' he said.

'I know.'

'Well, what you bin doing? One tap in an evening or even two we don't say nothing, but four, Gor blimey.'

Feather's tired disillusioned little voice whined back at him. 'I hate that tapping, Sid. I get so tired.'

'Aw, it's easy,' said Sid.

'Everything's easy when you know how, ain't it, dear?' said Ma.

'Can you give me a cup of tea, Corporal Dick Strauss?' asked Mrs Chance. The Jewish foreman in battle-dress behind the counter began pouring out cups of tea. It was funny about Feather being tired. It was a new factory problem for Dick Strauss, and one to be puzzled over. He was never tired himself. 'You married?' he asked Feather.

'No, she ain't,' said Alfred.

'Well, you got someone to look after you at home?' he asked.

'Yes, I have got that,' Feather said.

'Well, when you go home this morning, go straight to bed, see, and get someone to bring you yer tea, and don't you get up till it's time to come back to work; sleep on until about seven in the evening, see. Now, what can I give you to eat? Look, Ma, how about opening this tin of corned beef? mix it with some of these potatoes, see. I don't know what this fellow that's running the canteen thinks he's doing. I tell you straight I don't.'

Feather took her plate of food, picked up a knife and fork and walked over to the bench where she sat with Mrs Chance, Mr Peigne, the whitecollared worker of courtly manners, and another man we called 'the unemployed man', who had been working at Braille's for three weeks. He had come on from a Government training centre; he was a printer by trade, but for a long time before this had been unemployed. He did not wear a white collar but instead a red handkerchief round his neck; he also brought some thick bread with him in a knotted handkerchief. He sat quietly cutting it with a penknife. He very seldom spoke. This square-shouldered and rather red-faced man had a kindly, gentle expression. He did not seem to expect more of life than the bread, the two knotted handkerchiefs, the regular mechanical work and the day-time sleep. For a long while he had been without these things. His shoes were done up with blacked-over string instead of laces. He took his feet off the bench when Feather came along and smiled. Mr Peigne moved up to where the unemployed man's feet had been. Feather put her torch beside her on the table, and her small suitcase which carried her engineering gloves, work-hour book, teacup, soap, scarf, identification card, spectacles and money on the floor beside her. She sat down on the bench and began to eat her heated up corned beef and fried potatoes.

The North-country woman was sitting on the other side of

the same bench. She worked a very heavy capstan machine; this meant standing up all through the nine-and-a-half hour shift, except for this one hour when she drank her cup of tea, ate a sandwich which she always brought with her, and slept. Suddenly her whole mountainous frame shook itself awake. She said, 'How much did they knock you down for that, dear?'

'I don't know,' said Feather.

'I had the same; it was eightpence halfpenny,' said Mrs Chance.

'Eightpence halfpenny! They got a nerve!' said the North-country giantess, and fell back asleep again.

Her daughter sat beside the sleeper. She was a very pretty girl; she had only been in the factory a few days. Her mother explained, 'Lass's husband's gone abroad with his regiment, so she's come to live along with me; she may as well work at factory now.' The girl always read throughout her meal, and always one of two magazines, *Stella's Star* or *Maggie's Mag*. She wore a hair comb on either side of her dark hair and looked like a pretty beetle. Sometimes one of the factory hands asked, 'Wot's 'appening in yer book, dear?' and she would answer back, 'Oh, she's just planning to stab 'im to death. She don't know 'e' s 'er father yet, see,' and she read on. She did not look very interested in these stories, but she did not want anything more from the printed word than the usual formula, the same story with the names changed and slightly different pictures. As she read the hair combs moved ever so slightly with her head like the antennae of an insect on a hot day.

The white-coated men, the foremen, two charge hands, Corporal Strauss and two engineers on Home Guard duty, sat at their table near the food counter. Sid had his arm round Flash Jim's shoulder with the easy familiarity of a war comrade. There was no homosexuality in the factory and it seldom came into the conversation except as a music-hall joke about the lisp-hiss way cissies talked.

On the night shift there was no quarrelling or jealousy amongst the foremen and inspectors, but we were told, 'Now on the day shift it's another story.' It seemed to be not one story but several. The young engineers who came from the day shift to do Home Guard duty on the night shift used to tell us about this other life which went on in the same place but at a different time. For us the group of workers, who reached the factory each morning half an hour after we had left, were like the people of some distant totalitarian country whose methods we deplored and with whom we were always almost at war.

One evening one of the Home Guard boys said to Feather, 'I come from à Court's, you know, but I been here six months now, same as Jim; the yes-men that walk around at à Court's, it makes you sick, but it's the same here on the day shift, all these fellers will do anything to get ahead; I tell you there's no counting them.' He looked down at his own shiny brown boots polished like meerschaum pipes. 'A lot of good-for-nothing swankers.' He took off his tortoiseshell-rimmed spectacles. 'You ought to aim at inspection work,' he told Feather; clearly he thought she was a girl who was one grade up in refinement. He put his spectacles on again. 'Wouldn't spoil your hands, you know, the inspection work; of course it would mean your coming to work on the day shift. You should just see the scrum in the morning, the crowd trying to get on the bus, you know.'

'Why don't you bicycle?' Feather asked.

'Well, I don't want to ruin my machine coming up here on it. You see, it's a pretty good bike; it cost me nearly fourteen pounds.'

Feather asked young shiny-boots if it would not be possible for him to get to his work on an ordinary bicycle. 'Oh, no,' he answered. 'I wouldn't be seen dead on an inferior machine.' He looked down at his bright brown boots again. 'That's not my style at all,' he said.

This young engineer on Home Guard duty was in the canteen now. 'I seen you talking to him a few nights back,' Mrs Chance said. 'He's on the day shift, isn't he?'

Feather remembered the conversation again, the shiny brown boots, the tortoiseshell spectacles, the bicycle that was too good for riding to work and the one that was too bad to be seen dead on. 'What an idiot!' she said aloud.

The boys from the Government instructional institutes sat at a table near the door; there were half a dozen of these puppy-faced fellows all under nineteen years old. They ran backwards and forwards to the counter for cups of tea, asked each other riddles, laughing loudly at the answers and then, remembering that these were the same riddles they asked each other every evening, they stopped laughing abruptly.

One boy was very silent; he thought a lot about airplanes and the way they worked, but he was not articulate. He would say, 'I seen one of them Flying Fortresses to-day', and then he would blush. Sometimes one of the boys had 'trouble at home', and then he would be sunk in gloom right through the meal hour, silent and despairing. Sonny was the most articulate; he was not clear about the kind of life he wanted, but at least he knew that he wanted a better kind of life. Sonny's brother, the pilot officer, came often into the conversation. 'My brother was telling me some of the things they have to learn in the RAF are ever so difficult, they are really.' Sonny was most proud of his brother's capacity for passing examinations. 'He's ever such a clever feller, my brother is; much more clever than me.'

Mr Peigne, sitting near to Feather, looked thoughtfully at the food she was eating. 'Potatoes are very good for you,' he said. 'I planted potatoes on my allotment.' Mr Peigne used to like talking of the days 'when I joined the Volunteers'. 'It was near forty years ago when I was in the Volunteers,' he said; he thought the Home Guard was something of the same sort, and when they went clanking round the workshops with their guns and bayonets Mr Peigne used to say, 'We had some of those swanking kind of fellows in the Volunteers; think they're grown up just because they've got a gun.' He went to fetch a second cup of tea for himself. He was very courtly in his manner. 'Would any of you ladies care for a second cup?' he asked. We did not know very much about Mr Peigne, except that he was proud. Perhaps he had a tough wife who insisted on taking most of his wages; this might be the reason for his working so hard, eating so little and always taking the cheapest bus route home. 'That two hundred and forty-two,' he said, 'is a splendid ride for twopence, takes you right down to Tottenham; of course, they're few and far between, the two hundred and forty-twos, but they're worth waiting for. It's a real good ride for twopence, the two hundred and forty-two is.'

When he returned with the cups of tea someone said to him, 'So you don't eat anything of a night, Mr Peigne?' He shook his head smiling. 'No, I never have anything appertaining to dinner of an evening.'

When it was about four minutes to two, the workers collected up their torch lights and attaché cases; the giantess from the North country shook herself awake again, and we tramped out into the cold yard, calling out, 'Good-night, Ma', as we passed the food counter. Feather complained that she could not see her way. Sid shouted out, 'Well, I got a white coat on, ain't I, that's plain enough. Follow me.'

II

Soon after the midnight meal I finished the work I had started on my arrival. Alfred asked me if I thought I could do the next job. It did not seem possible to me that there was anyone who could not have done it. Hundreds of flat pieces of metal with a small ledge at each end had to be drilled through on each side of the ledge. It was easy, dull and monotonous.

As soon as I started this work Miss Peggy Perry came up to me. She was the white-faced girl with the upturned nose who gave the workers their check cards. She wrote down the operator's number and the number of the operation, tapping, drilling, filing, de-burring, milling or reaming. Sometimes she added a sort of sub-description such as drilling five holes, or de-burring two sides of metal. When the work was finished the operator counted the bits and the number was written next the column headed 'Output'. These check cards were kept, the details copied by each operator into the work book and this was handed to the foreman in charge each Thursday morning. We were also given duplicate sheets which were put with the work when it was carried over to the shelves near Alfred's desk.

Before Peggy Perry came to Braille's she had been a clerk in a small shop. She was able to make out these check cards in her neat, uncompromising handwriting, but as the night shift was small it did not take her long to do this work, and the rest of the time was spent in the various engineering operations.

Peggy Perry was not married. She was going to have a child. She did not speak about this often, but it was clear to us that she did not mind; she was neither pleased nor sorry, although she said once, 'It's all very unsettling.' Occasionally she spoke of her lover, 'Lewis, Mr Muir you know, is supposed to be getting leave soon.' Sometimes she said this the other way round. 'Mr Muir, Lewis you know, is likely to be getting back to London for a few days.' Peggy was inclined to superiority because she had been a clerk. In the canteen I had heard her saying, 'I always thought factory girls were a low class of girl; I was always told they were cheap with men, and continually getting themselves into trouble with fellers.' The words floated out from under the upturned nose which gave to her face an enquiring look although she did not enquire within or without, because she ignored that we were all working in a factory and that she herself was soon to give birth to a bastard. She sat near me de-burring some small pieces of metal. She did this by hand with a file.

Sweet-expressioned Nan said, 'Corporal Strauss says these machines are all too close together; he says it doesn't give the worker a chance, these machines being so near each other. Do you think Strauss is right?'

'Shouldn't be surprised,' the pretty whitefaced girl answered without any show of interest. We worked for a long time without speaking to each other. The air-raid destruction went on outside and the noise inside the workshop made me think of a ship which was always trying to leave port but never got under way.

Whenever we became aware that a bomb had fallen near Braille's factory, Alfred and Sid took their white helmets and ran down the stairs to see if any of the sheds outside had caught fire. Firewatchers were on duty in the street, but the two men in charge of the night shift sometimes felt compelled to join in the look-out work.

In their white coats with their helmets at an angle they looked like a couple of comic opera bakers. 'There goes old Adolf again,' they said, and were off down the stairs. They came back again in a few minutes. 'Couldn't see nothing,' Sid said. 'Adolf's farther away than we thought.' Flash Jim walked about on his inspection work more exasperated than ever, repeating, 'Wasting 'is petrol, that's all 'e's doing; there's no sense in 'is coming over on a night like this, no sense at all.'

Half an hour later Alfred said, 'Old Adolf's taken his Loofterwaffer off.'

'What do you mean?' Mabs said. 'They ain't never sounded the All Clear.'

'No, but they will.'

'Well, he's knocked off early to-night and no mistake about it.'

At four o'clock two of the women workers went downstairs to make the tea. When it was ready they brought it up in two great jugs, like the jugs used in Edwardian days for pouring hot water into bath tubs.

There was a notice on the board by the clock; it was written here that workers must not leave their machines and work benches, the tea would be brought to them; but when they saw the two jugs being carried in, several of them got their cups and went over to the tap near the doorway to wash them out.

One of the jugs was full of sweetened tea and milk, the other was unsweetened; there was no possible means of knowing one bath jug of tea from the other than by its position on the work bench. When the jugs got moved about several of the workers who wanted sugar did not get it and those who wanted plain tea got a sweet cup. So they walked about like dogs who have been eating grass — trying to chew the sweetness or the sourness out of their teeth and tongues. Each night the same thing happened.

Cups of tea were taken over to Alfred's desk and here the white-coated foremen, Sid, Alfred, Flash Jim, any other inspector who happened to be on duty, two or three charge hands and Corporal Dick Strauss sat drinking tea and eating immense flat sweet buns much bigger than a man's hand.

The personality of Mrs Lloyd, the Spanish worker, always

attracted hostility at tea-time. This was because she asked questions. Her first question was aimed at Nan.

'Have you finished your job yet?'

'No, I done all these, but there's still a lot more to do.'

Mrs Jove and her friend Chrissie were working on metal cylinders; they also got a question from Mrs Lloyd.

'How many have you done?'

'I don't know, we haven't counted yet. You see, a lot of them have got to be thrown out; they were started by that damn day shift and they do a lot of bad work.'

Mrs Jove had taken two layers of thick bread out of her attaché case; she began to munch; her face looked very thin, as if it had been shut in a door.

'What are you eating?' Mrs Lloyd asked. 'Sandwiches,' answered Mrs Jove, but as soon as Mrs Lloyd returned to her work Chrissie called out to Nan, 'Tea-time for us is question time for her.'

'Any time's question time for Mrs Lloyd,' agreed her friend Mrs Jove.

To-night was only Monday, the first shift of the week. The workers had stored up some strength during the Sunday rest. They could stand Mrs Lloyd's questions now, but as the nights went by and the end of the week was neared the scratching sound of the Spanish woman's inquisition became almost intolerable.

During the last two hours of the morning there seemed an even greater intensity of speed in the workshop; it took on the atmosphere of a newspaper office when the whole staff is trying to get the paper out. For the last thirty minutes some workers were carrying great trays of metal bits to the shelves near Alfred's desk; others piled up rounded bits of metal in heaps between the work benches so that they looked like empty beer tankards; the small tin cases filled with nuts, bolts and screws were put on Alfred's desk and Miss Perry made her pale-faced way round signing the work check cards. The operators cleaned the machinery with pieces of rag and took bundles of thread-like metal from the slabs below the machines and threw it into the salvage bins. At twenty-six minutes past six some of the workers were slowly making their way to the cloakrooms. There were only two of these wash-up rooms, one for the men and one for the women; both were small rooms with battleship-grey walls. There was always a thick line of grease and oil round the two wash basins, the roller towels were very dirty because it was not possible for anyone to get their hands and wrists clean in the depressing wash basin before drying them on the dirty towel.

The whine came forth from Feather's tired disillusioned little face, 'Every night I have to bring soap, a towel, a teacup, my work book, the check cards, an overall, a tin hat, a jersey, a coat, a scarf to tie round my hair, money, cigarettes, matches, gloves for my hands and I don't know what else.'

'Yes, that's it, dear,' said Chrissie. 'You need a portmanteau, you do really.'

The giantess from the North country tying on her red woollen hood was a displacement in the small cloakroom. Some of the women wore scarves round their heads; only two or three had tin hats. Mabs perched up a black hat trimmed with mauve flowers; its high crown sat there on top of her head in all its sad absurdity.

In these last two minutes before the clocking out and the journey home words were cast out casually like stones thrown into the sea during a walk along the sands.

'I suppose it will still be dark when we get out.'

'It was last Saturday morning, but the mornings are getting lighter now.'

'I wonder if it's raining.'

'This was one of my trousseau hats when me and Joe were married; I used to have a craze on hats.'

'I used to have a craze on shoes.'

'Anyway, there's no raid on now; that was a bit of a bang before we had our tea, it knocked the file right out of my hand.'

'Ar thought bomb was coming in at winder.'

'If I run down to the end of the road I can get a two hundred and forty-two, but they don't run often, the two hundred and forty-twos don't.'

'Sonny comes the same road as us now, until he takes his train, he does; he says he's getting used to us.'

The workers clocked out on the half-hour. Outside it was still dark; it took some time to get used to this after the glare-light of the workshop. It was a ten-minutes' walk to the cross-roads where the buses and trolley-cars stopped. A few more remarks were dropped into the cold air.

'It don't take me above an 'our to get back.'

'I aim to be home by half-past seven most mornings.'

'I'm just ready for a good long sleep.'

'I don't like to hang about, I always want to get back quick.'

'Anyhow it's not raining now, got to be thankful for that.'

The early morning journey was a trouble to be gone through in an automatic way; once out of the factory we were already home in thought, but there was still the struggle to get there, and the dispirited remarks we exchanged with each other were like whistled tunes taken up between tired soldiers on the march.

The workers went with blinkered minds swiftfooted to the cross-roads.

Tuesday

On Tuesday night I reached the cross-roads at half-past eight. I went into the café on the corner. It was called Hopp's café and was run by the hunchback Hopp. He was a short man with an abnormally large head; he told us there was not much to eat. 'I can fix you a sausage roll sandwich,' he said.

Two of the semi-skilled boy workers sat at one of the shiny grey-topped tables; we drank cups of Bovril and a deep depression settled over us. I did not know how so much hopelessness had been able to accumulate in this small room of Hopp's café. It was like a kind of bottled despair. More of the night shift workers drifted in. First Mr Peigne, then Feather followed by Mrs Jove, Chrissie and the giantess from the North country with her daughter carrying two new numbers of *Stella's Star* and *Maggie's Mag*. Mr Peigne was telling Feather, 'I come habitually to this café to see if any of the ladies would like to be escorted up to Braille's.'

'Has siren gone yet?' asked the giantess.

'No, he's not over yet.'

'But now we shan't be long,' said Mrs Jove.

And at this moment in quick-time answer to a prophecy the wail went out.

'Wot did I tell you,' said Mrs Jove. She had worked in a cabaret once, the dance-song life was with her still, the syncopated spindle-legging at the end of her thin body, she walked over to the white machine which looked like a refrigerator but was a pay-as-you-go gramophone. She put a penny into it and on the instant it lit up and blared forth with terrific brute strength, a noise that was far worse than shout, shot or cannon, a noise that could not be stopped or sorted out.

'Ere, now, not so loud,' said Hopp.

Feather's face had hardened into a box for a painful expression. With the best will in the world she could not stand the stale accumulation of shout and squalor. 'I think I'll go along now, I'm always afraid of being late.' She went out and on up the hill which led to Braille's.

At the factory the women workers came into the cloakroom talking, but as they began to arrange their hair and put on their overalls they sang snatches of song. One started, another joined in, and when they sang all expression went out of their faces.

'I had to pay threepence on the bus coming along,' said white-faced Miss Perry. 'Now, that's not right, is it? I don't mind anything else, but I do object to being cheated over transport.'

'I had to wait over twenty minutes for the bus, they knock off early on my route; now that's not right, is it?'

'Just we three, tra-la-tra-la-la,' sang Mabs, doing her hair.

'Just we three, da-dee-da-dee-da,' joined in Mrs Jove, tying on her overalls and all living look was wiped out from their four eyes from the first hum. But the painful expression came back to Feather's face.

'Oh, this day shift! They've been wearing our overalls again, they're always doing it,' complained Nan. 'I'm going to leave a note for them when I get away to-morrow morning. I'm going to write, "Wear yer own overalls, can't you," and I'm going to pin it up to mine so's they can see it.'

'That wouldn't stop the day shift,' said Mrs Chance.

'Blimey, I ain't clocked on yet,' broke in Mabs.

'Better hurry,' said Green-pants, 'or they'll dock you a quarter of an hour of your wages.'

'No, they can't, answered Mrs Chance. 'It wants four minutes to nine yet.'

The women trooped out of the cloakroom into the main

part of the workshop where Alfred and Sid were giving out jobs.

Two of the semi-skilled boy operators had been on the same job now for five nights; they had to level up some hollow, curved metal camera cases; they worked with a flat surface for testing and a file. I had seen Sonny take his dungarees off a hook near his work bench and get into them with that curious dip-at-the-knees gesture.

'It's funny us working on these things,' he said. 'We've been doing them for several nights now, but I don't know what part of the camera they are used for, that's the worst of industry, you do — oh, hundreds of the same thing, and you never know what they're for — monotonous, isn't it?' He laid the bit down on the work bench and started to tap it with his knuckles as if he was listening to heart beats. Then he began filing along the edges of this half-hollow metal case again. 'I ain't 'arf tired,' Sonny sighed. 'I took my girl friend to a theatre this afternoon, it was her day off. I've only had three hours' sleep since last night.'

There was another sort of metal piece which we often worked on. It was more easy to see how this could be used, because it was rather like a part of a camera which I had once owned. But this bit was stronger; it was made of a more tough metal, it was much bigger and more intricate, and on this bit alone there was a certain amount of precision work to be done. I had to ream through these bits and then run a 'go and no go' gauge through both sides and after this stack the work from end to end in large trays.

'It's easy,' said Alfred, 'but be sure you put a lot of oil on the work, then it'll run through easy enough.'

'This machine oil fair makes you sick, doesn't it,' the woman next to me said. She had greyish hair and was very thin. She looked like a tropical bird that has been suddenly woken up.

'I can't get rid of the machine oil, seems to get in your hair, in your clothes, in your skin.'

Someone asked her, 'How are you getting on?' This was a great catch sentence in the workshop; it took the place of 'H'y'ah', 'Good evening', 'I'll be seein' you', and suchlike sentences.

The answer came back now: 'Well, I'm not doing so good. I don't like it here; you see, I came on night shift because I was told it was good money, but we don't get what we were engaged to get.'

'Why don't you go to the Labour Exchange and get some other war work?'

'Oh, I don't want to go to the Labour Exchange, and there's many as thinks the same as me. Round at the Labour Exchange there are a lot of whippersnappers as never earned as much money as I have, and never will either. You see, I was a pastry cook, used to make five pounds a week then, but of course you can't get the stuff now, can you? Of course I don't say that *some* of them are not all right round at the Labour Exchange. Oh, well, maybe I'll get on here when I'm used to it. You see, I don't sleep so good in the day time, that's the trouble really.'

During these last few nights I had seen two members of the slightly higher class within the working class. They seemed to be very much aware of this one-hop-up stage of superior wage and living standard; but now they felt that they were being forced back from the small bourgeois life to the working class. I noticed that they only minded this at first. Once with the other workers they were glad of it like the bather swimming in cool water shouting to those still on the bank, 'Oh, come on in, it's lovely here.' Both Mrs Chance and the pastry cook were happy in the factory, or at least they were happy as far as social relationship went. It was clear that no one could enjoy making a tiring, cold and dangerous journey each night to a factory, to work at a mechanical job for long hours, sit for one hour in an uncomfortable shed and then work again at more mechanical work for a further five-and-a-half hours; and after this, set out in the cold dark morning, perhaps with enemy airplanes still overhead, to struggle through the tiresome and tiring journey home, and so on for six nights out of every seven.

Naturally, happiness could not be surveyed out in this rough territory, but all the same, these five-pounds-a-week women of former days were quick to forget the lost possession of the better living, and when they needed warmth of mind they wrapped themselves round in the grey blanket all-for-the-best mood of resignation. They hammered on, they hoped on, and like all the other operators they were glad when it was half-past six in the morning; they thought pay night was the best night, and Sunday the best day because then they were able to rest.

One of the hair-cropped trousered girls went by carrying a wooden tray of metal discs.

'Here,' shouted Alfred, 'that's too heavy for you to lift. Get one of the fellers to help you.'

'Oh no, it's not,' called back Green-pants. 'I've been in the Land Army, they put us to felling trees there. This is nothing to that, this isn't.'

At this time a curious kind of undercurrent of suspense swept around the factory; a whispering, a looking towards Alfred's desk. It was like the rustling of leaves swirling near the ground before a storm.

The girl next Feather said, 'That's not right.'

Feather thought the girl was speaking of the way she was doing her work and answered, 'Anyhow, this was how Alfred said it was to be done.'

'No, I don't mean about your work — I mean it's not right about Maree.'

'What's happened?'

'She's been given her cards,' Grey-pants said. 'That's a nice trick, sending a girl home this time of night, in an air raid too.'

Feather asked the reason.

'Well, Alfred said she was inefficient. Of course she is, but we're not supposed to be efficient after only two months' training.'

'It's not right.'

'They said she wouldn't do nothing the way they told her to. When Alfred told her she had done it wrong, she did it the same way again. She didn't like that machine she was working on, but he wouldn't take her off it.'

'She got on fine at the Instructional School. I was with Maree there myself. It's not right.'

'Fancy Maree getting back at twelve o'clock at night to her home and having to tell her Mum she's bin given her cards.'

'It's not right sending her home at this time of night. After all, Maree's only eighteen. They could get into trouble for doing that. They must have known before this; Alfred should have told her this morning, and then she needn't have come to-night. I should say something to them, they couldn't try that trick on me. Still, Maree don't know her way about, she don't.'

There was an intense atmosphere of hostility, loyalty, resentment and fear. Through the job that chink of light could be seen, the half-security. Being in a job was not full security, of course. There was still the cold cost of living, but at least it was like being able to see and know something of the warm sunlight through a partly opened door. Now the door seemed to be swinging closer to, the chill of the evening was coming up again and there was no warmth within the house.

'You don't know which of us it will be next.'

'It won't be easy for Maree to get a job after she's bin given her cards from 'ere, and she won't be able to say why, 'cos they don't tell 'er why.'

'I don't mind being given my cards, but I like to know the reason why.'

Feather said, 'Of course she'll get a job in wartime.'

'Do you think so?'

'Well, they want workers, don't they? I mean, they're screaming out for them on the wireless morning, night and evening — "Join up and make weapons for the air, the land, the sea and under the sea".'

'Yes, that's what they say. All the same, it's not right sending Maree off like that at a minute's notice.'

'I think they can do it if we're employed by the hour,' said the North-country giantess. 'You see, we're semi-skilled workers and we're not union members. Still, it's not right. Alfred ought to know better than sending lass home like that.'

After the hostile whispering from worker to worker they settled down again, but this time halfheartedly. In the canteen during the midnight meal, the conversation kept coming back to Maree. Peggy Perry came to our table. She sat there whitefaced but looking rather secure and prosperous. It was the fact that she was going to have a child that gave her this look. She sat square to the table in a matriarch manner. 'Fancy Alfred giving Maree her cards like that. Of course Alfred is a horrible man, there's nothing nice about Alfred. He's a horrible man, Alfred is.' She said this in her flat voice, looking in her white-faced way straight ahead. It was very strange that she should have done this, because Alfred was at the foreman's table only a few feet away and so he must have heard every word, but his face wore an expression of genuine indifference to the talk around him. This made Feather suggest that perhaps it was not his fault. 'I mean, he's only employed, after all.' She turned to Mr Peigne. 'Is it Alfred's fault about the girl being sacked?'

Mr Peigne answered, 'Maybe it's not his fault, but I am of the opinion that he had a lot to do with it.'

The unemployed man did not say anything. His feet always got tired at this time of the evening; he had loosened the blacked-over string that tied his boots. He put two pieces of bread back into his coloured cotton handkerchief and knotted it together again.   .

Mr Peigne said, 'You see, after an employee has worked here for a month they've got to give them a bonus. Well, it is not improbable that because the young lady's month was up they saw their way to avoid giving her this bonus. They're funny like that, the employers are, you know.'

'Well, we've bin here three months, Mrs Jove and me,' said Chrissie, 'but we haven't seen any bonus. At first we thought it was because we hadn't got past the probation period, but that's long ago now, and anyhow we aren't paid what we were told we were going to be paid.'

'Why don't you go and see the accountants about it then?' asked Feather.

'Well, you must all write a letter with me, one of these round robins. The wage packets are different every week. Two of the girls were twopence short only last week, but what's the use of me creating unless we all create. I can't create alone, otherwise they'll just think I'm the only one that is discontented and then they'll give me my cards and not trouble themselves any further. See.'

'That's right,' supported Mrs Jove.

The fantasy image of Chrissie creating slithered serpent-like through Feather's thoughts, but for her the joke was not worth a smile. Was she always to hear this hack talk of twopence halfpenny short, and one potato too few in the canteen shed? There was also the other talk in the same spirit. The more polished side of an identical coin, the petty boasts of Brown Boots of the Home Guard, with pomade in the hair and a shine on the bicycle handle-bars. It seemed to Feather that the working classes were sabotaging themselves. Why couldn't they call out altogether for what they wanted. This should be a shout that would break down the financial walls of that exclusive city of private property. But no such shout came, and instead isolated Lilliputians potted on haphazard with pea-shooters from somewhere well out of range of the fortress.

When Feather talked to me I could almost hear the prompting voices of several luxurious leftists — armchair sitters, Swan-pen writers, backs-to-the-fire shouters. Feather had seen them too often and heard them too long. They were keeping their comfort long after she had lost her peace of mind. Perhaps this fool, this girl called Feather, had expected and even wanted Red Weddin' heroics at the factory, but here she was getting the cold potatoes and the ill-formulated grumbling.

'When Maree came out of the cloakroom she was crying,' Peggy said, 'and Alfred came by, so he must have seen her crying. I wouldn't let Alfred get the better of me. I wouldn't let him see me crying, would you?'

'I don't know,' Feather answered.

Chrissie looked up at the clock; there were only three minutes before we must get back to the workshop and clock in again. She started the old factory joke: 'Ladies and Gentlemen', and all the workers sitting at our table shouted back, 'The King'.

Jim moved quickly towards the door: the unemployed man tied up his blackened boot-strings and followed us. Alfred nearby was talking to Flash Jim and Sid about food.

'You see, my Mother used to be rather well known in the

West End, and some of these Italians around Soho used to send us up dishes occasionally all cooked up and ready to eat. They were lovely cooking, you know, really well done up. These Italians do understand about cooking, they do, really.'

At the time of the four o'clock morning tea I noticed that two of the girls sitting by the work bench near the big bath jugs were filing some brass bolts as disinterestedly as children lifting spoonful after spoonful of tasteless milk pudding to their mouths without the will to stop eating, to protest or even sick-up.

'You see,' one of them said, 'we came here with Maree, and when Alfred told us he was weeding out some of the staff we told him back, as we didn't like him saying that, and now we can't take no more interest in working here after what's happened about Maree.'

And in the early morning before we clocked out, Alfred suddenly handed these two girls their unemployment and health insurance cards, so that they, too, were sacked. One of them had bought a steel helmet from the management for seven-and-sixpence.

'I shouldn't have got it if I'd known I was going to be given me cards,' she said.

Wednesday

On Wednesday night there was a storm. It rained, it hailed, there was thunder. Some of the girl factory workers came in like cats from a damp garden, shaking the raindrops from their hands and feet.

Nan, taking her card from the rack to clock on, said, 'There isn't no air raid on now.'

Mabs's husband, Joe, said, 'Well, what more do you want. We got near everything coming down but snow.'

The North-country giantess unknotted the ends of her red woollen hood. 'Ar think snow's better than air raid.'

Nan put her card back in the rack. 'I wonder if they've got rain, hail and all in Berlin.'

Mr Peigne arrived in good time. He carried an umbrella which he folded up in a neat way and hooked over his arm as he stood in front of the clock. He was like a well-to-do club man, strolling in to see if there were any letters for him. There was a notice up on the board to tell us that Mr Patterson from the day shift would be coming in to help with the reorganisation of the night shift, and so would the workers please do their best to co-operate with him.

Mabs said to her husband, 'Co-operate? I thought that was a word for going with a feller.'

'Co-operate don't mean that, softie.'

'Well, I thought that was the word. One of them medical words it was. Anyhow, if it wasn't that it was something like it, I know.'

Mr Patterson was already in the workshop, but he did not seem to have anything to do. He kept picking up bolts and nuts and staring at them. Sometimes he talked to Alfred or Sid, but this was not easy for him because the two foremen were always moving round at a great rate.

Flash Jim told one of the charge hands, 'I don't know why they sent Patterson up here. Why can't they leave him where he belongs, on the day shift. He doesn't know anything about the night shift. Alfred and Sid have reorganised it already and they don't want a feller like Patterson messing about. Well, the employers are always blundering. You can't expect anything better from them, really.'

'There's not a lot of sense in it,' said the charge hand.

It was true the time weighed heavily on Mr Patterson. He picked up a hand reamer and stared at it in melancholy. He took a silver screw and seemed to get nothing but loneliness from it. He put it back and looked at a box full of brass bolts as if he would like to pour vitriol over the lot.

Mr Patterson walked with his hands behind his back down the shop. The boy next Sonny imitated his way of doing this so that the others laughed, because they thought of him as an intruder on the night shift.

'After all, we got Alfred and Sid and they do work hard, they do really.'

Patterson went over to Mr Peigne who was working on a large milling machine, turning the various handles in different directions, watching the work very carefully, so that sometimes as he stared down at this work he made me think of some pier Peeping Tom, getting the story of 'what the butler saw' from a penny slot machine.

Mr Peigne had been put on piece work. He said he reckoned that if he could do seven or eight added pieces in the week, it would work out at between three and four shillings extra on pay day. 'I could do with a bit coming in like that at the end of the week.'

'I remember when I was first put on piece work,' said Mr Patterson, 'I was working in a factory up North then.' For Mr Patterson the night shift was like a foreign country. He was glad to come across a pleasant acquaintance. Mr Peigne did not want to make friends of his work-mates, but his pride also prevented him from being offhand or ill-mannered. He was almost the professional pleasant acquaintance.

'How shall I address you, in speaking of you to my colleagues? How would you wish me to refer to you?' he asked.

Mr Patterson listened in patience and then said, 'Call me Pat', and walked on round the workshop.

Mr Peigne told the North-country woman, 'That, how shall I call him — er — executive from the day shift is all right, he has no side about him. I can do with a fellow like that, a fellow that has no side about him.'

'Of course he is better than the works manager,' chipped in Mrs Lloyd. 'Does the works manager look at you men as he does at us women, as if we were dirt?'

'I don't know how he looks at me,' answered proud Mr Peigne. 'I have never observed his manner of looking because it would not affect me. I am perfectly satisfied with my own private life away from here, thank you, so any works manager can look in any way he pleases. He can't see as far as my home life, and he can't interfere with it either.'

Towards the end of the evening Mr Peigne worked ever harder at his milling machine. He took a little black cap out of the pocket of his overalls and put it on his head. When one of the operators asked him, 'How are you getting on, Mr Peigne?' he replied, 'Oh, I think I'm just about drawing level now.' With the little black cap on his head he seemed a symbolical jockey. 'Will Steeplechaser Peigne get first past the piecework post, will he win the race for the bonus or will the hoofs of Time, Death and Fatigue come thundering up and overtake him. Look for the result in next week's wage packet.'

Mabs had started to work on the drilling machine near me. Most evenings she said, 'Oh, I'm fed up,' but to-night she said, 'Oh, I don't know whether I'm fed up or not yet.' Nan, tapping some metal bits on the other side of me, gave one of her long shut-eye winks. Mabs looked round the room in her dreamless green-eyed way, and so staring she broke the drill. She reached down for the scarred blue leather bag by her feet and took out another drill, which she fixed into the machine immediately.

'I hope it's right,' she said. 'It doesn't do to let them know how many you break.'

This was the cue for another wink from Nan.

'Every time she sees a drill on the floor she picks it up and puts it in her bag. Then her husband sharpens them for her. She'd get her cards if they saw her, and him too.'

'Joe give me this bag after we had a bit of a row,' said Mabs. 'He said he was going to give me a bashing, but he give me a bag instead.' As soon as she started to talk about herself a light got into her green eyes. Mabs had a bad mouth with teeth like a rake, but her brown hair was very soft.

'When you're married everything seems so much the same. Night and day alike. When Joe was courting me it wasn't so bad, but that's almost six months ago now. It was ever so funny the way me and Joe got married. I never thought we should. A feller that I used to go with before said the same thing. "You won't never marry him," he said. "You'll go with him for a bit just the same as you did with me." This young feller I was telling you about, Ritzie — I called him Ritzie, see, because his name was Writson, Mr Writson. Well, I saw him one day in the street. He was in uniform but he was on leave, see. So I said, "Hullo, Ritzie," and he says "Hullo, Mabs." Then he says, "I often thought about you, Mabs. Wot you doin' now," he says. And I says, "Oh, I don't know, Ritzie, nothing." I didn't tell him about Joe, so he says, "Well, I often thought about you, Mabs, like I told you. I'll come round and see you." Well, I didn't want him to come because of Joe, but I didn't say nothing, and the next day when I was sitting home talking to Joe, I heard a knock at the door and Joe says, "There's a knock at the door, ain't it?" And I says, "Oh no, Joe, it's nothing"; but the knocking started again, so Joe says, "Well, that's a knock all right," and I says, "It's the man next door knocking his pipe out against the chimney. He's always doing it. Smoke, smoke, smoke, that's all he lives for. He's a regular chimney hisself." Of course I knew really it must be Ritzie and after a little while Joe says, "Well, aren't you going to answer?" So then I says, "All right, I'll go down. It's probably Mrs Feline for Mum." That's a friend of Mum's, see. So I went down and there was Ritzie outside. He come into the kitchen and started talking to me. I told him I was going with a feller and Ritzie says, "Wot's his name, perhaps I know him," and I says, "No, you don't." Well, he says, "Where is he now?" and all this time Joe was sitting upstairs and I was afraid he'd come down and when he saw Ritzie, he'd bash him. So I says, "Well, how do I know where he is. He works," and Ritzie answers, "Well, so do we all, don't we?" And after a bit he says, "Well, what's his name?" But I didn't tell him and then he says, "Well, I've got a present for you, Mabs," and he took out a powder puff in a handkerchief and give it to me. Then I could hear Joe walking about upstairs, and after a bit he comes down, and when he sees Ritzie he says, "'Ullo," and Ritzie says "'Ullo." And Joe says, "Mabs and me are getting married." "That's all right," Ritzie says, "I used to know her. I just come round to see her as a friend." So Joe answers, "Well, that's all right then," and soon he says to Ritzie, "Well, hadn't you better be going?" and Ritzie says, "Oh, I'm going, but I just come round to have a chat with Mabs and talk over old times," and when he went he says to me at the door so's Joe couldn't hear, see, he says, "Get rid of him to-morrow afternoon, I want to talk to you, Mabs." I told him as me and Joe were getting married, and he says, "You two will never get married, you won't," and then he says,

"Well, Mabs, I'll come round at two o'clock to-morrow when he'll be out." When we got back upstairs I told Joe Ritzie was going back to his regiment, and later on in the evening Joe says, "What you doing to-morrow afternoon, Mabs, because I can get a day off." So I told him I'd be busy, helping Mum with the washing and mending. "Well, I can come round and talk to you while you're doing it." "Oh, no, you can't," I told him, because I knew Ritzie was coming round, see, so I says, "How can I do washing and mending, Joe, with you sitting there jawing?" So he didn't say nothing then, and the next afternoon at two Ritzie come up, but after he bin talking to me for a bit, Joe comes in. And when he sees Ritzie he says, "Wot, you again?" and Ritzie says, "I only come round friendly like," and Joe says, "Well, I'm not stopping you from going friendly like either. Me and Mabs are getting married," and Ritzie says, "I don't suppose you ever will." But soon after Ritzie did leave and he says to me, "Good-bye, Mabs, I'll see you soon," and Joe says, "That's not probable," but Ritzie took no notice. He told me, "I'll write to you, Mabs," and so he went, but I was afraid Joe would bash him, I was. You know my Mum was cross with me when I gave up Ritzie. She said, "Fancy giving up a nice steady young feller like that," but I always thought he was a bit slow for me. Joe's more alive, you know.'

At this moment Nan asked, 'Wot happened about Joe and Ritzie?'

'Oh, Joe didn't say nothing. Ritzie rejoined his regiment. My, it's one o'clock, the time seems to have gone much quicker to-night. I expect that's because we've been jawing; it always goes quicker when you have a bit of a jaw.'

Mabs liked to think about her power over Ritzie and Joe. Her talk was like a pump which worked the life up from a well of consciousness through the deep mud of despair. Death was with her already, but still she wished for death.

She did not know that she wanted to be killed. Perhaps she was a murderee. She took off the mauve turban and ran her thin hands through her hair.

After she had clocked out and we were walking through that underground passage on our way to the canteen shed, Mabs ran after us. 'I forgot to tell you,' she said, 'Joe found the present wot Ritzie gave me and he threw the handkerchief on the railway line and the powder puff down the lav.'

II

Mrs Lloyd sat at one of the benches in the canteen with Chrissie and Mrs Jove. She talked about wages, when the bonus was due, the overtime money and the trade union rates. There was something of the stupid schoolmistress about Mrs Lloyd. She always mistook resentful silence for interested attention. A girl at the next table was frowning. 'There goes Mrs Lloyd laying down the law again,' she said. 'No wonder there was a revolution in Spain if she was there. It's silly her telling us about when we can get the war bonus and overtime and all that, because she doesn't know. Nobody knows, so it's no use talking, and anyhow we haven't got it.'

Mrs Jove went to help Ma behind the counter, seeming to have a wish to make herself indispensable. However tired she was she helped to cut the bread and hand out the plates. She took her singing way from the eating bench to the cooking counter. 'No kiddin', I'm just savin' all my love, just savin' all my love, honey, for you-ou-ou,' such bearded notes came out from her poor thin pretty face. She sang as deep as the red-hot momma and as nostalgic as the black-suited, red-scarfed White Russian women in the nightclubs of last war days. From behind the counter her head and shoulders showed, a lock of hair had fallen to the centre of her forehead. Waiting here for the workers to come up and get their tea she looked like a lonely colt staring out over a stable door. Soon she started to cut bread and butter at a great speed. She thought she did this better than anyone else. She thought, too, that it would give her a sort of staff status. Sometimes she went and sat beside Sid or Flash Jim or Dick Strauss. She put a thin arm round one of their shoulders and swung her legs backwards and forwards under the bench in time to some tune she was humming. But the white-coated men never responded to her; perhaps it was because they knew that she could not get much rest from the lifelong 'rather rough deal'. The knowledge that she had started 'a bit far down the street' came back often in her memory. There was a sort of tough martyrdom about her which might have become a psychological snare, she might enforce a fierce militant loyalty because she was so quick to complain. She would come up to one of the white-coated men and say, 'That feller over there has been making the same old pun on my name. You know, "By Jove!" Oh, I'm sick of him', and Alfred would answer, 'Did he, by Jove, Mrs Jove!' A few hours later she might storm Alfred's desk again. 'Look here, is it necessary for those two girls to take so long making the tea. Chrissie and I brought it up in ten minutes last night and they've been down there half an hour', and Sid would answer, 'Here they come now, bringing the tea along they are', so that Flash Jim said, 'Good old Sid staved off another shindy.' Mrs Jove was not a troublemaker, but quick tempered because she had not been free from anxiety long enough for her to ease up on this surface hostility. She worked hard at Braille's, hoping to make a success and get on to a higher pay roll. She was putting in for a stretch of security.

When she had finished helping with the bread and butter and handing out the food, she came back to the eating bench. Her friend Chrissie was sitting bland-masked while Mrs Lloyd talked. 'Let me see, who is absent to-night?' She looked round the room. 'Oh, the young wife is here, she stayed out a night last week; but the girl they call Feather isn't here. English people are very lazy.'

Mrs Jove opened her attaché case and took out a beef sandwich.

'What are you eating now?' Mrs Lloyd asked.

'It's a sandwich,' said Chrissie.

'English people are always eating.'

Mrs Jove took out a second beef sandwich and ate it with angry jaws.

Chrissie was helpful to Mrs Jove because she was more calm, and the reason for this might be that she had more security in her life. She looked less tough, but she was in fact less vulnerable. She had a gay carefree manner, a facile kindliness.

A uniformed sergeant on Home Guard duty was shaving over the counter with a white towel flung over his shoulder. Mrs Chance complained. 'Well, fancy shaving like that in here. What will they be doing next?'

'Oh, well,' said Chrissie, 'Sarge hasn't got any other place to shave; he's just a big kid, Sarge is.'

One of the women called out, 'Say, Sarge, we ought to pay entertainment tax for you,' and Mrs Jove said suddenly, 'The sergeant is a naughty boy; when I came in to-night he kissed me.'

Her friend Chrissie laughed 'Ugh-huh-huh' on a high note as if she didn't believe it, as if it must be an extravagant joke.

Mrs Chance was talking about an air raid. 'They got a shelter — every one of the people maimed or killed. Then there was another crash, and I told my husband "That's no ordinary common or garden bomb", and it wasn't either. It was a bomber plane they brought down. They took the crew prisoner; most of them were young boys.'

'They're just a lot of kids,' said splay-hearted Chrissie.

When we got back upstairs Mabs was next to me on the

same job. She went straight back into the talk.

'Let me see now, what happened after that,' she said. 'Well, I went with a good few before I met Joe and started to go with him. You know my sister Evie is going to marry Bill. He used to be Joe's mate, and I used to go with him. That's how I met Joe, see. Funny him and Joe being in trade together, and now he's marrying my sister Evie. Course I didn't trouble much about him after I met Joe, that was how he and Evie got talking and sort of got along together. My sister Evie was evacuated to the country, now she wants to come back. Our Mum don't want her back. She's always a trouble. We've had some peace since she's been away. Our Mum wishes she'd stop away. You see, Evie sort of resents me because I used to go with Bill, can't forget it like, she can't. She's always making trouble. She said that Bill told Joe, they used to be mates like I said, she told him as Bill had told Joe about me, see. How I'd been with a good many and wouldn't stay with no man long, and she said, my sister Evie did, that Bill hated me now, couldn't bear the sight of me, she said he couldn't; but that's not true, because he always speaks to me when he sees me. I've a good mind to ask him straight out, to say to him, "Look here, Bill, how is it you speak to me if you can't bear the sight of me?" But somehow I never have asked him.'

Mabs didn't stop talking, but Nan on my other side gave me another of her long, slow shut-eye winks.

'And another thing about Evie,' said Mabs, 'she's always throwing out snacks. When I was getting married to Joe, you know when I went with him, when he was courting me, see, she made my life a misery for a fortnight, always throwing out snacks. You see, I wasn't married in white, we had a quiet wedding Joe and me, because nobody has these white weddings no more in war-time, they don't. Well, there goes Evie talking about how she's going to be married in white, how she's going to have blossoms in her hair and attendants and two page boys to follow. Well, she'll be too old to be married at all by then; she'll be a grandmother by the time she gets all she wants. Still she goes on with her talk, making me miserable. I don't mind someone who says something straight out, but not Evie, that's not her way, always throwing out snacks she is. Of course, if I wanted to be nasty I could say to her about Bill, "You're only getting left-off goods, seeing as how I used to go with him before I threw him over for Joe." I could say that if I wanted to be nasty.'

Mabs got back to the chronicling of her life with Joe. It was a series of true stories about a lot of lies. Mabs's voice took on a half-dead tone now as she ploughed back over the arable of lies. 'See, one day I said to Joe that I was going to work at the factory, not here, but the factory I worked at in peace-time. Course, I wasn't going to the factory at all that day. It was only what I told him. Well, he come up to meet me outside the factory, seeing as I'd told him I was going to be there, and blowed if he didn't meet a girl what worked with me. So he says to her, "Mabs come out yet?" and she answers, "Mabs ain't been to work to-day, she hasn't, and she don't come Saturdays." "You sure?" he says. "She told me she was coming up today." Well, soon after this I come out of the pub and when I sees this girl saying good-bye to Joe as she got on the bus, I thought "Oh, Gawd, she's told him." I wasn't 'arf frightened. I began to run as steady as I could because I'd had a drop too much, and when I caught up to him he said, "Why did you tell me you were going to work to-day when you never," and I said, "Well, I bin there, honest I have, Joe." And then he told me that my friend had said as I didn't go Saturdays, so I said, "Yes, I bin there, but she never seen me because it's a small shift on Saturdays and I was in another part of the building." And he said, Joe did, "Now you can't lie yourself out of this. I won't 'arf bash you when I get you home, me lady."'

Nan listened and I listened. Neither of us knew the reason for the endless speaking out of lies which had become a part of Mabs's life. Perhaps it was all for the sake of a bashing which never quite came off — the bash to be — Joe was a good hearted boy. But Mabs had a deep despair in her. She felt she was only half a person. In some way the bashing might kill her and so take from her the responsibility of life which was too great.

Mabs finished the job of work. She started to read us some letters from Joe.

'I said I would bash you, but I won't. I love you, my darling wife; if anything happened to you, I don't know what I should do. I only said I should knock the daylight out of you because you made me wild. Why do you do it? that's what I can't make out, why do you do it?'

'You see,' said Mabs, 'Joe said he would bash me, but when I got home I found this note instead.' Mabs put the bits of metal into the tray ready to take to the shelves near Alfred's desk. While she was counting them over, Nan said to me, 'Fancy showing them letters. I'd rather die than show a letter what someone had written me, wouldn't you?'

We noticed now that Joe was watching us from behind a milling machine at the end of the room. He looked round in a one-eyed way like a pirate in a film. He held a spanner in his hand.

'Lor, there's Joe,' Mabs said. 'I've got a recipe for a bread-and-butter puddin' here, so I shall pretend I was showing you that, instead of his letters, see. Here it is. "Soak puddin' well for two and a half hours."' She walked over to Joe.

Nan said, 'She talks about him and he talks about her. She's a funny girl, she's screw-ie. I think they both are.'

I was curious to know what Joe would do when he found out that Mabs had been reading his notes aloud to her workmates.

'Oh,' said Nan, 'he won't 'arf annihilate her.'

In a little while Mabs came back. She spoke in a low toneless voice.

'I showed Joe the recipe for the bread-and-butter puddin'. I told him it was that we was reading.' Her green eyes were without zest. 'He berlieved me,' she said.

Nan began to sing, 'You'll be a Woolworth heiress yourself some day, don't you berlieve it.'

Mabs retied the mauve turban round her head; she leant towards the machinery as if inciting it to murder. There had been a night when her hair got caught in one of the wheels. She had been dragged closer to the machine at a great speed. 'One of the fellers turned it off quick. I didn't 'arf scream, but it took a lot of me hair, look.' She opened the blue bag and took out a great tuft of hair. 'I never want that to happen again, so now I always wear the turban,' she told us in a cast-out, lonely voice.

'Here,' said Sid, 'haven't you got a job? Oh, you've finished them. Well, there's something over there wants doing.' He walked down the workshop at his usual intense speed. 'Follow me.'

When we went home in the morning it was very cold and dark. There was a thin drizzle of rain. We waited for the bus, we saw lights flaring up in the north.

'That's air raid,' one of the workers said.

'You said that yesterday morning.'

'He says that every morning,' Green-pants remarked.

'It's Tube station,' said one of the North-country operators. 'Tube station always shows lights like that, I reckon it's electricity and cold air; don't you reckon it's that, Sonny?'

Mabs and Joe stood waiting for the bus. She wore the mauve flowered hat. She kept twisting the mauve turban round in her hand. She was very cold and her rake-like teeth chattered together. She leant near Joe, saying, 'Wish we was home, Joe.'

'Here, Mabs,' he said, 'stop that shivering; it's cold, we know, but you don't need to shiver like that. Stop that shaking, Mabs, you'll shake the hat off my head.'

Thursday

The next night some of the workers failed to clock on at nine. This was because they were unable to get through the heavy air raid.

Flash Jim was two hours late, Mabs and Joe were absent altogether, but Feather had arrived at half-past eight. She walked in well equipped with top coat, haversack and the 'tin hat' which was slung over her right shoulder by its chin strap. Her hair was newly done and it chickendowned round her head in a way that was not as simple as it looked.

Sid was getting one of the machines into good running order. 'Hullo, bin on your honeymoon?'

'I couldn't get here last night. Bronchitis,' Feather explained.

'Never heard of him,' said Sid.

After Feather had got into her overall she found Sid again. He was setting up some work.

'Do find me a job. I got here hours early this evening.' Sid screwed up his eyes to stare through the smoke of his cigarette at the micrometer in his hand. 'I just seen you come in,' he said.

Feather was in an exalted mood of high optimism, she was pretending to be a forewoman. 'What! this job not finished yet,' she said to one of the operators near her. 'What do you think you're paid for? Don't you know there's a war on?' and the woman answered back in the same charading tone. 'You've said it, Mam, like hell you have.'

Feather worked on a lathe; the work she did was really five operations, but in a little while she worked with such smoothness that it seemed to be only one simple action.

A brown-skinned woman who had worked in a boot shop stared at Feather. 'I got to do that same job as you,' she said, 'Sid's just setting it up for me,' and then she said, 'Excuse my saying so but your hair is done lovely to-night, it is really, you look ever so well. I think it done you good staying out last night.'

'I had this sore throat, no wonder the English people are tough. Look at the winters we go through and still live.'

'That's right. How are you off for cigarettes, dear?' '

Feather gave her a handful.

'Oh, I only need one.'

'No, go on, I've brought plenty this evening.'

'I hope I'll be able to get some in the canteen and give them back to you, if not will tomorrow evening do?' The girl read the name on the cigarette. 'Don't know if I'll be able to get these though; what sort do you like, dear? Those I had last night be all right for you?'

'Yes, I like them.' Feather remembered the time when she had first come to the factory. Any of the workers would have given her a cigarette then, but they would not have accepted one from her; in those early days they would have said 'No thanks, I've got some smokes of me own', but now it had been decided in silence that Feather was well liked. At times she was given over to these bouts of irresponsible, irrepressible high spirits. This pleased the people around her because it gave them a veiled view of some other sort of life of grace and leisure, an existence free from that endless economic drag that was like an ache of the inner stomach.

Feather thought that her workmates reacted in an instinctive way towards strangers which was more dignified than the manner of the bourgeois world 'where you get so much talk going on for or against an individual and nothing decided at the end of it'. Feather also said to me, 'Have you noticed the way they all act here towards that questioning bore Mrs Lloyd, when she looms up with one of her useless questions they don't answer, they simply walk away; it's much better, quicker and cleaner.'

Soon after eleven Flash Jim came in. He clocked on, got into his white coat and began walking round on his inspection work.

A young day-shift engineer who had just come off Home Guard duty was talking to Nan at one of the lathes near the end of the centre work bench. She had been laughing as she worked and listened to his talk, but now her face wore an ill-at-ease expression. The Home Guard boy was leaning over the machinery like a caricature of a drunken guardsman breathing down a barmaid's neck, and then suddenly Nan slapped his face, quick as a cat at play. Nan's slap was not a hard hit, but it was a boomerang blow, so speedily sent and quick to return that it was difficult for the boy to be sure that Nan's hand had ever left the lathe. He went on talking as if nothing had happened, but the memory of the slap stayed like a brake on the back of his mind.

Feather, who had happened to look up and see this happen, thought, 'She's like those high-class cricketers who can field and throw back in one movement.'

Jim walked by Nan. 'Can't you go down to the canteen or something, or do your Home Guard duty outside? Have you been talking to that girl all night? Why can't you let her get on with her work?'

The boy answered, 'All right, Jim. I'm just waiting for Corporal Strauss to give me the key of the cupboard downstairs so's I can get some Oxo heated up.'

He went away, using the butt end of his rifle on the ground as an emphasis to his going.

'These fellers get on my nerves,' said Jim, 'always underfoot. I don't know what they'd do if they found themselves stranded on a desert island.' Jim said this so often that we wondered if he had ever been on a desert island himself, but no one had the courage to ask him this. We had to be content with knowing that he would at least have liked to be shipwrecked and live for a time as a lonely 'Crusoe' pioneer, cursing the crew that brought him back to civilization.

Feather came up to Jim. She walked rather on her toes because the exalted mood of high spirits was still with her.

'The bit of work I was doing has bent the knife of the lathe. I have fixed it again myself but I'm not sure if it's right, because I haven't got a micrometer. Could you help me?'

Jim answered, also smiling, 'I'd do anything to help yew.'

He shuddered as another Home Guard boy went clattering by.

'This noise gets on my nerves,' said Feather.

Sometimes it was like that in the factory. The machinery noise never ceased, but it was the sound of a squeaking boot or a dropped cup, the noise within the noise, the unwarranted attack that was so painful.

'Those fellers get on my nerves, too,' said Jim. 'That one that was over there shouldn't have been in here at all by rights. He's supposed to go downstairs when he comes off his Home Guard duty. Nan should have told me that he was getting objectionable and I'd have given him a punch on the nose. That's all she had to do, just let me know and then he'd have got his punch on the nose.' So spoke thin, well-dressed Jim, as if the punch on the nose was something official, like a confirmatory copy of a telegram: 'That's quite in order. You'll receive your punch on the nose in the morning, Sir.'

Feather talked to Jim in her high-life teasing voice.

'I notice that you didn't come in at nine o'clock this evening, Jim.'

'No, as a matter of fact I was in two minds about coming in at all to-night.' Jim was dealing with the bit in the lathe like a dentist with a delicate tooth. 'I don't think you use enough oil when you're working on this. Don't be afraid of it. Splash it on with this brush before you switch the machine on, it gets too hot otherwise. Well, you see, we had an incident down our way tonight. There was some people trapped in a building that had been hit at Croydon where I live, so we were getting them out, but I didn't fancy it. I had my crash helmet, so the others seemed to think that I could go in, but to tell you the truth I just didn't fancy it at all.'

'Did you get the people out?' Feather asked.

'Yes, we got out five of them — two were all right, one was badly smashed up, but the other two were dead.'

'Were there any more left in the house?'

'I don't know. After the Civil Defence people arrived I didn't hang around to see.' He said again, 'I didn't fancy it somehow', and walked on round the workshop on inspection.

On these nights the North-country woman and Mr Peigne worked near each other, she on a large capstan machine and he with a milling machine. Sometimes she brushed the sweat from her face with one of her great hands and pushed the straight hair away from her eyes. She seemed then like some member of a strange half-bear, half-woman tribe. Near her, Mr Peigne, black cap on his head, continued to look closely at his work. They did not have to ask the white-coated men for any help. They went through the ninehour night shift, and then in the early morning the North-country woman put on her red woollen hood and Mr Peigne took off his black cap and overalls, hooked his folded umbrella over his arm, clocked out and walked down to the cross-roads to wait for the home-going bus. Feather, whose moods alternated between exaltation and despondency, had long bouts of fatigue and boredom before she became high-spirited again. She was affectionate to people and then suddenly they got on her nerves. She was too concerned about herself, but now as she watched the North-country woman and white-collared Mr Peigne being able, in such a quiet way, to do what they had to do, working as they were asked to work, she felt a deep respect for them. The trouble of getting to the factory, the long hours of work, the sickening smell of the machine oil, the noise, the bad and inadequate food, the jazz-hum singing of the girls, the buses which stopped before the night shift started, the long cold journey home and the monotony of the work all seemed worth while to Feather at this moment, because she was proud to be with people like Mr Peigne and the North-country giantess. This was not a lonely night for Feather, because her high spirits carried her along. Sometimes she had been aware of a sense of loneliness; at Braille's there was no one with whom she had ever shared the same sort of life. She had often been poor, but her way of being without money had been a different way to theirs. Feather had had a bad time on not much credit, and they had had a bad time on no cash. It was the difference between restlessness and fatigue.

Later on in the canteen some of the workers had news of the girl who had been sent home. 'Maree's got a job again,' they said. 'It's a job nearer her home. She likes it all right.'

This seemed to cheer them up. 'She likes it fine!' they said.

Mrs Jove and Chrissie had become so tired of the Spanish woman now that they moved away from her altogether. They had taken to sitting at a bench near the doorway beside Green-pants and Grey-pants, but this did not daunt Mrs Lloyd from her talk-questioning. She shouted across from the bench where she sat alone to the one next her. Feather had some sort of tonic capsules prescribed for her by a French doctor. She always forgot to take them at the right time, so that now she swallowed one quickly with her second cup of tea. Mrs Lloyd said, 'So you take a pill, eh?'

Feather replied, 'Yes, that's it, a pill.'

'What is it for?'

'I don't know,' said Feather.

'You take a pill and you don't know what it is for?' Mrs Lloyd gave out her wide-mouthed demanding laugh.

'Why should I know, I'm not a doctor.'

Mr Peigne told them now that he did not believe in doctors. He thought that either they took your money and did nothing, or else they experimented on you for nothing. 'Since I've given up doctors,' he said, 'I've several pounds more in my pocket at the end of each year and I've kept my health as well, so I haven't done so badly.'

The unemployed man, seeing that time was getting on, took his boots off the bench. A gentle smile flickered across his face.

Feather had read the notice which had been put under the clock: 'I have taken it on myself to postpone the meeting for ten days, when I will put the Union proposals up to the Board and will bring you back acceptance or amendments. Signed: Chas. Cartwright, Works Manager.'

She asked what it meant.

Sonny said, 'Oh, just something Chas is trying to fix up.'

'But I thought this was not supposed to be a Union shop.'

'It isn't really, but some of the fellows are Union members all the same. You see, Union shops won't employ non-Union men — but it works the other way round, if you get my meaning. A non-Union shop gets a lot of Union men working for them. I think Chas is a Union man himself. Anyhow, he tries to work in with them and get everyone a square deal.'

'Then he's not so bad.'

'Who?'

'Chas.'

'Oh, he's probably a very decent fellow, but I don't like him, of course, just because he *is* the works manager.'

Sonny was very fond of Feather. This was because she was gay and also because she was never able to work out the right bus route from her home to her work. Sonny was always telling her how to get from one place to the other and this made him feel grown up.

Feather said, 'I don't think Alfred noticed that I wasn't here last night.'

'I did,' said Sonny.

Feather smiled. 'So did Sid, unfortunately.'

'Anyhow, the office upstairs will know that you didn't clock on. They'll dock you the evening's pay.'

'I don't mind that so much. An evening's sleep is worth the world to me. But what I do mind is losing my pay and getting these lectures from the white-coated men as well.'

'That's right,' said Mrs Chance.

Suddenly Sonny started to speak about the Austrian, German and American boys with whom he had made friends.

'You've heard of the Youth Hostels, well, some of these foreign fellers stayed at ours. There was all sorts that came and stayed there. Belgians, Italians, and all. They're a good thing, these Youth Hostels, honest they are a good thing. I met an American University professor at one of them and I still write to him and he writes back to me sometimes, all the way from America. I want to travel right over the world like this. You see, it's the only way for people such as us. I shouldn't care to be like my Mum and Dad. They've never been away from the place where they were born, almost not been out of the street they lived in since they were married. I shouldn't like that.'

Alfred was showing the other white-coated men a trick with two pennies and a saucer. The noise of the pennies scratching against the saucer was almost intolerable to Feather.

Sonny began to speak about his friend John. 'You see, my friend John went to fight in Spain. I saw him off at the station. It was a foggy night, but all the station was lit up so that somehow it did seem bright and hopeful. He went with the International Brigade. We thought everything was going to be different. John thought him and his friends fighting would change things. Funny how you see things all different sometimes. Seems as if it can't last, not at that pace it can't, and everything has got to slip back to the old ways again. John was happy going off and I wished I'd been with them. That night when I got home I wrote in my diary, "Saw John off to Spain to-night. Wonder if I've seen him for the last time." He came back after he got ill in the trenches. Some sort of chest complaint, it was. You know, we never spoke of that night at the station, seemed as if we couldn't find the words for all we'd hoped then. Not that I'm one to get myself mixed up in politics, mind you. All the same, I wish I'd gone with John and the other fellows. Must have been a good experience being out there and knowing what it was all for.'

The North-country woman woke. She sat up as if she'd been on a long train journey and was happy to be arriving in a new town.

'Ar always think second half of shift is better than first,' she said.

Back in the workshop Alfred told Feather, 'I think he's gone off, Adolf has. I shouldn't be surprised to hear the All Clear.'

'I should,' said Feather. 'We can't hear anything in this noise.'

'Oh well, one of the fellers on guard will tell me.'

Alfred was wondering again about Feather and what she had done before the war.

'Do you know we have all kinds of people here. Why, there's a girl on the day shift who in private life is —' Alfred paused, catching his breath to get back his composure before speaking out on the high note of good life. 'She is or was a receptionist at the Grand Gild Palace Hotel.' He did not say, 'What do you think of that?' but he let the thought smash through the lenses of his spectacles. For him it was strange and rather romantic to think of a girl grand-hotel receptionist coming down to the tough workshop of machines, dirty overalls, oil, bits of metal, noise, the canteen shed, the old cooked-up potatoes, bubble and squeak, and instead of two veg. only two Home Guards sleeping on a bench, while the sergeant shaves and one of the boy workers calls out, sucking his teeth in between the words, 'Any steak-and-kiddley puddin', Ma; any steak-and-kiddley puddin'?'

'Of course,' said Alfred, 'she's on the day shift.'

'Oh, the day shift.'

Alfred knew that Feather had been abroad. He wanted to ask her about it. After he had tested the work, he went away; but in a little while he came back again. 'Can you speak any of the languages of these places you've been to?'

'No, not much. French with fluency, a very mediocre German and some slang Italian. That's about all I know.'

'I've always thought I could speak languages,' Alfred said, 'I seem to be able to pick up words and pronounce them easily.'

Alfred carried a monster file in his hand. He looked down at it now as if from embarrassment he might begin to manicure his nails with the 'Frankenstein' file. 'I've always wanted to travel, but for that you need a lot of time and a lot of money. I've hardly ever been abroad, only to Belgium and once we went to Italy for a week. Of course, I've been nearly everywhere in England.'

This conversation seemed strange to Feather, because she too was continually thinking that she wanted to travel. She did not consider the capitals of Europe, or the small fishing villages where smartness had long since overtaken simplicity; or Salzburg in season where the vulgarity of the rich visitors made the life seem like delicate food eaten off an ornate plate.

Poor Feather feared discomfort and until now had shied away from it. She felt doomed, as if she had been born at the wrong time in the wrong place of the wrong parentage. As she worked she had to stare straight at the revolving knife and the face plate which was also spinning round at a great rate. They moved much faster than the signalling system between eye and brain, so that they seemed to be two almost still surfaces as quiet as a lake in a large field.

Fatigue loosened up Feather's thoughts, so that she became conscious of another film of memory being run through her mind. It was like re-living some scenes from her life while swimming under water.

Feather could not select these scenes at will any more than it would have been possible for an audience to alter the sequence of a film while it was in the process of being run through. For a long time she had censored any thoughts of her early life, but now through this haze of fatigue there came to her again a clear image of the house owned by her father and mother.

In those days it had been possible for her to look out of a high nursery window down a long avenue of trees through a park. At the end the sky seemed like a large expanse of sea and the cars which bobbed along a distant road strange boxshaped sea craft. In this privately owned land, grandiose and spacious, the cattle appeared as small as dogs and the pet dogs themselves dwindled down to rats.

Now, free from the anxiety of childhood, the early life scenery observed from the present took on a Walt Disney friendliness. The moorhens speed-boated across the lake, the green-headed drake waltzed sideways near the water's edge, and the swans dreadnoughted slowly round without accepting the passing of time. The girl herself rode about the gardens on her wooden bicycle. The birds sang, dragon flies airplaned overhead, the pet dogs Pluto'd across the lawn in their clumsy friendliness and the cats smiling broadly prowled down the paths.

Feather's cousins came swooping down to stay when their parents were abroad, and as was natural to children they all had a confused idea of ownership. They used to think that the motor car which the other servants called Mills's car really belonged to the chauffeur Mills. They supposed that of his own free will he took their parents out in it from time to time, and that this was kind of him.

The children also had a great admiration for a red-haired gardener called Reynolds. They were impressed by his strength, his skill and good looks. They used to watch him working, but when he grew tired of their following him about through the greenhouses and into the potting shed with their wearisome questions, he would say, 'Nah, then, slide orf afore I cop yer one acrost the ear'ole.'

It was not until the children were much older that they realised their parents would have been deeply shocked had they known the employed man talked in this way to the 'sweet young sahibs'.

This inherited country place was like a principality, Feather's father and mother, minor royalties, and her eldest cousin, a princeling who early showed signs of developing all the traits of a bad king. In the village the men and boys sometimes fought with each other; there were several drunkards, a few cases of incest, and even an attempted murder, but in the idiom of the day 'it was all amongst friends'. Up at the big house the land-owner was supposed to be responsible for the villagers, beyond him there was the king and England was an island; then there were the Colonies, the Empire itself and afterwards God, who was also a sportsman and, no doubt, spoke English at all times. This seemed something like the general ideology of those times.

However, it did not last. Feather's father and mother could not get themselves into the field of change. They quarrelled, drank too much and set an ever increasing store by their, now ill-suited, standards.

Feather had grown up painfully in an atmosphere of confusion, disorder and fierce warring egoisms. Her parents seemed to be enslaved to a desire to destroy each other. Their quarrels crescendoed up in shrillness. They argued about money, troubled about income tax and gave themselves up to the anxieties of land tax, overdrafts and the difficulty of letting their large house to rich tenants.

There was a grand good-bye to it all at the time of the wedding. Feather's cousin Sarah married an incredible young man called Charlie. He did not seem to be able to trouble about anything except the way he played golf and whether he did it better or not quite so well as the last time he had walked round with the clubs. He also liked to leg it round a racecourse looking at jumps, and on a large map of his home shire he marked the places where his horse's hoofs had landed in, or out, of a particular field. Charlie looked sleepy, with half-closed eyes, but out of this slow mask there came forth from time to time a great neighing laugh.

Because Charlie was rich he decided to lease a house for himself and his bride, while Feather's father and mother took themselves off abroad to continue their quarrelling and money-talk in a more confined space.

As it turned out, there was concealed inside this apparently cardboard character of Sarah's husband, an extreme, although inarticulate, sensitiveness. One day out shooting he suddenly threw his gun to the ground and waving his arms up and down at a great speed, while standing on tiptoe as if trying to fly, he screamed, 'I'm a pheasant, shoot me, shoot me!' For a long time after this incident Charlie had been in a lunatic asylum and Feather wondered if he had ever got well again. She thought now that of all the people she knew who were able to boast of their unhappiness, hardly any of them could have a card to play against the inner misery of unsound, inarticulate Charlie. Since then the country house had been taken over as a home for inebriates, and all this life was finished.

As these memories flicked through Feather's mind, she knew that she could never be disturbed by them again because she knew that she was no longer the same person who had lived through this. None of it could happen again. It was not only a dead life, but one that had been lopped off from her present existence like a useless tree branch.

The factory workers were stacking up the metal pieces again. Miss Perry was on her way round with the check cards. There were only ten more minutes before the hour of clocking off. Mabs, her teeth chattering with fatigue, was droning through them her early morning theme song, 'Roll on half-past six; oh, roll on half-past six'.

Friday

Friday night was pay night. The pay was brought down from the office by one of Braille's daughters and handed over to Alfred.

Alfred walked round in his white coat looking like a nursery gardener with little pay envelopes like packets of seeds in a wooden tray. I was glad to get the money but there was something I dreaded about pay night. After Alfred had given over each wage packet with the operator's name and the sum enclosed written on the outside, an atmosphere of resentment and hostility went up quickly like a rise in temperature.

Mrs Jove looked carefully at the written figures on her sealed envelope. It was fourpence halfpenny short. She counted the money inside but it matched up with the outside figure. 'Wot the hell they playing at!' The brown-faced woman from the peace-time boot shop said, 'Every bloomin' time the wage packets are a bit different; well, you don't know where you are, do you? All I know is, I'm not being paid what I was engaged for. Last week I clocked in one night at ten past nine, only ten minutes late I was, and that was because the bus coming up swerved to avoid a dog and ran into a lamp. We got out, the railway men going on night shift and all, and the bus wouldn't start up again, so we had to wait for another one to come along. You don't expect that, do you — a dog loitering across the road as lah-de-dah as you please when a lot of people got to get to work of an evening.'

'Maybe he didn't know there was a war on,' said Chrissie.

'Well, I ran up the road and got in ten minutes after the hour. Of course, I knew they'd dock me the quarter, but I didn't expect them to take off half an hour. It's not right, is it?'

Mrs Chance asked Feather, 'Is your wage packet OK, dear?'

'Yes, I think so.' Feather didn't have to trouble about these questions of fourpence. She had never had to do this. She had owed sums of money in which no fourpence had any place. 'You see,' Feather said, 'I was absent a whole night this week, so of course I miss that.'

Green-pants said, 'We don't get overtime and we always work Sunday mornings. Last week we worked Sunday night instead of Saturday, but there was no talk of overtime pay. And what about bonus? the war bonus, production bonus, or whatever it is? We ain't seen none of that. There was a piece about it in the papers last week, but we ain't got no production bonus here.'

Always it went on, this petty preoccupation with petty rights, with petty packets of money, when one letter, one interview or one conversation could have straightened it out. But they preferred to peck on like nervous birds; these women preferred to peck and feared to bite. The skilled engineers did not grumble about their wage packets, nor the semi-skilled boy workers. They knew the problem was open to discussion and a settlement could be reached, and in the meantime, although they were not getting high wages they were at least getting their agreed wages.

Mr Peigne said, 'My wage packet was inaccurate one week so I came up during the day and saw a young lady in the office. I explained to her what was wrong, and it was put right. Of course, I missed my sleep, but it's always better to know where you are.'

On this pay evening Alfred sent Peggy Perry on her white-faced way round the workshop asking the women if their wage packets were right or wrong, and where they were wrong. She took down notes of what they said, and during the second half of the shift, the rumour raced round that those workers who had got through the probationary period and whose production output was up to standard, would become due for the war bonus and also for a piece-work bonus.

In the canteen the North-country woman had shown us a second wage packet in which was an extra seven and sixpence for piece work. 'I never expected that neither,' she said, 'but when I saw I was getting two wage packets this week I had to say it was welcome.'

Mrs Ex-Pastry Cook said, 'It isn't as if they paid our fares. For me it's fourpence halfpenny a bus ride here. You've got to think of all that too, haven't you?' She began to work out sums in her head. If the war bonus came in and the piecework bonus and the Sunday overtime as well as the overtime which we were already getting for night work, it would be possible on the sixty hour week to reach a wage of just over £4. 'Then as you've got to take off fares and food, that brings it down to £3 5s. you're actually getting. Me rent's 19s. 6d, a week, that leaves £2 5s. 6d., which at the present cost of living is worth about 25s. I've got to pay for all me clothes, heating, light and cigarettes — it don't leave much for going to the pictures of a Saturday afternoon, do it?'

One of the younger girls told us, 'I've got to give twenty-five shillings a week to Mum.'

'When you come down to it, there's not a lot in it,' said sour-faced Green-pants.

'Of course,' said the brown-faced boot girl, 'there's prospects here. Oh, definitely. The longer you stay the more you get. This is considered to be good money. Girls at my training centre said there weren't many factories giving as good money as Braille's, I mean not for semi-skilled workers. Most of them only manage to knock up two pounds a week with overtime and all.'

'Goodness,' said Feather, 'I thought Braille's was a sort of swing back to Victorian factory life.'

'In one sense yes, and in another sense no,' Mr Peigne explained. "Course they haven't any of these modern comforts here, like they have in the modern factories. But

Mr Braille isn't a bad fellow. I come up in the bus with him one night. There's no side about him, you know.' Mr Peigne looked thoughtful. 'You seen any of these modern factories,' he said. 'I went up to look at one. They've got a welfare worker there, a nurse. You know what I mean, one of these sisters in uniform to deal with accidents, influenza and suchlike. They got a restaurant for your time off and the lights are shaded just right on to the machinery so as it doesn't make your eyes ache. Besides this, they've got beautiful cloakrooms with hot water and soap and all.'

'Well, we've got nothing like that here,' said Mrs Jove.

'We did ought to have it,' said Green-pants. 'We did ought to really if others have it. There's no rest room here, no food, no sister in uniform, no nothing. It's supposed to be a Government order, but we ain't got it all the same.'

'Oh, well,' spoke up one of the semi-skilled men workers, 'isn't that democracy all over for you.'

'Yes, it's a mucking muddle.'

'Well, people are better off than what they'd be under Hitler.'

'We know that, but it's a mucking muddle all the same.'

Yet, with each day the workers became more happy. There was the hope of better money and with it the hope of being able to just 'manage along'. There was a great capital of comradeship to be drawn on. Mrs Chance was quickly ceasing to regret the better living which she had lost. She would call out to the workers, 'How ya doing, sister?' There was Sid, who had a saintly and poetic nature without jealousy or self-interest. There was Mr Peigne with his decency and patriotism, who never missed a minute of his time at the factory and worked on his allotment all Sunday.

'I haven't studied these new-fangled ideas on politics. All I know is that the Germans are still the Germans and we got to beat them again, otherwise nobody's going to get a chance of a decent life.' Even Mrs Pastry Cook had become more cheerful, so that sometimes she threw out to her workmates a thin smile, a smile like a woven net.

As we went back upstairs from the canteen on this evening, Mrs Jove two-stepped along, singing:

Good King Charlie had Nell Gwyn,
Rudyard Kipling had Gunga Din,
But I ain't got nobody,
Nobody at all.

She put her arm round Feather and waltzed her round.

Alfred called out, 'Quiet, please. You know he's still over.'

'Well, even if he is, he can't hear us singing all that way up there,' said Chrissie.

Feather had to finish her tapping job. There was something the matter with the belt of the machine. Sid started to mend it. Balancing on the ledge like those circus animals who are taught to stand up on a tennis ball, he stared down into the base of the machinery, twisting the belt round, switching the machinery on and then off again. Bitter-smiling fair-haired Flash Jim was walking by on inspection work. He thought Sid looked very funny.

'Well, Sid, how are you?'

Sid looked back at Jim through the smoke of his cigarette without saying anything.

It seemed to Jim that Feather was too fond of the second foreman in charge. 'Say, Sid, why can't you let her mend her own blooming machine,' he said in his exasperated way.

'Well, you know how it is with these blonde Venuses.'

Jim's teeth showed in his resentful smile. 'Are yew a blonde Venus?' he asked Feather.

'So says the second foreman in charge,' Feather answered.

Her gloves were torn and soaked in the machine oil. She took them off now and put them down on the ledge of the machine.

'Why didn't you tell me,' Sid said. 'I got some old gloves over there you could have had.'

I was sitting at one of the machines between Mabs and Feather, so I heard this three-cornered conversation between Sid, Feather and Flash Jim, who now walked away on his work looking as acid as if he had been nourished on vinegar fed to him from the end of a hat pin.

In the early part of the morning Mabs and Feather and I were all working at the same job; it was called reaming. We had to put each metal piece in the vice to hold it firm before twisting the reamer through it. The iron vices on the work bench had been set close together and so we could talk to each other as we worked. Feather was still in the same high spirits which even the monotony of this work could not kill.

Alfred came round to supervise some precision work of one of the boy-workers on the other side of the same bench.

Mabs's hands were so thin that they looked transparent, she was very tired and a depression had settled down on her spirits. 'He's still over with them damn bombers,' she said. 'One of these nights he'll get this factory and then it'll be curtains for all us poor saps.'

'No, don't you worry about that,' Alfred told her. 'There's lots of other factories besides ours for him to be after, only he don't know where they are.'

'Are they so well hidden?' asked Feather.

'They are; I could tell you where there's factories all over the countryside, places you'd never suspect, only of course I can't say where they are.'

'I thought you just said you could.'

'No, I could, but I'm not allowed to. See.'

A sudden concussion shook the metal bit out of my hand.

Feather said, 'It's those damn Fascists with their blasted bombs.'

Alfred looked puzzled. 'Fascists,' he repeated. 'Do you mean the Wops? We've had some of them over, I know; that was the last word, that was; we can stand anything but the idea of Wops coming over London; still, I expect old Mussolini will soon pack up altogether.' Alfred looked round the room as he talked to watch that the work was going well and that no one was in difficulties; he looked over the heads of the operators, stretching up his neck to see the far distant points of the workshop. He reminded me of those photographs I had looked at in doctors' waiting rooms, printed in shiny papered periodicals, the men and women of 'good family' photographed at steeplechase meetings. One of my aunts had a scrap-book made up from these illustrated papers; she used to cut a part of an advertisement out and paste it on to a part of one of the photographs and there you had the racehorse observer with caption below: 'Over the sticks. Sir William watches his horse round the course'; but why did the well-fed fellow wear a tweed coat over a pair of Victorian bicycling bloomers? Well, of course it was because my aunt had been at work with her scissors snipping from other pages. And now Alfred wore plus fours and over them his white coat and on his head the white helmet, because he had just been out to see that the sheds were safe and he had forgotten to take off the tin hat, so he had something of the same look as those composite pictures in the scrap-book of my eccentric aunt.

Feather asked Alfred if he was a pilot.

'No, but I should love to be. I should just love to join the RAF and get myself trained up to meet those fellows, those Nazis up there.' There was a great strength of sincerity in Alfred's voice when he said this. He was not politically conscious, but he wanted to try his strength in combat; he knew there was a certain vitality he needed which was missing from his life;

71

he felt he had been deprived of something to which he had right. 'But there it is, you see, I have to wear glasses and I am married.' He remembered about the white helmet now, he took it off and went back to his desk.

'Well, fancy old Alfred wanting to be a pilot,' Mabs said. 'I wish he'd been a pilot the night they come over the East End, I'll never forget that night. Yer see, we heard the airplanes coming over, but we never thought nothing of it cos they'd bin over before and done nothing, and then it started. Oh, it was wicked — my Mum screamed and my sister, the houses were coming down, I saw people's possessions lying out in the street and they had to watch their houses burn. They couldn't do nothing.'

'Why?' asked Feather. 'Weren't there enough fire engines?'

'Not for that lot there weren't. You see, we hadn't never had it like that before. My two friends wot worked with me at the factory were killed and their Mum too; it seems terrible when it's people you know and people you've worked with too, and a friend of my Mum's wot lives down the road she was killed, she'd got her nephew home on leave and his Dad and the three young children — they was all killed; oh it was wicked. I reckon they didn't ought to build houses round the docks like that. Well, of course he's bin over again since then. We was bombed out twice, me and Joe, and now we're going to live up this way; it's better to live near your work these days. But it's never bin as bad as it was that first night when he come over. It was wicked; I reckon if he was to come down in the East End after all he's done to us, there wouldn't be one single bit of him left.' This was the talk of Mabs. For her, Hitler was like a personified god of evil, this symbol was very strong. He was over, he was bombing the East End, he'd gone away again, he'd got tired of sending down flares and suchlike and gone off home, but he'd come back again to-morrow night. In the battle of Britain he came over, but one of them not-so-fine-nights he got a punch on the nose so he spun round and went back to Berlin damn-quick to have another think. Besides this great 'He', this fire-breathing, bomb-throwing, stinking jack-booted son of sweat, there were a variety of smaller enemies called 'they', only 'they' were much closer, always under foot or just round the corner; a set of empowered rats who built bad houses, muddled the insurance schemes, wilfully ignored the cost of living and were maliciously given over to making life more difficult.

After Mabs had been telling us about the night in the East End there was a long silence from talk. The operators went on with their reaming. An hour or two dripped by, this tedium of mechanical work, these sloe-eyed girls with their bent heads, their thoughts in an inner haze made me feel as if I had been transported to an oriental bazaar of the kind I had seen on the cinema before talk and colour got in. Mrs Lloyd was on the other side of the work bench rolling thin metal casings, like chop sticks, on a flat surface plate for testing. She had to bend her head over sideways to see if the chop-sticks were rolling evenly on the plate; with her black hair scraped back, her skin, which looked yellow in the factory light, and her wide mouth, she had the appearance of a native at work. These rounded pieces of metal were always a trouble. Mrs Lloyd had to hammer on the spots where they limped along instead of rolling evenly; it became rhythmic, hammer, hammer, roll along the surface plate, stare, hit, hammer and stare again.

Although the operators were so near each other they had no heart for talking now. They were very tired. It was six o'clock in the morning, it was Friday, the fifth night of the week. The first words I heard came from Mabs's rake-like mouth: 'Oh, roll on Sunday, day of rest, roll on'. When Mrs Lloyd heard this sung-out sentence, the prying expression crept back into her eyes. 'We have to work to produce the arms for the airplanes to fight the Nazis.' She had the tones of some home from-the-seas politician giving a world-to-day lesson over the air for tiny tots.

'We know that,' answered Mabs. 'But it don't prevent you getting tired, do it? Besides, although it's war now, I worked in a factory very much the same as this, in peace-time, see.' Everyone frowned on Mrs Lloyd, there was a convention against easy heroical talk and pat-off patriotism in the workshop; that way of yapping-out was all right for people who did not work at all, read in the newspapers sitting well back in their arm-chairs and thought, 'We are all in it together' because they listened to the radio news four times a day.

'After all,' said Mrs Chance, 'we work here to get away from thinking about the war, so what does she want to start in talking about it like that for?'

'Oh, just laying down the law, you know what she is.'

Mrs Lloyd did not hear what was being said about her because the hammer, roll, hit rhythm did not make her receptive to outside impressions. Sunk back in the semi-orientalism of mechanical work, she missed a sentence or two that might have set her questioning again.

Peggy Perry came round with the check cards to make up our production output. She had become friendly with the pastry cook and it was only to this woman that she ever spoke of her lover. 'It's ever so funny, when I'm going to see Mr Muir, Lewis you know, I feel sort of sick, strange isn't it how you are. I suppose it's just nervousness, really; perhaps I'll get a letter from Mr Muir when I get back home, but I always think I shan't, so then if I do it's a nice surprise.'

We handed Peggy our check cards. Mrs Lloyd stopped the infernal rolling of the metal chopsticks and started to count them over.

Feather dance-walked to Alfred's desk carrying a tin box full of finished work, but soon she came back slow-stepping and sad. 'I've only just heard about the unemployed man; to-night they gave him back his health and unemployment cards; they say he's not skilled enough, but I hear he used to be a skilled printer.' It was clear that Feather was deeply distressed by this news. The unemployed man had seemed so quiet and happy working by a kind of forge in the centre of the shop. 'I never quite understood what his work here really was,' said Feather.

'Oh, it was moulding; they say he's not skilled enough, but it's unfair on him, he done everything they asked him.'

'Funny, isn't it?' said Mrs Chance. 'Working in a place where you don't know rightly what's going on; first there was that young girl that was sent home in the air raid, and then the Scotch girl and her friend, and now this pore old feller.'

'Yes, might be one of us next.'

When Mr Peigne went out Feather went with him. They walked down the road together towards the bus. 'It's not so cold this morning.'

'No, do you think the unemployed man was very upset about being sacked?'

Mr Peigne shifted his umbrella from one arm to the other before answering. 'I'm inclined to think so, he had tears in his eyes when they told him. He seemed to like the work here all right and the night hours suited him. He was just getting into it and he'd been out of work a long time before this; he's a very decent kind of working man.'

The North-country woman overtook them. 'Lass has gone home the other way, she wants to stop in for breakfast with her auntie and uncle over Paddington way.'

Feather felt as if she also was out with her aunt and uncle by the seaside now. Mr Peigne and the North-country woman seemed suddenly to have become· very old, perhaps it was only their natural dignity which gave them an appearance of age.

'I don't know if the unemployed man will get another job.'

'Surely that's easy in war-time.'

'It's hard to say, mostly they want these young fellers under eighteen, they're strong and they don't need to pay them full rates.'

All gaiety had gone from Feather. 'Did you notice that he'd bought himself some new boot laces,' she said. 'He wore them for the first time to-night.'

Saturday

On this night I was free from the factory. Some of the workers were needed for the Sunday shift, and my name had been on the list.

I lived in a furnished flat in a street not far from the factory; most of these flats were empty now, so that the remaining tenants had to give one half evening each week to firewatching.

On this night there was a severe air raid, so that for a long time afterwards it was spoken of as 'the Saturday'.

There was a full moon and the two dogs locked in the flat of the woman next door, who had not yet come home, howled up at the sky through the open window, but soon after the siren sounded the dogs were silenced by the usual orchestra of city bombardment.

Through all the noise I could hear the clear notes of a penny whistle being played by the street musician who stood, each evening, at the end of the road where the shops started.

With incredible nonchalance he continued to go on with this work as if the happenings around did not concern him. It was a sad thing that a man, old and alone, should have to earn his living in this way, but now the whistling had taken on an enduring sound like the treble tune of thrush heard through a thunderstorm.

At this stage of the evening I was without fear, or else fear had not reached me yet. I knew the air-raid formula well in these days; after the siren sounds got crescendoing up it was often a little while longer before the bombing and the fires started.

When the first incendiary bomb fell at the back of the street the tenants came running along with stirrup pumps and buckets of water to put it out; it was quickly done. A sergeant-pilot on leave joined us. Someone said to him, 'Well, chum, I suppose you're almost sorry you ever came on leave.'

And he answered, 'Oh, I don't know, I was beginning to think I was never going to see an air raid at all.'

We stood in front of the street of houses watching the battle; the sights and sounds of air bombardment were constantly changing, the people near us tried to interpret them now. 'We don't hear so much of that gunfire these days, do you remember the old days when the barrage first started, that was something like a row, that was.' The few months ago in war-time so soon became 'the old days' so that already we looked back on the first months of war as on remote memories of adolescence. 'Well, I suppose it's because our night fighters are up that they lay off the gunfire.'

Soon we heard a sound like the crackling of dry twigs burning. 'That's machine-gun fire, that is, shouldn't be surprised if Adolf got something he didn't like to-night.' A long-legged leisurely girl watching on the terrace said, 'This is not my lucky day, it isn't really. I was out this afternoon and got caught in the rain. I had no mackintosh coat, no umbrella, nor nothing. I was drenched to the skin; first the damp day and now the noisy night. What a game!'

Some of the barrage balloons looked silver, some white, but the moon itself shone through the trees the colour of amber. The sergeant-pilot said, 'Funny this yellow moon, ain't it? I ain't never seen a moon like that before.'

I went up to the top of one of the empty houses and looked out over London. All around us there were fires, seven or eight of these bowls of flame were near, so that we seemed to be existing in a small camp. In the sky there were intermittent flashes of anti-aircraft gunfire. They looked like stars and took their place amongst the other stars which never went out.

I came down again and toured round the street. Someone called out to me, 'Looks like we're in for one of those old-fashioned evenings all right; there's a crater at the end of the road here, so no more traffic won't be able to get by.' Each time I heard the pre-sounds of near falling bombs I sheltered in one of the doorways. This happened often.

At the back of the street there was a small sooty garden, the railway goods station overlooked it but the trains had ceased to run soon after midnight. That was one sound less, the sound of the penny whistle had stopped too; it was some time since I had heard it, perhaps the street musician had been killed.

The time of my firewatch duty would soon be ended, in five minutes it would be three o'clock. The doors of the ground-floor flats were all kept open during air raids so that the wardens and fire fighters could deal quickly with flames. I walked slowly through one of these empty flats from the front of the street to the back, where I met the wife of a railwayman who was to take over from me.

'You can't expect to get no sleep in this,' she said. 'Seems like we've got a free firewatch tonight; he don't usually knock off much before six o'clock these nights. Look out, 'ere comes another.' We leant against the staircase of the house. I watched a lamp that had been hung up in the hall swing backwards and forwards at a great rate and then slow up until it was almost still again. 'Funny thing,' said the railwayman's wife, 'when one of these bombs come down it puts me in mind of the boat I was on when I went to Ireland with Paddy to see his Dad; oh, it was rough on that boat, shook something terrible, it did.'

I went back to my own room. I rested on my bed. I had found an old book; I was reading a description of the upheaval in a certain man's household on the arrival of a Frenchman, when a piece of plaster from the ceiling fell on my forehead; a wave of anger swept over me. 'There'll probably be a bruise in the morning.' I could hear a man outside saying, 'They ain't 'arf copped it in Austel Street, seems as it's all afire; talk about blackout, the nights are lighter than the days with all these fires showing up the whole blinking place.'

I went downstairs again and watched from the front of the street. Two women were talking together, one of them was telling the other that she could sleep through heavy gunfire, 'bombs and syreen and all don't wake me, but there's one sound I can't abide, and that's the barking of a little dog. My sister-in-law had one — oh, it was a yapper. It got on my nerves terrible, I couldn't sleep nights. I thought I should have to leave London, but she went away about five weeks ago and took her dog with her so there's peace again now.' At this moment all the windows in the first house broke, scattering their glass along the pavement. The two big dogs broke out in howl-protest again.

Outside my room there was a stove, above it in a rack I kept the china plates I needed for my meals; from time to time they chattered together, but none of them got broken.

I thought of the way in which we lived by sounds and in my mind I began to go through the sounds of the evening. The penny whistle, the siren wail, airplane hum, gunfire, penny whistle again, howling of dogs, a tear-sheet sound of bomb, crackling sound of fire, running feet, dragging of a stirrup pump along a floor, human voice giving out directions, water jetting against burning rafters, the stones of a house falling in quickly, talk, ambulance bells, fire-engine bells, breaking glass, patter of shell splinter like fine rain, boots brave-walking along a street, machinegun fire in the air, shell splinter on the ground — a noise like a barbed wire rug being rolled up, wardens' whistles, firewatchers' whistles, auxiliary fire-engine wheels and shouted orders. And so these same sounds again in two-sound, three-sound time, altogether or separately.

This higher method of counting sheep lulled me to sleep

for ten minutes, and when I woke up the goods station had got a direct hit. A rain of fire came down in the sooty garden behind the houses, every few minutes there was another muffled explosion as oil and spirits caught fire. When this happened lighted pieces of paper flew up into the air and floated down on us, but they had no power and went out as soon as they touched the ground. We were able to walk in the garden like miracle men and women through this fire rain. It was harmless but must have looked very strange.

The All Clear sounded out. I walked down the road; policemen were patrolling about in twos like men going out to bat at a cricket match; the firemen still worked on burning buildings, otherwise the streets were almost deserted.

The gas cooking stove did not work now, but I knew a café where I thought I should be able to get breakfast, so that after I had eaten I could come home and sleep until it was time for me to dress and get ready for the Sunday night shift.

The extremes of fatigue brought about by long hours in the workshop and air bombardment could make an individual into another person, a half-conscious creature removed a little way from the things which were happening. All through this night people had been killed, buried, suffocated, made homeless, burnt and trapped beneath buildings, but as soon as the All Clear sounded all those no longer concerned with active civil defence work went to their beds and slept. Tiredness took over.

Now as I roboted my way along this street of gutted-out houses my fatigue enclosed me. I looked at the firemen, grey-faced, sitting on the pavement half asleep, their legs and arms sprawled out as if decentralised from their main will and I thought, 'It is happening somewhere, but not here.'

It was Dick Strauss who had impressed on me the need to eat breakfast before sleeping and, listening to him telling me this, the other workers had said, 'Listen to old Straws; he does know how to look after hisself, Straws does. Trust old Straws.'

I slow-walked on, in unwilling compulsion as if I knew that at the end of my journey I should find something pre-known but dreaded.

The trolley buses had started. I got into one of these, it was filled with railwaymen on their way home from work. Sometimes they talked, but on this morning they were silent, staring out into the grey day.

Fatigue had a great strength, perhaps it was stronger than love or hatred, because it could produce a mood which no insults or sorrow could reach.

I got out of the trolley bus and made my way up the road which led to the café. Looking listlessly to the left I saw a mass of smoke coming from Braille's factory, and when it cleared I could see flames. At first, because the whole scene had such pantomime unreality, I did not realise that Braille's factory was burning.

Braille's had been built in two parts, two towers were joined together by a stone passage, and this was burning very fast now; it was bright red with the intensity of the heat, and flames waved out of the high windows at the top of the two towers. We had never been in this part of the building, the offices were there and the larger workshop for the operators on the day shift.

A small crowd of people were standing in the road watching. This group was like a revue sketch crowd of actors carefully made up to seem absurd. There was a fat man wearing a blue serge suit, his tin hat rather far forward over his eyes, also a silent kilted soldier, a good-looking but phlegmatic milkman and a black-dressed old lady of the vague-mad-decent school. A man walked by, he wore a brown suit, a homburg hat, and he carried over his arm a raincoat carefully folded. He said,

'Excuse me please, what is this building burning, could you tell me?'

The milkman answered, 'It's an aircraft factory.'

The man said, 'Thank you', and walked on.

The fat man walked about looking down at the ground. 'I put out some incendiary bombs here the first air raid we had, perhaps the marks of them are still on the road; it was just hereabouts.' He searched like a man looking for a lost coin.

The milkman said, 'Must be thousands of pounds worth of stuff gone up there, thousands of pounds worth of stuff.'

'I suppose they work on production at nights there,' said the soldier.

'They won't do no more production to-night,' the milkman told him.

All these watching people had the cardboard look of people who are too tired to be either awake or asleep.

A part of Braille's building crashed in and at this same moment a bird began to sing. The old lady in black looked at me in amazement. 'Did you hear that bird singing?' There was a second sound of falling stones, the note of the singing bird became more clear. 'That bird is really astonishing,' said the old lady. 'Fancy through all this, too.'

'Yus, he carries on all right,' answered the milkman.

A girl came running along the road, her high heels half tripping her up so that her ankles turned inwards and she stumbled; she held on to her hat by its brim, it was decorated with flowers over the crown. We both stared, trying to recognise each other through flames and fatigue. I knew it was Mabs, but I had to wait for the slow signal to reach my brain.

'They got Braille's,' she said.

'I know, I can see it.'

'I never bin to-night, nor Joe neither; we was bombed out, a

door hit Joe acrost the head, I went with him to the hospital.'
She was looking towards the burning building. 'They say as
Joe will be all right, but he don't remember nothing, don't
know me nor nothing, he don't. I wish we could get up to
the factory.'

'You can't do that,' the milkman told her. 'You're near a
quarter of a mile from it here; it looks close, I know, but it
ain't, the whole road is blocked up with firemen, ambulances
and suchlike; you can't do nothing, so it's no use thinking you
can. There's nothing much to be done against a direct hit like
that, you know.'

Mabs's rake-like teeth were chattering together. 'They
brought Straws into the same hospital as Joe, but they
couldn't do nothing for him, he was gorn, pore old Straws.
Fancy him being the first to go like that. I wish I bin there,
I wish I bin there to-night with the others.' She went away
on the words as quickly as she had come, running along the
road, her transparent thin hand holding on to the brim of the
flowered hat.

'Poor girl's scatty,' said the milkman. 'Wishes she been in
all that to-night, don't know what she's talking about, she
don't.'

The bird went on with its song, the tired people drifted
away, they dropped out like children getting off a slowed-up
roundabout. I too went back home. The policemen were still
patrolling the streets, they gave an impression of permanency
as if the possession of life could never be lost. The cheap
Union Jack flags were already appearing from the windows
of half-bombed houses or rising from the street rubble where
houses had been. Women were sweeping up glass into the
gutters as in peace-time they had swept up dirt, some small
shopowners were hammering boards across their broken
windows, and out of all this grey-grime there exuded forth
national pride. These people who hated heroical talk did

not think of themselves as being superior but through these events they had learnt that, all the same, they were superior.

When I got back to my own rooms I saw that an almost undamaged return ticket to Tottenham had floated in through the window; it rested now on my bed.

I remembered again two clear sounds, the penny whistle at the beginning of the bombardment, the bird singing at the end of it. Between these two sounds there showed a chink of light through which I could see the start of a more hopeful life, a future in which the courage of people could also be used for their greater happiness and well-being.

The names and faces of my workmates on the night shift ran through my brain and before my eyes. I saw them now, outside their own everyday existence and lives, and before fatigue fell across my mind like a final blanket it was quite clear to me that each one of them had been worth a second chance.

It Was Different At The Time

by Inez Holden

The text for this edition of *It Was Different At The Time* was scanned from the first edition, and was silently corrected for typographical errors and punctuation consistency.

1938

April

My sitting-room window looks out on to the well-kept grass of the rich woman's lawn. Most of the morning a gardener, wearing a green baize apron, ambles round the flower beds keeping everything up to a high pitch of excellence. My bedroom window looks out on to the street, and to-day a boy is bicycling towards us, whistling, steering with one hand and holding, in the other, a false foot in a black leather boot. He is bringing this to the lame refugee who lives on the ground floor.

My limping neighbour is 'a business man in a small way', but since escaping from central Europe he has found it increasingly difficult to keep up his connections abroad. A few weeks ago he got married to a tall, thin woman from the Balkans. She tries to earn a living by selling face creams. They keep a small black kitten which gets lost every night, and after dark I can hear them calling out in the street, 'Kitty, Kitty, Kitty, kom here', and after a while one of them wails, 'Our katchen ist lost once more.'

The man with the false foot limps down the road to the post-box, but whatever he sends out he is disappointed at not getting much back, because when I go down to get my letters from the ledge in the hall he opens the door of his room to see if there is anything for him. 'Oh, Madame, you have so many letters continually komming to you — always so many — I am quite jealous of them.'

The letters which 'continually came to me' yesterday were of the kind which are sent out alphabetically. Some from the deathly sweet centres of charity printed on shiny paper, gold-edged — a ball was to be given in aid of this or that, So-and-so's well-known band would blare out, and some of the balance from the evening's high boredom would finally filter through to an institution named at the bottom of the announcement. These announcements of supper and champagne came at one like maniacal laughter from behind dry-rotting wainscoting in a collapsed castle.

When the street door opened the boy handed the refugee his false foot and then remounting his bicycle he went whistling away. The sun shone through into my room. The large house on the other side of the lawn had the sun blinds drawn down, the long windows were blinkered.

From Friday to Sunday last week I stayed at J's country house. Acquaintances in the four-figured income class gyrated round the grounds to slow conversation. They seem to think a great deal about money, to talk money, and to brood over it. The possibility of the money getting any less preoccupies them, but on this subject the conversation is always kept within a certain radius — far outside the poverty of the mining districts. Distressed areas, malnutrition, and unemployment are all subjects before which the blinds of the mind must be drawn down quick. But to these members of a chain-gang of house parties there is a kind of money-lack which seems romantic and worthy of talk; this is the gay Bohemian thanklessness of artists, writers, musicians, and the like. The well-set-up guests at J's country house last week seemed very interested in some sort of slightly removed stratum of existence; they troubled about how it could be made to work, while semi-enjoying their own incomes — only semi-enjoying because there seem to flicker at the back of their minds disturbing doubts. 'After all, one never knows these days, there's all this Communism, Fascism, Nazi-ism, Radicalism, and the Reds' — a vast international army these

Reds, who won't take off their shoes in the sacred presence of private property. All these Bolsheviks are menacing the future so it's as well to be on the safe side, although there may come a day when no side is completely safe and where will the income go then, poor thing? This sort of thinking brings the bright landowners to a quick search through their acquaintance list for the names of those of good up-bringing with no fixed incomes. 'After all, old So-and-so has no apparent means of subsistence and he gets on all right, he was down here last week-end, and as for Such-and-such he also lives in good style without any regulated rate of pay, if we can get a few tips from them about how it's done it may be all right on the night of reckoning.' So much for the ideological outlook of J's guests.

Two days ago Felicity came to see me here. She wore a straight black dress and some sandal-shaped shoes; she has a forehead fringe and when she talks her eyes move restlessly from side to side. It was as if I had a girl-Eddie Cantor galloping round my room. She told me that her sister Sally goes to a gymnasium class for health and beauty. 'She takes a terrible attaché case with her and changes in the boot-hole and then goes bending and high-kicking round an immense hall. They have a magazine too, full of bright chat about pupil-teachers and old girls. When I got hold of it the other day the very first sentence I saw was something like this: "Tilline, our instructress, is adored by all her pupils. As soon as you see her you feel that at any moment there is going to burst upon you a happy, hearty laugh, and then Tilline will be gone with a leap and a skip, leaving behind her an impression of two blue eyes set in that smiling face 'neath a sheer bedlam of golden curls."'

Felicity, I suppose, is almost an average girl of chaos, but it is difficult to be clear about the compulsion under which she acts. She is seldom free from something phoney — fortune teller, quack medico, meretricious magician, cheap mystic, lecturer on the occult or what-not. Even for Sally, Felicity's sister, contemporary life seems such a strain that she is transforming herself into a whimsical Amazon.

May

To-day I was in a bus with Felicity. A brown-hatted man was in the next seat. He had thin long hands and a sheep-like face. He was well-groomed and wore a black beard — probably a psycho-analyst, genuine or self styled. Beside him there was a thin, clean Cosmopolitan woman pouring into the well-washed ears of Black-beard-sheep-face the subterranean stuff of her subconscious. Preferring some Latin form of release she was using French as a medium. *'J'ai l'impression de vivre ma vie en arrière.'* She was explaining how this was like existing inside traffic which was shunting backwards while she herself was being carried forward. It was very complicated. We only heard half sentences here and there. 'Crossed swords … music at night … and death the only goal.' Sheep-face listened, crossed his long thin legs left over right and then uncrossed them and again the recross right over left. In a little while he got up and with his elegant companion went walking down the whole distance of the bus. They went out like people leaving a restaurant.

Felicity suddenly said: 'Oh, look at that — a banner with a strange device, if ever there was one!' A white banner was hanging from a high window. 'Exhibition of Mystic and Clairvoyant Pictures' was red-embroidered on it. Felicity's brown button eyes lit up. She was after the occult again. Out of curiosity we went into this gallery, but even Felicity took a step backwards before taking one forward, for here was such a hotchpotch of a hundred old maids' fancies, the inside of a thousand spinsters' skulls.

On the walls were water-colours painted, so it was claimed,

in vision, trance, clairvoyance — and especially dreams. But what a bad advertisement for dreaming, trancing, and the having of anaemic visions! Tall poppies grew from nowhere and without grass; golden-haired children gazed into the future from one vacuum into another; purple and green had been generously splashed about within ornate frames, and a tall, Norfolk-jacketed man with skin the colour and texture of an undercooked and tepid potato was pacing the gallery and talking, talking, talking to a woman wearing a woollen dress and a knee-length feather boa. 'I said to her, madam, I said, "your conversation only gives away the interior of your mind." And, Madam, I said to her, "let me tell you it's no credit to you, madam, it's a crowd mind you've got."' He went on talking of some public holiday as he had seen it from inside his psychic sedan. 'Everybody was wonderful, and everybody behaved. And why, yew may ask? "Influence," I answered. "Influence again and again. That's how it works. We know these things, others don't. Why not? Because they've never drawn back the psychic veil. They've never seen the vast beyond as we have. But there it is — the whole vast scheme of things and life, life, life."'

We moved on quickly to another part of the room, but here it was not much better. We found a gentle knitting lunatic who had painted some garden scenes, vaguely washing into them pixies, nymphs, elves, and every other hopping whimsy. She said: 'That's a beautiful garden, isn't it?'

Felicity asked: 'Where is it?' and got back the answer, 'Venus — I go there every night.'

'Do you really?'

'In my dreams of course.'

'Of course.'

The knitter stopped a little while, peered short-sightedly to pick up a dropped stitch, and when she had got the hooked wool back on to her wooden needles, she went on: 'There's music in that picture, you know — the bells of dancing pixies. Can you hear them?'

We made towards the door, but Norfolk-jacket was too quick for us.

'Is there anything you ladies would like me to explain?'

Felicity said: 'Explain? I don't think so. You see we're late for an appointment, but we'll come back another day.'

Felicity's voice was getting up on a high note of hysteria, different altogether from most of the voices in the gallery, which were droning on now, gentle, drowsy, never high, never low, no sense and no silence.

'Yes,' said Norfolk-jacket, his teeth passionately in the argument, but in his pale blue eyes an elsewhere expression. 'Yes, yes, I shall be happy to tell you everything about the real meaning of life. Every Tuesday at half-past two we have lectures on the great and only truth, and on Wednesday a short talk on Wisdom and Self Expression. Not so much a lecture, you understand, as a social, when Cosmic Wisdom is given to guests free, gratis ...'

At the side of Felicity's face I saw two drops of sweat, and when we got outside we realised we had been running the last few steps. From the swamp of illiteracy the streets seemed very safe.

September

Now the days in England begin to be numbered by war crises. This has been going on for a long time, but it has become more apparent. The radio helps with regular news bulletins, and people ask each other, 'What does the news mean? Is it better or worse or only a repetition of the last news with the hours of aeroplane takings-off, landings, and adjournments for lunch added?'

Last week Margaret asked me to have a drink with them. Her husband, Ambrose, had been doing everything according to instructions, and more. He has dug a trench in the garden and ordered a vanful of air-raid precautions. The hall was a paraphernalia of sand, spades, buckets, hard hats, and hose-pipes.

People kept coming in to drinks, to heroics and hiccoughs — and most of all to talk. Several showed up in their true colour — a ghastly grey. 'Thirty thousand will be killed in the first air raid on London,' said one Grey Face. And as no one answered, he went on with the figures rising rapidly towards the million mark. Grey Face was wound up. 'Like a watch, isn't he?' Margaret said. 'I mean, like the springs of a toy that won't stop until it is run down, and heaven knows when that will be.'

A friend of the family arrived. He was a popular doctor, a slick specialist; and with him, his wife. Walking on his way through the wards of hospitals this doctor had clearly become a little troubled. He got his money from the rich patients whom he despised, his rather unreal manners from going to the theatre too much, and his handsome sunburn from a sort of powder sold in a box, probably at half price to medical men. Altogether he was a smart surgeon for a smart audience, but he was now looking forward to the changes which were coming into the world. He hated the rich, he loved the poor — well, at any rate he did on this evening when it seemed to him as if medical work might be on the way towards nationalisation. And as for his wife, she was thinking about security and the importance of it to herself and her children. She wanted to Heil Safety for all she was worth as soon as it got back within heiling distance. All these international crises were not her style at all, and if they went on the cradle would rock … She was really very much afraid it would.

Smart-Surgeon and Mrs Surgeon had always got on very well together. They had almost made a business of it; but now, suddenly, it was all changed and they made heavy weather of it. She began to tell him a thing or two … the way he had been talking for the last two years. Oh yes, he had … 'Is he a God-damned Communist or what, she would like to know.'

My friend, Margaret, was very interested in this mid-Munich quarrel, because she was usually quarrelling with her own husband; but now she watched intensely, as an actress taking her afternoon off in the stalls might watch a drama.

Ambrose tried to calm everyone down. He was tired dealing with the staff at his office and digging in the garden at home. The Surgeon told his wife: 'Poor old girl, you're overstrung, that's what it is …' He said it several times, 'overstrung … overstrung …' as if speaking of a piano de luxe.

'To-day has been too much, really I can't stand any more,' Mrs Smart-Wife-and-Earthy-Mother moaned. 'After this is all over I shall go to Canada and take the children with me.'

During the evening Margaret's old aunt came in; a well-fed widow in a porridge-coloured serge dress, with eyes of a cold blue steel shade of snobbishness. She carried an umbrella made from a second best silk, and her hair was an arrangement of well-ordered wisps. She had returned from a farm in Sussex, where she had gone on the threat of the crisis, to collect her things before the bombing started.

'Of course it won't be before another twelve hours,' she said, as if speaking of the time the next train was due. 'Do you know, when I arrived at the farm I was treated as the first refugee.' She saw herself as a figure of some national importance — not only the First Lady of the Boltons, but also the First Lady Refugee of Horsham. Later on she said: 'Oh well, I've no sympathy for the Czechs. My cousin was in Prague last year and she said that the Czechs were not at all friendly. In the streets they were always treading on her heels.'

This naturally needed no comment and everybody weighed it with a heavy silence.

The Surgeon's wife was talking about her daughter Dollie. 'I took her to her dancing class myself, she's as keen as mustard although only seven … points her toes better than any of the other children, and now she can waltz as well.'

The voice of the Surgeon was rasping out: 'One must treat them toughly, very toughly, these political thugs …' And then his wife again: 'Dear little girl, Dollie … and now she wants to learn ballet …' The Surgeon was saying: 'There will be some drastic changes … some of these rich idlers will learn about life — and not such a bad thing either.' Then his wife began to cry: 'I can't bear any more. The nerve strain of these last days …' The husband goes over to her, gives her a pat on the shoulder: 'There's a girl …!' 'Oh, Teddie, I'm not one of your damned patients!' Bing. Bang. She hits him twice, as quick as two cats' paws. A dull red angry blush appears on his cheek. She follows her hit up with some straight-from-the: shoulder talk. 'Oh, you're always on about your Communist ideas. I wish you'd find yourself in a Communist world, and then you wouldn't be showing off to these fine girls all the time.'

Teddie answered back in the same soothing voice. 'Now, dear, it's all right … Dollie's quite safe in the country … you're tired, I know, but there's nothing to worry about.'

'A lot you care about your children … always look bored when I talk about them.'

'Well, dear, after all we're on the verge of a great national upheaval — I mean international crisis. It's not very interesting for everyone to have to hear about Dollie's dancing class.'

The quarrel was on again.

'A lot you care for my happiness … only think of yourself and trying to show off!'

'Stop it, old girl, stop it! Stop all that talk!'

So the argument for two egoists — crescendo, allegro, and piano. The other guests did not take much notice.

Although disliking the things people around me were saying, I had become sensitive to the sound of their voices, so that now I seemed to be hearing several conversations at once, and each of them acutely.

Margaret was trying to construct a picture of her future war-time life. 'l suppose we shall work in shifts,' she said. 'We shall all be nurses, but it will be dark, won't it, in the streets? And bombs will be raining down from the skies, the sirens sounding and houses coming down with a run — so how shall we manage to get back to our houses from our hospitals when the day's work is done? I mean, with the darkness and the air raids it will be a bit of trouble moving from one place to another ...'

Several more people came in to listen to the latest news from the radio. There was a quiet girl who said she had no opinions — nothing to say, so tired was she of people's personal ideas. There was also a rather athletic girl who had already joined several brigades — women territorials, ambulance, first-aid, Red Cross, and so on. She seemed to be worrying about whose worker she would be on the day of war declaration. There was a Frenchman who said: 'To think we shall all 'ave to be soldiers again, my de-ar.' He rubbed his brow like a man who has just finished ploughing up a bit of rough land on a hot day. 'I 'ave been a soldier once already,' he said, staring at Surgeon and Mrs Surgeon as if there was something very distasteful about them. But the quarrelling couple had become silent. Their vague hostilities and obscure antagonism had been brought up from the depth of their two lives, and now countries and nations could only be for them symbols of a personal inter-bitterness long hidden by ready-made smiles. As two exhausted armies the human couple faced each other, wondering how the conflict could have started.

Ambrose told us about a man he had met in a pub down the road. It seemed that this man was one of the vast army who sustain themselves through the giving out of news and rumours. He was quite content to sit in the pub from opening till closing time getting into conversation with people. 'As a matter of fact, it isn't generally known,' he had said, 'but the fighting has already begun!' His earnestness and, indeed, his whole technique, Ambrose told us, was that of the racing tipster who writes down the names of all the horses and sells a different slip to each client, so making sure of getting at least one winner.

'These 'ere aerial torpedoes will go through anything,' the man had told Ambrose. 'Well, with reference to these 'ere aerial torpedoes, I seen one with my own eyes go through a great building like it was no more than paper!' He seemed, Ambrose said, to derive great satisfaction from this thought, and ended the conversation with the words: 'Well, it's begun good and proper now. (Thank you, I don't mind if I do 'ave another Bass.) As a matter of fact, sir, it's not generally known, but I don't mind telling you that at this very moment they're over Dover!'

Margaret's aunt remarked: 'Of course the first air raid will be before the first.' And the Frenchman, staring at her, said: 'Surely you h'exaggerate!'

'Perhaps the second air raid will also be before the first,' Margaret's aunt went on, and the Frenchman, exasperated, asked: 'But 'ow can that be?' It took some time before any of us understood that Margaret's aunt meant that the first air raid would be before the first of October, and perhaps even the second air raid would be before the first of October.

All this time the radio was giving out a kind of timetable of news bulletins.

Miss Trudgeon, who worked as secretary to Ambrose at his office, told me about her mother. 'Mother has never liked Mr

Chamberlain,' she said. 'Mother thinks Mr Chamberlain's a fox.'

A terrible apathy had fallen on my limbs and mind, as if I were in a kind of dream, in which the strangeness of events and their ill-arranged sequence gave me a desire to escape, yet it was as impossible to move as if I were in a half-conscious state of sleep, weighed down by heavy blankets.

'Mr Chamberlain into fox ... They're over Dover ... The second air raid before the first ... Dollie's dancing class ... Stop it, old girl — stop it! ... The Czechs were always treading on our heels in Prague last year!' And all through it the broadcast voice giving out the times of aeroplane landings and re-takings off. '"Once more unto the 'plane, dear friends, once more!" Another season, another reason for making Munich!'

The driver of a van who brought up a further set of ARP materials stared at Margaret's house and said: 'You could kiss good-bye to all this in an air raid,' and then, leaving his queer cargo at the door, he drove off, sucking his teeth and saying: 'Well, if this ain't a fine how-d'you-do!'

There was no lull from news bulletins coming through the radio; the French stations told how the English people were digging trenches in Hyde Park, and the English stations told how the French were calm and ready for anything.

Miss Trudgeon talked about life at her office. 'Really, the office didn't seem like the office to-day,' she said. 'People think that every day is the same in an office. Well, of course, many of the days are the same, but not all. There are always gala days — Royal engagements, holidays, the time when one of the employees won a Football Pool, or when they got the news that the daughter of the boss had come in first in the Ladies' Point to Point race.' It seemed that on those days the office staff didn't talk about the weather at all. It was true that you still had to receive instructions from the young

Assistant Manager, who sat in his swivel chair with one drawer open, and that the one he put his feet in. It was still necessary to make cups of tea and to say: 'How many lumps of sugar, please?' and 'Fancy!' and also 'Sorry' — when you bumped into anyone going up or downstairs; but during this time of international crisis at least people didn't talk about the weather any more. They spoke a great deal but always as if they were not quite ready with what they wanted to say, and so their words did not always add up to any sort of sense.

The porter remarked: 'The news is bad — worse than ever I remember it since 1914!' And the American-influenced typist — the one with the cute sideways look — said: 'The way I look at it is that it isn't a question of politics at all. It's one of religious revival.' And Miss Trudgeon told us: 'And the way I look at it that young typist was talking nonsense!'

The under-manager, assistant-manager, boss, head-clerk, and all the partners talked right out of character, too.

'What are the politicians doing about this?' or 'What are the world's monarchs doing about it? Why doesn't the Church stop it? … The women ought to get together … It's the fault of the Fascists … the fault of the Communists … the fault of the Jews!' And all who felt disorganised themselves imagined some menacing organisation elsewhere.

Miss Trudgeon thought it was funny now to talk of plans and hopes and the way everything pinned on to the future had become so suddenly unpinned. Waiting to die with dignity was a difficult job; being blown up with hundreds of others was not a dignified death and nothing would make it so, but in the waiting there was some dignity. And besides this, there were a great many things Miss Trudgeon would rather not be than dead — which came to the same thing as her saying she would rather be dead than many other things. For instance, Nazi ruled or Fascist ruled.

'Certainly better dead than either of these. Not the slightest doubt about it, and Mother agrees with me, and I agree with Mother. Oh, well,' said Miss Trudgeon, 'how I do run on to be sure!' And she picked up her gloves and umbrella and prepared to depart.

'Well, good-bye, Miss Trudgeon. We hope tomorrow the news will be better.'

'We hope so.'

Miss Trudgeon went.

Munich made a change in people. It brought out the talk in them. They shouted it out in politics, they had to do it. The rain of Munich had raised a mushroom field full of Miss Trudgeons and Mr and Mrs Surgeons and aunts with silk umbrellas. They were to be seen everywhere. They were to be heard hammering out this idea and that. The words went round and round and came out all the time. Perhaps the aunt with the heavy silk umbrella school was one of the most viciously verbal. She had believed that with the fixed sums coming in to her on quarter-days, everything disagreeable could be kept at a respectful distance. The troubles of poor people of no fixed financial status should be like the bells of Hell which ring-a-ling-a-ling for you but not for me!

My friend Felicity had a different kind of problem. She needed to belong to a group, but could never get a group to suit her. At the time of Munich she felt that she wanted to come out violently for some group — but which one? That was the difficulty. There she was, instinctively against certain sects of people, and these, like the objects of unhappy passion, attracted her most. She attended political meetings. Apparently she did not go to these meetings because she liked them, but because she hated them. But being in the company of only two or three individuals was for her like having to sit through a long and tiresome recitation. She became dull, dumb, and deaf with disinterest. Only groups got her, it had to be a group or nothing, so each week — usually on Sundays

— her marching feet, her heartache, and her hatred of humanity got her within hail or clench of some community. No doubt there are many people like her now. Perhaps soon there will be still more.

October

I saw Victor, recently returned from Spain. He arrived in England by aeroplane just after Munich. He had been to some large London store to order a few biscuits and a small tin of coffee for his breakfast. He found the shop assistants rushing about in an hysterical way, bumping into each other. When he asked what had happened he learned that a woman had ordered a hundred pounds worth of ham against the crisis — not a hundred pounds in weight, but a hundred pounds in money. Apparently after Munich the woman wanted the store to take all the ham back again.

Victor told me about his speech in an immense London hall when he had asked for money for medical aid for the Spanish Republicans. He had never spoken to an audience of thousands before; he says his fear was almost like an animal fear. A piece of paper on which he had written some notes shook so much in his hand that he was obliged to fold up the notes themselves and speak out entirely from memory. He heard a sound which he supposed to be the storm outside — it was several minutes before he realised that this sound was the applause of his audience.

Victor told me about the Basque children in a camp near the sea. They were bathing when the Fascist aeroplanes came over, and as soon as they heard the engine sound they set up a sort of whining — like a lot of little animals — and ran out of the water; this was doubly dangerous, because they could be seen more easily from the air — a close clump of people for the Fascists to machine gun. Victor shooed them back into the sea, even going out fully dressed and swimming with them. After the aeroplanes had gone away Victor went round the camp with a tin of sweets; the children held out their hands for the sweets, they were all laughing and singing again and had completely forgotten the events of a few minutes before. But every time the enemy aeroplanes came over they reacted in the same way. Many of these children had seen their parents killed in earlier raids.

November

The 'quiet dinner' with D and her husband turned out to be a small party; one of the guests was a German with some National Socialist's paid job. D told us before he arrived that she had asked him because she wanted some news of her family in Germany. Everyone said that they would not have come to the party if they had known this man was invited.

The Nazi came into the room like a Labrador dog on the wag, half sideways, fawning, and smiling. He wanted to pat people on the shoulder, put out his hands to touch them, but not at all costs to risk the refused handshake.

Very thin fingers and professor spectacles gave the square-headed Baron a sinister look which did not go well with his yearning calf-love personality. The women smiled, the men bowed, and the dinner party went on.

There was a pinkish, vote-catching Liberal with a leaning towards asking questions, but every now and then D spread out her hands with a nervous gesture as if over a troubled bowl of water and said: 'Please, no politics to-night!' — and yet the political talk did go on. This was the way the Nazi talked:

'Of course it's nice to talk things over in a friendly way like this. Our leader wants to smooth out difficulties. He likes Great Britain. He's going to cut out whole pages of *Mein*

Kampf altogether. But in any case the alterations are no longer necessary. The atmosphere is radically changed. Our Fuehrer loves France, too. Why, Mr Daladier came out smiling all over the face as much as he could, and in Munich the German people cheered in the street. No, he has — I mean our Fuehrer has — absolutely no interest in Spain. He will be glad to withdraw the few thousand of broken-down troops. The Fuehrer just sent them there for the sake of Mussolini's blue eyes. Of course he thinks it good practice for our airmen.'

This was the first time we had heard anyone speaking of killing civilians from the air as being 'good practice'. Airmen machine-gunning a few thousand non-combatants as a pianist might run over scales on a newly bought piano.

Was the Nazi-boy Square-head unconscious, a merchant ready to get himself a good living at any price, or what was the matter with him? It was difficult to tell because everything seemed to be wrong with him. The faces of the people round the dinner table seemed to show something of the sick sensation in their stomachs which even the good food could not settle down; but of course the whole subject was not one for this sort of evening, and it must have been quite clear to all the guests then that, sooner or later, we should have to shoot it out with machine guns.

Meanwhile the Nazi, smiling at his food and picking downwards at his plate, was asking everyone about the Royal Family and the English attitude towards them. The guests got bored with this conversation and naturally nobody said the same thing.

December

For the sake of a commissioned newspaper article I had to go to Mosley's meeting. It was being held in an exhibition hall. Mosley was on for nearly two hours. Also he was on the top of a giant rostrum, and on Sir Oswald were two spotlights. When the stamping, shouting, 'Hailing', *'Heiling'*, and saluting ceased, there was a sudden silence in which you could have heard a bee buzzing in a bonnet.

The beginning of the speech was given over to attack, the words 'Revolution', 'Triumph', 'Blood', 'Purge', and 'Perish' poured down on to the audience from this Premier Black Shirt up above the world so high, like a boxer in the sky. For the first hour it was an outward show of anger against invisible enemies, especially that poor old shadow-sparring partner the Jew. But afterwards Sir Oswald seemed to be saying that he stood for increased production and increased markets within the British Empire. He shouted that no one had dared to come forward and contradict him. The reason for this may have been that so many of the contradicting classes themselves had been advocating the same policy from various platforms and various parties ever since Mosley was knee-high to Hitler.

Possibly Sir Oswald does not want to save the world so much as the Aryan world. Of all myths, the racial myth must surely be the most obscure. I don't know if we are Aryans, but if we are we cannot help it, so I suppose we shall have to make the best of it. But whatever an Aryan is, no one would want to be one after listening to Sir Oswald. Sometimes there appear on the political horizon men who see strategy instead of suffering, politics instead of people. Men who have a kind of tone-deafness to humanity. I think Mosley may be one of these. Such men are dangerous.

A certain number of people left the meeting before the Fascist leader had got down; for them it was 'Bye-bye Blackshirt' and home to bed, but most of the followers stayed on. Amongst these I noticed personable young men, friendly, fresh-faced young women and middle-aged women of an income-group able to squander their surplus money on domestic animals such as Pekingese dogs and long-haired Persian cats. Some wore badges, several hummed the Fascist hymns, and altogether an audience that was amiable enough but not adult enough brought to this evening of higher soap-boxing a co-educational college atmosphere.

1939

February
Mêgève, France

I came here the day before yesterday to stay in a wooden pension half-way up a steep hill leading from the centre of the town. From my window I can see dark-clothed children ski-jumping over a kind of natural precipice; they never get tired. Below them a few languid figures on the skating ring gyrate to music. They seem to be tired all the time. On the higher part of the hill a row of coloured flags have been arranged in a vertical line. The young men and ski-professors practise turns here; their lives are rather like those of well-trained hares.

In the pension the other 'guests' are an uncompromising Frenchman, two serious knitting old ladies, and three trousered young ladies, each with a touch of melancholy. There is a snooker table in the hall, and the click of billiards balls heard up in my room produces a definitely depressing effect. The mountains are generous and beautiful, but the lights of the little town below make everything seem artificial.

When the sun shines I walk alone through several small hamlets; in the afternoon the school bells suddenly ring out and the children rush from the gates of their infant schools on skis and go bouncing along over the snow with all the grace and charm of Walt Disney characters. A few sleighs drawn by raw-boned horses trot through the town to the tune of the chatter of their cargo of visitors and the bells on the horses' harness.

***

In the compartment of my train travelling by night to Paris there was a gentle professor with a silky beard and three silent skiers wearing black berets; when I wanted to sleep one of these coarse mountain animals lent me his cloak and wrapped it round me. My health seemed to have improved so there was no need to stay any longer in that energetic ski-ing but sleepy-thinking town. All the time I stayed there I never heard the slightest hint of any political talk.

I lunched with Georges in Paris; he is clearly very unhappy about the present events. He was in Barcelona during the Spanish war. The proprietor looked at the newspaper Georges was reading and said: 'I suppose now we shall have all these Spanish refugees coming here and we shall have to feed them.'

When we got outside the restaurant, Georges said: 'That was all he thought of, the abject creature! Only the idea that these people would have to be fed and it might, even indirectly, cost him something; if he had not been a menial I would have slapped him on his face.'

April

In Trafalgar Square I walked right into a colossal meeting. The band players walked in front and after them marchers carrying banners, only a few to each banner. A tall shaven-headed man wearing a Norfolk jacket carried the highest banner.

The people must have come from somewhere, but it did not seem as if they were going anywhere — only round the square and round again like stage soldiers who walk over and under the stage to suggest a vast army, until the audience begin recognising faces so that there has to be a change of scene. Something of the sort happened here because the procession suddenly centipeded itself into the arena and then the whole insect broke up into separate individuals in shopping-clothes, handing each other chocolate, exchanging gossip, and peering in their homely way at the plinth of the Nelson Monument, now well stocked on three sides with leaders, speakers, camera men, journalists, members of Parliament, and the whole what-have-you of any political get-together.

The crowd on demonstration Sundays stands so still watching and waiting for a move from somewhere; the chairman was talking a bit on the provocative side with his 'Why don't you boo when I say that', and 'Why don't you cheer when I tell you this', and 'I was never so ashamed as when that happened', and 'Never so proud as when this came about'.

Next to me stood the bowler-hatted man in the trailing mackintosh coat. He could not keep silent for long. His straggling moustache was no barrier to his speaking out, his eyes were as gentle as a pet pony's, and he often spoke in kindly encouragement: 'That's right, mate', or 'True enough, chum'.

Two blue-suited boys stood on either side of a banner with their feet square-planted down on the stone of the plinth. In the distance beyond them there was a sudden movement as of leaves taking off from the ground at the start of a storm. One of the blue-coated young men came to life. He said to me: 'Why don't you come up here, comrade?' He leant down and, with his left hand, as from one Alpine climber to another, pulled me up on the plateau.

'You can see them better from here,' he said. 'It's the International Brigade.' And on this moment there came the cheers. The voice of the Labour leader was no more now than a gramophone sound played in a drifting punt and heard from a fast-travelling speed-boat. A small squad of men from the International Brigade marched round the Nelson Monument. They wore everyday clothes but carried a few flags from Spain.

There was a tremendous cheer and, in the echo of their own cheering, the crowd seemed to live a little while in a last fight for liberty against all organised machinery of death. These few survivors swept past very soon.

I saw poor Gentle-Pony-Eye putting on his bowler hat again, the crowd turning politely back to politicians — so far from slaughter but so near to shouts.

On this stone platform those who moved about outnumbered those who stood still to speak. There was the man in the fawn-coloured coat who walked up and down like an ocean traveller, but thinking his thoughts in tune to voices instead of to waves; there were also the four schoolboys, the little girl with false flowers falling over the brim of her hat, the coloured man, the cripple, the old lady with a walking-stick, and the tall turbaned Indian with no overcoat.

A political speaker had asked for money for the Spanish People's Medical Aid. Money was showering round us. The people had thrown it up on to the platform in instant response. Pony-Eye had been quick to empty his pockets, and it was his half-crown that hit me on the head; and this, together with a second florin from Pony-Eye, was picked up by the coloured man quick as a conjuror. 'Dat's wan more, Sister!' He dropped it into one of the long cloth bags which the collectors carried, scurrying about, dwarf-like, as they picked up the money.

The lady with the walking-stick said to the flower-hatted child: 'Want to go home now, Duck?' and the girl, shaking back the curls from her Shirley temples, answered: 'Don't know, I'm sure.'

'What is the danger that has been facing us?' the speaker was asking, and Pony-Eye called back suddenly: 'The Popular Front.' Then, as if in politeness taking a neighbour or two into his confidence, he added: "Course it is. I remember the days when we were all chased round this very square by Liberals!'

The speaker hurried on, knowing he must get his own

answers in pretty quick after his own questions, but no fast talking could keep such a conversationalist as Pony-Eye at bay for long.

'Oiland!' he called out; and then again: 'Oiland.'

'What is that man down there saying?' someone asked and the blue-suited boy with the banner explained: 'He's talking about Ireland now.'

Well, once was enough, twice was repetition, and the third time it was something like an interruption; and, as the word 'Oiland' rose up again, a policeman walked forward with heavy tread. They went away together, poor Pony-Eye as sadly quiet as any ill-behaved child who gets led from the room so often that it expects nothing better from the adult world.

'A copper's come and shifted him,' explained one of the blue-suited banner-bearers.

'Who is the enemy of the working man?' a speaker was asking. He expected no answer, but all the same he got one. From the bowler-hatted interrupter retreating with helmeted policeman there came back one last answering shout: 'The working man, of course!' After this it was rather difficult to have any clear idea of Pony-Eye's political policy.

The meeting went on. There was emotionalism, political conscience, a kind of ill-balanced optimism, perhaps a yearning towards a more hopeful future for the majority, but quite suddenly all these impulses seemed to separate and then be switched off, the people broke up into little knots, and everybody went home to tea.

August

Personally I have never doubted during these last years that we should be at war very soon, but now that it seems as if it will break out within a few days I find a certain reluctance to accept something which I always knew must happen. I find the same attitude in several of my friends. They would be appalled at the possibility of a second sell-out — as at the time of Munich — but there is just this difficulty of making the mental jump from even phoney-peace to the start of slaughter near us.

A few days ago I heard J the journalist say: 'I don't mind telling you that I don't think there will be war. After all, it stands to reason, if someone asked you "Which would you prefer, to be given several million pounds or be blown off the face of the earth?" Well, you wouldn't find it very difficult to choose, would you? No more will Hitler.' The radio blares out the foreign bulletins all day; it sounds as if a stage manager is endlessly telling an audience to keep their seats while, at the same time, informing them that the auditorium is on fire.

September

I thought that at the outbreak of war there would be an instant air raid in which thousands would be killed, and that those who survived would be very shortly overtaken by pestilence, and famine would follow fast. We should make our way through streets with bombs falling, mounted police galloping about, and straggling, homeless people wandering everywhere, and all through the night lorries with grim-faced mechanics at the wheel would drive through the darkness at a great speed.

I did not seriously believe that anything like this would happen, but it was just a kind of panic picture photographed on to my mind and afterwards rejected as being altogether out of focus.

However, many people seem rather relieved and say, 'If it's got to happen let's get it over with, the sooner it starts the sooner it'll end.' TD asked me to stay a few days in a house she had been lent in the country. It was difficult to make a decision, but as it was near London I decided to go and return at once if war was declared. At the time of Munich I had become a member of the Red Cross and passed the elementary examinations, and now I was pleased about this.

TD had a family friend called Billy with her, also the refugee boy, Klink, the nurse, and two children. She seemed to be rather weighed down with the responsibility of the children, but they were jubilantly happy at the shaking up of their normal routine. They chattered and charaded right through the journey.

Klink is an immense Italian-Jewish-German, with black burning eyes and high spirits. He is fond of imitating English colonels. He said: 'It's difficult to know what will happen now. I thought that never again could humanity be so foolish as to involve itself a second time in this colossal slaughter — but all the same, I think it must happen. After all, I know nothing!'

Klink has been in concentration camps in Germany and in Italy, but he has never been actively anti-Nazi, so he was not subjected to great physical cruelties, and in each case his sojourn was short and he was released. He is a lazy, good-natured fellow, a kind of Berlin playboy.

I drove most of the way to the country with Klink in the second car, and just before dark we arrived at a well-to-do house on a hill. Billy, the friend of the family, was carrying suit-cases indoors; the children had been helping TD to make the beds, and they came out on the lawn still in high spirits. We tramped in, feeling ill-at-ease and awkward as if we had no right to be there. An uncouth butler-footman house-steward continually came into the sitting-room to ask TD 'May I speak to you?' Each time she got up, went out and, when she returned, told us what he had said.

'Shall I bring the food in and let you serve yourselves?' TD had answered: 'Yes, yes — of course!'

Klink got very hungry and asked several times: 'Ven vill vee have supper?' This annoyed TD, who said afterwards: 'Everyone else was just as hungry, and *they* didn't keep asking for supper!' — but possibly Klink's size and general sense of insecurity gave him a greater hunger.

The uncouth steward came back, and TD had to follow him out again. When she returned she said he had asked: 'As the kitchen sink leaks, shall I send for a plumber?' — and also: 'There are no eggs left; ought I to order more?'

Once he came in, wanting to speak to Billy outside. This time it was about some beer. Should he bring it in or not? He explained that he thought that a question dealing with drink should be asked of a man, but the repeated appearances of the unsound steward, and his habit of calling us out in turn, got on our nerves, and once Klink said: 'I don't like his eyes!'

We listened to the radio for each possible batch of news — almost always a repeat of the last news, which gave us the impression that we were fixed half-way between past and future, and might have to stay for a long time in this cleft time-stick.

Rather late in the evening the steward came back and called TD out again, and she returned after a few moments to tell us that he had said supper was ready. We left the vast arm-chaired room and made our way down a long passage. The room chosen for supper was the nursery schoolroom. The walls were decorated with nursery-rhyme story pictures. All the furniture was small, and a bright blue kiddy-car stood in a corner. We had the illusion of having returned suddenly to security and childhood, and even the refugee became quite happy. The two children — Charlie and Louise — came down in their dressing-gowns. Eight-year-old Charlie said: 'The *Bremen* has been stopped and searched in New York harbour.'

Klink asked: 'How does Charlie get hold of such an idea?'

The boy stared at the kiddy-car in the corner: 'They found a whole lot of prisoners battened down in the bunkers,' he said.

'Nonsense, Charlie!' TD shrugged her shoulders. 'Children are so mad!' — but much later we did hear the rumour that the *Bremen* had been stopped and searched.

The word 'they' came a great deal into the conversation at supper. There were two 'theys' — the Nazis and the owners of the house in which we were staying — so the talk switched from 'they' to 'they'.

Whatever happened, it would be the cracking up of their regime, so surely 'they' would not be so foolish as to make war. Also 'they' will be coming back soon. Already 'they' had reached Switzerland. 'I bet they won't be able to bring the Studebaker with them,' said Charlie.

'Well, with or without their car, they will be back soon, and when they do arrive I hope you won't keep on interrupting with your silly statements,' TD told her son. The small boy Charles smiled in a good-natured way. He had hit on this wide smile, which worked very well, and seemed to make him master of any situation.

Klink and the kind family-friend, Billy, went back to London that night.

I did not wait to see the Studebaker-owning 'they', as I was going on to stay with A, who was at her house near-by. When I arrived, A's daughter of nine years old was riding round the garden on a tricycle, singing: 'O! for the wings — for the wings of a d-o-o-o-ve!'

A few days later war was declared.

The child, only half-understanding, but seeing serious looks on the faces of the adults, ran out of the room, her eyes filled with tears — but, tripping over the step as she ran, she began, in that instant, to laugh.

Somebody said: 'I shouldn't be surprised if we saw an air-battle over here to-night.'

Outside, the child was singing: 'O! for the wings — for the wings of a d-o-o-o-ve!'

December

We are now in the period of war-silence called Sitzkrieg. I am working the necessary hospital training hours at a large LCC hospital. It is in a suburb which has what is called a residential district. There is one large pretentious, genteel hotel. I stayed there a few nights.

The residential district is more than a mile from the hospital and so refined that no buses approach it. There is the difficulty of reaching the hospital each morning and getting back in the evening, and also the difficulty of having to eat in an airy but too large dining-room and having to hear tired commodores and their wives talking about golf and about money.

The hospital is a great square building; our heels echo along the stone passages when we go to the operating theatre, the various wards, the dining-room, or to what is called the 'gate' for messages.

Before coming here I had a fixed idea that every hospital matron was half Fuehrer, half Florence Nightingale. But the matron in this place is no such composite character. She is more like an Edwardian hostess, rather remote and with an affectation of graciousness, and the hospital itself seems to be divided up into a kind of local government of staff sisters.

Whenever the matron comes round the ward, the staff sister tells us to turn out the lights in the sluice, in the bathroom, and by the men's beds. We watch the matron making her hostess way down a long line of beds, rather like royalty, with a word for everyone, although, however well chosen the words, they are never very well received.

After she has gone, one of the men says: 'Did you hear what matron asked me? She asked me what the Russians will do next. Because she knows I've been in Russia, see? Well, how can I answer a question like that? Nobody knows, so how should I? Huh! And her supposed to be an intelligent woman!' The others smiled in indulgent agreement, and the staff sister says: 'Got to have those lights on again now, otherwise the patients can't see to read. After all, they've paid their rates, haven't they, same as everyone else!'

On the day a dozen Red Cross nurses arrived, the matron gave them a short lecture in her office. She spoke about tact and good manners and, altogether, her talk was along the same lines as a lecture on deportment at a finishing school for young ladies. After this, one of the women orderlies — a terrifying personality called Maggie — took them to an upstairs room where they could put on their uniforms. Maggie watched them pinning on their caps, and said: 'Take your time, ladies — take your time!'

After I had been introduced to the sister in charge, a young nurse asked me if I would like to help her make up some beds in the office at the end of the ward, because two bad accident cases had just been brought into the main ward.

At this time there were between twenty and thirty patients and one or two extra beds in the centre of the ward; three or four convalescent patients hobbled about on crutches and helped with the wheeling round of meal trays. There was a sister in charge, an auxiliary staff nurse from one of the LCC schools, two other nurses, a probationer, and two orderlies.

The nurse who had asked me to help her seemed to be a terrific egoist. She said: 'Oh, gee! I remember the first time I ever made a bed. Oh, la! I thought it would never be right! I wonder who's going to be in this bed. Will he be young or old, I wonder! I think I like young men better than old, don't you?'

I gave a vague answer, for fear of offending two very old

men who were sitting on their beds in their dressing-gowns near us.

'Except, of course,' continued Miss Egoist, 'when I marry, then I want to be an old man's darling. I want to marry a parson of sixty-one years old. An ageing clergyman would be just the right husband for me. I mean it, honest I do.'

The two old patients laughed in their good-natured way.

The men in the surgical ward were very pleased about the Red Cross nurses. When I was helping in a minor way with two dressings, one of them — a rather cultured taxi-driver — said: 'You're the first Red Cross nurse I've seen. It looks nice.'

And the man in the bed next to him said: 'It looks a treat!'

The pale Jewish boy in bed 18 lay quite still with his eyes closed, but after a while he said: 'Nurse, can you get me a hot-water bottle? I'm frozen — simply frozen I am!'

Nurse Egoist — whose name is Paterson — tidied up number 7 bed. The ill boy with a rather high colour told her: 'I just feel I want to be left alone.'

'Now, now,' answered Nurse Egoist, 'we must make you respectable, you know.' She smiled at him. 'You don't much care, I suppose?'

'Well, not at the moment.'

'When I was ill,' she said, 'you should have seen me, you should really. I had erysipelas, you know. When I was brought into hospital I had six pairs of pyjamas — beautiful silk ones they were — but they all had to be burnt. Erysipelas is terrible on your clothes!'

One of the accident cases was being wheeled back from an operation. After all, they had not had to amputate his foot.

'He'll be coming round soon,' sister told me. 'Will you sit with him and see that he's all right?'

I could hear Benny, the pale Jewish boy in bed 18, talking to a friend who had come to see him.

'That's the trouble with my brother-in-law,' Benny said.

'Always the same. Don't try to make himself happy, never sees no one.'

After his friend had gone Benny started again: 'Oh, nurse. I don't never seem to get comfortable. I can't explain how terrible it is — the sickening monotony. Here I lie, day after day, and all I see is the same things; just people lying ill in bed.'

Unfortunately for Benny he had Miss Egoist nursing him.

'Excuse me asking,' she said, 'but are you Jewish?'

'Yes, I am.' This question did not seem to show a great perception, as the patients' names were written over their beds, and above number 18 was 'Benjamin Isaacs — aged 24', and then the details of his case.

'Now you know one of my greatest friends is Jewish,' the nurse told him. 'Ever such a nice boy he is.'

'Some people don't seem to like them,' said Benny in his pathetic voice.

'Oh, I think we're all the same,' the nurse answered.

'We're a very scattered people, us Jews,' said Benny. But the young nurse did not want to hear about scattered people, she only wanted to speak about her scattered self. She started to tell Benny that her father was half-Austrian, but she was naturalised, and as she had travelled a great deal it seemed to her that she 'had the best of both worlds'.

''Course in Germany,' Benny said, 'there are many people who are fair sickened by the treatment the Jews are getting, and if they say anything against it they are shot. And anyhow, they're all starving, poor devils!'

When the operation case was becoming conscious and beginning to groan, Nurse Egoist lost interest in Benny.

'You're all right,' she told the man in the next bed.

'That's what you say,' answered the operation case.

'You know,' said the nurse, 'I have a boy in France. He's out there still. Think of what the chaps in France are getting!'

'Thank you,' answered the operation case. 'I'm quite satisfied with what I've got myself now!'

In the sister's office two of the nurses talked about Miss Egoist. 'She had a date last night.'

'Oh, she'd go out with anything in trousers.'

'She's making up to number 7 as well as number 26.'

'Oh, well, number 7 is just like a big kid. I can't understand her about number 26, though.'

***

At first sight the men in the surgical ward all looked so seriously ill; their faces were a kind of grey; yet one got used to this. The same thing happened when I first saw the inside of a factory. The people there looked ill and grey, too; but after the first shock was over it seemed a part of the environment, as if we were all living under the sea. The routine of referring to the various patients by the numbers on their beds is a convention. Number 4 smiles in a saint-like way. He has a hunched back. A book from the hospital library was brought to him and he read it very slowly, running his finger along the page. 'You know,' he said, 'I was miles away in this book … My, they did have a time there! See this, about travels to Mongolia. Do you know, not only is it very cold there, but it's also boiling 'ot as well! My word, I shouldn't like to go through what the chap that wrote this book has been through, with 'is pals!'

Number 4 has worked as a porter all his life. He has been seriously ill with some sort of spinal disease, lived in poverty continually, and carried great weights on his back.

'I shouldn't like to go through wot 'im and 'is mates went through!' he said again.

Number 4 was always pleased about everything. 'Of course I feel nearly a hundred per cent. better,' he said.

He has a damaged foot, too, and he said of the cage round it:

'Wonderful thing this cage, ain't it? It's worth twenty pounds.'

A nurse near us said: 'Lucky it doesn't cost what it's worth, then!'

This was the sort of joke that always appealed to the patients, and several of them laughed about it. Their reaction to money was often like this — money was either awful or funny.

The man in the centre bed smoked a cigarette while the wagon of surgical dressings was wheeled up near him. He made a great effort at being casual, but it was quite clear that he was extremely sensitive to physical pain; he had a great dread of these dressings.

'Of course it's a nuisance about this 'ere foot,' he said. 'Sometimes it feels worse like as if it had still got the piano I dropped on it — but it can't be helped. It probably saved me from something worse. That's what mother said to me, "This 'as 'appened to save you from something worse," she said!'

About this time a man called Jerrold, who had been five months in the hospital, became very pale, and vomited into a kidney bowl. Two or three of the other men in the ward called out: 'Lor, look at Jerrold! He's worth seeing, he is; never a dull moment with old Jerrold about!'

***

Back at dinner-time in the large suburban hotel, this kind of conversation goes on: 'How are you this evening, Commodore? Did you win your game of snooker?' and 'I was reading in a paper last night what a lot of people are killed on the roads. Do you know I'm surprised that there are so many people alive as there are!' Also: 'You do have to pay a lot of income tax nowadays — but if you understand it you can get out of it sometimes!'

In the lounge there is a colonel, whose body looks like a ramrod in a bolster, holding over his two hands a skein of wool which his wife untwines.

It was better to leave the hotel and to continue with the hospital work from London. It meant getting up early and catching a series of trains and buses to reach the State Hospital in Suburbia, but it was less of an effort than listening to the slow talk of Commodore and Mrs Commodore.

The men's surgical ward was a very long high-ceilinged room, and there was quite clearly contained within the radius of each patient's bed a separate life of associations and ambitions, hopes, and disappointments; one became dimly aware of this. The ill people managed, without moving, to exist like much-travelled cosmopolitans who had touched first this world and then that. The kitchen, with the green-aproned orderlies, and the office opposite, with the two or three extra beds, were also like other countries, although only divided from the wards by a few feet.

The conversation of the cleaners, sweeping round the kitchen, was of a different material from that which went on in K–1 Ward. A man from the dispensary, who was always flattering the nurses, came into the kitchen, and a tough cleaner said: 'Aw, I know what's wrong with 'im — 'e's girl-struck!'

K–2, the ward opposite on the same floor, was again a completely different territory, and even Nurse Egoist said: 'I don't like going in there. They're different there. They're ever so cheeky in K–2.'

Sometimes the doctors arrived with the slight swank of dictators surrounded by a bodyguard — sisters, X-ray men, a nurse, and perhaps a listening probationer.

The green-overalled orderlies who wheeled in the heavy trolleys and handed out cups of tea gave the appearance of gardeners.

Naturally nurses have a certain amount of power over the patients, but most of them seemed to be much more preoccupied with keeping on the right side of sister. They said: 'Sister's ratty to-day …'; and 'I don't know what's wrong with sister — she's been ratty all this week!' There was a considerable amount of talk, too, on what sort of pudding they were going to eat at the mid-day dinner, and whether or not it was possible to have two helpings.

At certain hours the relatives came into the wards, carrying their gifts of flowers, fruits, and sweets. They moved silently and confidently to their appointed bedsides.

The convalescents limped about. Sometimes a long-skirted Roman Catholic priest went rustling round, or a jolly-voiced Church of England parson. There were stretcher bearers, too, and occasionally an attached hospital helper from outside, nervous of invisible officialdom and awed by the presence of pain.

The ward itself, like a hotel, a theatre or even a Government building, had developed an illusive personality of its own which influenced, to a certain degree, the talk and behaviour of the various people who existed and suffered there.

We went downstairs to meals, past the operating theatre, into a large dining-room where about a hundred nurses sat at small tables. The conversation was usually about time off.

'I'm off duty at half-past two to-day. I think I shall go down the town and look at those new scarves at Shepperton's.' And food: 'When I was at St Ignatius I never had a second helping the whole of one week, because the sister there never asked me. I think she had something against me. I don't know why, but she never asked me to have another helping.' … And friendship: 'Have you heard anything from Jenkinson since she went on to Durham? You and she used to be such friends, didn't you? "Out of sight, out of mind." There's many like that around, aren't there?'

This was the rhythm of some of the first-year nurses' talk. It seemed to be slightly subnormal, but hours of duty are very long, and the pay very low. Many of the nurses were more alive than this, and all the staff sisters were intelligent women without pettiness, able to carry a great weight of responsibility with grace.

At the nurses' dining-table there was a good deal of tiresome refinement and ceremony. 'May I pass you some more potatoes, nurse?' and 'Excuse me stretching in front of you, nurse!'

Back in the ward a staff sister said: 'Now where is Nurse Paterson?' A second-year nurse — the one with the clean blank face and gold-rimmed spectacles — answered: 'She's done the disappearing trick again. That's Patty all over. Never there when you want her!'

At this moment Nurse Paterson came along. We went round the wards on the routine of tidying beds. The patients in these few minutes often tried to tell us something which could amuse and make us smile, to bring the brief illusion of companionship into their own lives, or else they tried to speak swiftly of something that was on their minds.

The porter in bed 4 was reading again, holding his book almost to eye-level, and seeming to look more through than at it, shutting one eye, as if it were a telescope. He put it down when we came round and said: 'I've never been a lover of reading.' Nurse Paterson responded to this remark with one about herself.

'Funny you saying that,' she told him. 'When I was thirteen I read almost everything. My Mum was always saying "Read, read, read! Never seen such a girl for reading!".'

O'Hara, the Irish lorryman in bed 22, lay still and looked straight ahead of him. He had just got through his first dressing after the third operation on his arm. 'Oh, well,' he said, 'I'm not so bad, except every dressing half-kills me. Still, I suppose I've got to get on with it.' O'Hara's eyes had dark lines of pain beneath them, but it was the convention of K ward to say that everything was not so bad.

'I know just how you feel,' said Nurse Paterson. 'I ricked my arm getting on to the bus this morning. The conductor looked at me kind of comical — oh, he's soft, that conductor is! But my arm did hurt. I couldn't speak for a few minutes — really I couldn't!'

The boy in bed 17 said: 'I feel considerably better. Something like a human being, which I didn't a few days back!'

'When I'm in bed, I always lie back — it gives me more rest,' said Nurse Egoist. 'But you, number 17, you're always sitting up.'

'Well, it's because I've got these stitches, see?' he answered, 'and if I'm sitting up already it doesn't hurt me to be moved.'

'Oh, you know a lot, you do!' answered Nurse Paterson. Number 17 instantly looked deeply depressed. 'Oh, maybe I don't know much,' he said. 'It was only an idea of mine.'

On this night when I reached London the room in my flat seemed clean and quiet; the walls were white, and everything in place, like a calm clinic. Outside there was the gentle largeness of the park, and opposite the great green empty house of the rich woman.

In the evening I went to a party given for two people who had been living together for twelve years and had just decided to marry. In the early part of the day they had gone through the formal wedding ceremony, and the man had met the relatives of the woman. Guests came into the party looking old-fashioned in war-time. They wore shell necklaces, turbans, and all the rest of it, and said to each other: 'It's a long time since I've seen you', or 'It's so-and-so many years since I've seen you!'

There was a girl living upstairs who had been in a car smash; she came down to the party wide-eyed, with a broad ribbon in her hair. She wore a flared house-coat and walked on crutches. She migrated towards the table of drinks, holding first on to this man and then on to that.

When I returned to the hospital in the morning I felt as if I had been away from it for some time. Deputy Dougall, the tall sister with the high Tudor cap, was on duty. The beds had been moved about since the day before to make way for new patients. Benny Isaacs was in the first bed now. He smiled his self-conscious, self-pitying smile, and told me: 'I don't think this sister likes me. It's a funny thing, but my young brother came to see me the other day. All the way from Risboro' he came. It's true he arrived a few minutes late, but she wouldn't let him stay. He'd only been here about a quarter of an hour when she told him it was time for him to go.'

Then Benny said — quick-proud: 'It's not the fare, or anything like that — just that I wanted to see my brother.'

The other men in the ward did not dislike Benny, but they seemed to wish to dissociate themselves from his whining. Also they wished they could be free from the incessant talk of the little boy in the centre bed. He had a damaged shoulder and stitches in his head, but no neurotic memory of the accident. He seemed to have forgotten it except as something gay and of interest — a funny event.

'I'm going home to-morrow,' he sang. 'To-morrow — to-morrow — to-morrow!' The small boy sang continually; he hummed, too, and talked almost always nonsense. He was intoxicated by words and the idea of being able to use them. He didn't trouble himself much about the sense of the words themselves. It was the magic music of words — any words —that appealed to him. There was plenty of time in the far-distant grown-up days for him to discover the meaning. He went on in his sing-song voice: 'This hand's all right — that's the one that's hurt. That's the one that's hurt — this is the one that isn't. I'm going home to-morrow ... Do you want a sweet? I've got tuppence — I've got sixpence. My name's "Jim" —a little girl pushed me dahn right in the road. I've got tuppence — sixpence — sixpence ... sixpence. I'm going home to-morrow!' And so on and on and on. The men never got cross with the boy, but they often asked him to be silent. It was of no use.

A few mornings ago there were several operations in K–1. Wearing their operation shirts and the triangular bandages round their heads, the patients sat up looking pathetic. Many of them had been in the operation theatre before.

'When are you going down, Bill?' asked number 28.

'Oh, I don't know,' answered number 33. 'I've been waiting since ten o'clock.' The white triangular bandage gave a greenish look to his face. 'It don't make much odds if I wait a bit longer,' he said.

The child in the centre bed sang to himself — still drunk with words without sense: 'You mustn't hit his hat, you must hit his bat, he's a sailor-man. You mustn't steal his cat, or else you get a smack.' It went on over and over again.

One of the men said: 'I've bin down a fortnight ago, and they tell me I've got to go down again next month.' His leg had been operated on five times, and this had earned him a reputation of importance.

As for 'going down', the ceremony is always the same. The aquiline, silent stretcher bearer arrives; the stretcher is put on the trolley. It runs along on its tyres all too easily. The nurse goes with the man into the lift and down to that other bright-lit world of an operating theatre. After an hour or so the man comes back, a screen is put round his bed, and for a while there is a sickly smell of anaesthetic. Later on he sits up, a bed-rest behind him, but he sleeps most of the time, without troubling about anything; the other inmates of K–1 ward say: 'He's bin dahn, and 'e's come rahnd. 'E's all right now, ain't doin' so bad.'

'That's right.'

'Pore ole chap.'

In the office room at the end of the ward there are two or three extra beds, the sister's table with the notes, and a few X-ray photographs; also the curly-headed boy with the stitches in his side and thigh. He looks through his comic papers and talks about them at the same time. The only other patient is a thirteen-year-old boy wearing a camel-hair dressing-gown which is the same colour as his own hair. His damaged arm is almost well again, although he still wears a sling. He is bored with the younger boy. The four years difference in age makes a great gulf between them.

Camel-hair says: 'Oh, shut up, you, can't you?' And then, catching the eye of one of the orderlies: 'He's always talking, this feller, morning and night he talks. I get fed up with him.'

Camel-hair likes walking about in the men's ward. He likes to wheel trays about and be sent on errands. He insists on an exterior life. The inner life of the imagination is not for him.

'Several going down to-day, I see,' he says, staring with his clear untroubled eyes at a white-coated stretcher bearer. 'Cor, that's a heavy man! It's taking three of them to lift him on to the stretcher. Last week there was one wot took four of them to look after, and he screamed something terrible all night.' The boy does not change his conversational tone: 'He kept me awake till the morning — and then before breakfast he was gorn.' In the boy's voice there is no note of horror, no inquiry into the nature of death. 'Funny thing, a lot of them went last week,' Camel-hair continues in the same matter-of-fact voice: 'All from one side of the room, too. I think there were six or seven of them.' Camel-hair walked about, helping, with his one free arm giving out cups of water, and when this was done he asked: 'Ain't you got another job for me?'

A man recovering from the anaesthetic was breathing heavily. The oxygen cylinders were brought up to him. There was a heavy hammering going on at the end of the ward where someone was trying to open another oxygen cylinder. The sound of hammering did not last long, but it must have been very disturbing to anyone in pain.

The man who had just been given oxygen had a Ramsay MacDonald-shaped face and a heavy moustache. Number 28, in the next bed, looked round the screen from time to time, and asked in a quiet voice: 'How is he getting on? Is he coming round all right?'

Number 27 moved about moaning; he waved his arms with a sweeping outward movement. He stared but saw nothing clearly because, for him, the room had not yet fallen back into its usual outlines. He flung his left arm outwards. His hands had to be put beneath the blankets again so that they should not get cold, and also he was told to be quiet and not to move. He smiled and nodded, but number 28 looked through the screen and said: 'You've got a job on, you have!'

A little farther down K–1 another man was coming out of the anaesthetic, and a nurse was slapping his face to bring him to. The man with the sweeping arms woke up again now and began to cough, spit, and vomit into a basin. I had to wipe his lips and forehead with swabs dipped in cold water. Soon he smiled and went to sleep.

Number 28 said through the screen: 'Poor old number 27! He's all right.'

A quarter of an hour later number 27 started to talk indistinctly. 'He says to me "of course the carriage can't get by" — "how can it?" she says, and it went away, right away.' He waved his arms high in the air, and began once more to tell me the same story without word sequence.

Deputy-Sister Dougall said: 'It's all right — you can leave him now. It's time for you to go down to your lunch, isn't it?'

Another nurse near said: 'Come on — dinner time!'

When the man in the bed began to moan again, I asked if we should leave him. The nurse looked at me rather coldly.

'My dear, when we're off duty, we're off duty — and that's all there is to it!'

Two new nurses came into the ward, putting on their cuffs with a quick-snapping movement. We went down the stone stairs and along the passage, past the Medical Superintendent's office, past three operating theatres, a massage room, and an X-ray room. A dark Irish nurse gave me her cape. 'I've got an extra jersey — and these passages are very cold!' She wrapped her cape round me and we went into the dining-hall. There was a notice up on a board behind the door:

> Will anyone who can play any musical instruments bring them to the Medical Superintendent's office to discuss the forthcoming Hospital Concert.

This was followed by the names of those who had passed examinations, lists of lectures, and a notice to say that first-year nurses, auxiliary, and Red Cross nurses must attend a lecture on blood transfusion in the evening.

In the afternoon it was arranged for me to go to the operating theatre with Charlie, a man who had already been in the hospital for thirteen months, and had no definite idea of when he would be discharged. He was rather an important man in K–1 ward because of the amount of times he had been 'down'. To-day it was only a dressing. The white triangular bandage round his head made him look pale, but he was not very nervous.

We had to wait for the lift for a few moments, and the orderly called out: 'Ere, send that lift dahn — there's a pieshent w'itin'!' It came down abruptly, and the stretcher was wheeled in.

Experienced Charlie reminded us: 'Whatever happens, my foot mustn't get cold.' A first-year nurse re-swathed the thick blanket round his leg. The stretcher bearer was as silent as a messenger from another world. He wheeled the stretcher along the passage towards the theatre. It seemed suddenly to go much faster so that we all three almost ran along to keep pace with it.

The theatre nurses moved about very quickly. We got our overalls and masks, and Mr Robb, the surgeon, arrived. Charlie was brought in and put on the operating table. A bright centre light shone downwards. There were four nurses, a white-gowned man, probably a visiting student or a war-time auxiliary, the surgeon himself, and two people who came in at different times with messages. It must have been tiring for Charlie to have so many people round him, but there was also something about the whole ceremony which seemed to make him appear at his ease, as if he were a host and, although tired, determined to be gracious to his guests.

The surgeon talked all the time, but it was difficult to hear what he said because he had a low sing-song voice, and it seemed as if there was always a humming sound going on in the theatre. There was also the noise of another patient being brought into the anaesthetic room behind us, and a tap was turned on.

Charlie's leg was greenish and had the appearance of marble. The surgeon took the dressing out. Soon the bone was exposed through a deep hole in the side. The skin round the wound was clean and neat, like the wide, white lips of some sea animal. There were a few small pieces of white dressing that had to be got out with sharp instruments like pliers. There was only one moment when it was painful for Charlie, and this moment was over very quickly. More dressing went into the wounded leg, layer after layer. The surgeon continued to talk in his low sing-song voice, and sometimes asked the war-time auxiliaries questions.

Charlie became rather high-spirited. He knew from his experience of 'going down' that it was now all over bar the wheeling back upstairs.

The surgeon said: 'We shall give him the green drug about six o'clock. He will turn green and blue and all kinds of colours.' He said to the war-time auxiliaries: 'Perhaps you would like to see the green drug.'

When this dressing was done we took off our masks and gowns, and threw them down the chute. One of the theatre nurses gave the young first-year nurse a shove and said: 'Now you're in the way — hurry up and get out!' The ward-nurse moved into the ante-room where the clean linen was kept, and cut the tapes off the mask. 'I can't bother to undo them,' she said, 'but I hope she don't see. Not that I trouble much about her!' We went away just as the next patient was being wheeled in.

When Charlie had left the ward to go down, the other men had called out: 'Good luck, Charlie', and 'See you back soon, Charlie!' so that in this being wheeled away from K–1 ward there was something splendid, as if Charlie were a king being carried on his litter into battle; but when he returned they seemed not to notice him at all; from a certain sacred respect of recent suffering they all pretended a deep interest in the books they were reading and the flowers which rested in the tall glasses above dark wooden lockers.

In the early afternoon everyone was quiet. Some of the men went to sleep. They slept sitting up. They had learned to do this in the way that tired horses can sleep standing up, or journalists write in a room of intense noise and bustle. There were one or two visitors, the barber, the man from the dispensary, the long-skirted Catholic priest, and the jolly, red-faced parson, of whom number 32 said: 'Another of these sky-pilots. He must be after you, nurse!' and number 35 answered: 'Oh, well, poor old b—, it's his job. I s'pose he's got to come round here.'

The parson stopped beside the bed of the lorry driver with

the broken foot, only to be told: 'Look here, sir, a man's only got one good friend!' The clergyman asked who it was — hoping to get back the answer that it was 'HIM' — but the lorry driver said: 'A man's purse, that's his only chum in this world.'

'Now you don't mean that,' said the clergyman in his jollying voice.

'I mean it,' said the man, 'and what's more I've proved it.'

Later the relatives came in. 'I suppose it's all right for me to go in, nurse … I know where he is!' Or 'I'm just waiting, nurse — he's got the screens up!'

A working man in a black suit and bowler hat said: 'I'm Harry's father. He's the railway man that has hurt his arm. I've only just got the news. Is he very bad, could you tell me, nurse?'

The man had already been operated on. His arm had not had to be amputated after all, and it was going to be all right.

'You see I only just heard about it, nurse, and I come up to the hospital as quick as I could; but his mother's in hospital, too. She's been there at St Ignatius for five months now, and I think she's finished — she won't come out again.' And then he said: 'I'm so lonely these days. It feels like I can't carry on sometimes. There's not a soul at home.'

Harry was out of the anaesthetic now, and his father took off his bowler hat, walked into K–1 ward, right up to his son's bed and said: 'What you want to go and do that for? I won't half cop you one when I get you 'ome, my boy!'

I was sent over to the women's ward on the other side of the hospital to tell Sister Moncrieff in ward D–2 that the green drug was going to be given to a man at six o'clock in ward K–1, and would she like to come over.

Ward D–2 had a more optimistic look than our own ward. There was more colour here. The women wore bright blue, green, and red bed-jackets to give themselves some sense of luxury and escape from the drab diseases which imprisoned them.

Sister Moncrieff was very tall, and had a rather high colour. She was thin, and gave an impression of great strength. There were three children's cots in her office at the end of the ward. The tallest child, with fair hair, jumped up and down in its cage like a young calf on the way to market. The second one, only three or four months old, smiled and stared at nothing. The last child was asleep. This one was very small, with exact sharp features. Sister Moncrieff asked me: 'What do you think of Bobby Dugout?'

'Who is that?'

'The child, of course,' she said. 'The one that is asleep. His name is Bobby Dugout. "Bobby" after the policeman who found him, and "Dugout" from the air-raid shelter where he'd been left. The policeman brought him in to us.'

'How old is he?'

'We don't know exactly — probably about eight weeks. He looked about three weeks old when he was found, and he's been here about five weeks.'

We returned to the talk about the green drug. 'Just my luck!' Sister Moncrieff said. 'I'm off at five to-day — and I did want to see that. It's always the way, isn't it. When you're off there's always something on!'

I returned to ward K–1, and went round straightening the beds with a tall strong Irish sulky nurse. A surgeon came in to give the green drug. Number 35 said: 'He's a nice man, isn't he, the surgeon. A man you really can have confidence in.'

All the men who were able sat up in their beds. The giving of the green drug was a ceremony rather like a coming-of-age party. Charlie smiled as self-consciously as a shy twenty-firster. Mr Robb talked to the sister in his low sleep-inducing voice, while the drug — the colour of *crème de menthe* — was being poured out. The nurse put the rubber tourniquet round the man's upper arm very slowly. The hypodermic was injected. Charlie did not care, did not stop smiling. Only the slightest trace of his being exaggeratedly at ease suggested some vague anxiety.

Almost at once Charlie's face began to turn green. This greenness started from his chin and as quickly as a blush it spread. Even the gums round his teeth got green.

'He's a better colour than what he were yesterday,' said number 28; and number 29 said: 'I shouldn't like to meet him on a dark night!' From the other end of the room another man called out: 'Puts me in mind of Lon Chaney, the film actor. Did you ever see him?'

'No, I never,' answered a neighbour.

Green-man Charlie sat up in bed smiling. Green skin, green gums, and ginger head. He smiled on even after the surgeon and nurses had passed his bed and were going on their evening round.

Leaving hospital in the evening, I walked down the road carrying my suit-cases. All nurses are continually confronted by happenings of great horror, but this ghastliness is yet made endurable by a routine so exact that it can dull down suffering, pain, and death. So, in spite of everything around, the hospital seems like a large enclosed space of safety, and a nurse's life, in a sense, a very sheltered one.

Travelling by bus and train homewards through the cold black night, I thought again of what one of the hospital orderlies had said: 'So different here from outside, somehow!'

New Year's Eve

The Canadian actor who lives in the next house came to see me to-day. He has volunteered as an auxiliary war-time policeman, and has been taken tramping round the district with an inspector.

A wooden table on which I had been writing was too high, and the Canadian actor brought a saw and sawed several inches off each of its four legs. He said that this gave him the idea of writing a play in which this incident of cutting down a table should happen. He thought it was exactly the kind of thing that pleased an audience. He could imagine them saying: 'You must go and see that play. A real table is sawn up every night!'

I went out to dinner in the evening, not realising that it was New Year's Eve. We sat upstairs in a gloomy old-world grill made much grimmer by favours, streamers, and rather forced gala smiles. A good deal of jazz-drumming and whoop-singing went on in a downstairs room. In the streets beggars followed us, selling toy black cats and miniature bottles of coloured water made to look like whisky, with a label round the neck on which was written 'Good Luck!'

Just before midnight we looked in at the pub opposite. A sailor was playing a concertina and two others were dancing a kind of bunny-hug round and round the room, their caps bobbing up and down like coloured corks on stormy sea water.

1940

January

I have been finishing my hospital hours in a casualty ward. This is altogether a different world from the other wards; a long empty room with two rows of beds, the left side for women casualties, the right for men. There are curtains round each bed, so that when a casualty is brought in he or she waits there for a doctor, boxed up in a kind of cubicle.

Casualties average about thirty a day. Telephone calls come through from the gate. About five minutes later swing doors open at the end of the ward and the ambulance men bring someone in either on a stretcher or in a kind of invalid chair. I have to take down particulars: name, address, occupation, date of birth, whether married, and so on, also a list of the patient's clothes, which he signs. It makes me nervous to ask ill people — sometimes in a state of mental distress — these kind of questions, although of course many of them have been in hospital so often that they know the routine well.

They have to wait a little while for an interview with the doctor before being parcelled up in blankets and taken by stretcher up to the allotted ward. Some of these people walk into the casualty ward themselves, and nearly all of them have one or two members of their family or friends waiting in a resigned way at the end of the long room. One man came in quite alone. He wore the old-fashioned kind of corduroy trousers tied round at the knees and a thick homespun waistcoat, and his hair fell in a thin fringe just above the eyes. When he was asked his address and next-of-kin, he answered: 'I ain't got no relations.' The doctor said: 'But surely you must have some.'

'Oh well,' the man replied, 'I did have a son, but I ain't seen 'im for ten years. 'E went away — didn't see 'im no more. The last time I 'eard, 'e was somewhere near Northampton, but that was eight years ago. I did 'ave another son, too, but I ain't seen 'im for fifteen years. Don't know what happened to 'im.'

The doctor said to me: 'Ask him if he's got any friends.'

'No, I don't think I've got any friends,' the man told us. 'Did 'ave one once — feller called Alf that used to come round and see me, but I don't know where 'e is now. I ain't seen 'im for some years!'

The curious thing about this man, free from all friends and relations, was his apparent happiness. He was uninhibited, without fear, smiling, and strong.

One day a child of about ten years old was brought into the casualty ward suffering from some sort of spasms of the muscles. Her hands were clasped and doubled up. They were exceedingly thin. Her eyes — which were pale blue — only reflected an unreasoning terror, and her teeth — which were almost transparent — were serrated like a saw. The doctor was preparing her arm for an intravenous injection. I myself have an inexplicable horror of an intravenous injection. I have often been given this kind of injection, but never got over the 'phobia against it, so I shared something of the girl's fear. In a few moments I remember being in the kitchen at the end of the ward, although I do not remember walking out. It seemed as if I were physically unable to stay there a second longer, though no doubt it would have been possible for me to do so if it had been really necessary. When I returned, the child had been given the injection and was quite calm, except that when she had a drink of water she was unable to swallow it and was instantly sick. The parents, who had been sitting at the end of the ward, came up. They had been rather amused at the crying of the child. They were a wooden, sub-human gipsyish rather syphilitic-looking couple. They stared at their child and she back at them, without any interchange of affection between them. I went up in the lift with the sub-human couple. I think that they were pleased that their daughter was in hospital, and that they were rid of the trouble of her.

The sister had told me that the child's nervousness was a symptom of her illness; in any case it was not likely that she would live much longer than a few weeks. No doubt it was a better thing for this child that death should come to her, and that it should come quickly, but it was pitiful that she should have had to go through these painful ten years of early life for nothing.

In the casualty ward there was an iron routine which produced a sort of sleep-walking tedium. There was a Civil Service atmosphere, too, in the use of letters for words. 'Go down to the gate and get two DLs.' These were the Danger List Forms which enabled relatives to come in and see patients out of normal visiting hours. 'Take this note down to the MS' — Medical Superintendent. And so on.

A girl of remarkable beauty who came into the casualty ward suffering from some mysterious violent attacks gave me her name and address. She said she was Emily Woods; her husband, Charlie Woods, a baker by profession; living at 28 Oslo Street. Later, the sister-in-charge, who had seen the girl's mother, asked me why I had written this down in the book — because, in fact, the girl's name was Margaret Taylor; she was married to Sam Taylor, in the building trade, and they lived at 14 New Street.

When I explained that the girl had given me the particulars I had written down, the sister shrugged her shoulders and said: 'Clearly an hysterical case.'

The assistant matron and the sisters were all spontaneous and friendly. Of course it is not possible for a Red Cross auxiliary to understand very much of the professional part of hospital life, because she has neither the basic training nor the experience, and, in a sense, she can only be there on sufferance. The impact of hospital life is probably the same intense impression one might get from working as a scullion in a grand hotel for a few weeks. In the hospital I realised the immense difference between being a patient and being a nurse. This sounds obvious, but the difference is so great that although patients and nurses breathe the same air in the same few feet of territory, hear the same conversation, and see the same faces, it is as if they were each living in a completely different country. An LCC hospital could, I suppose, be called a State hospital, and I left it wondering why all hospitals were not nationalised. In the hospital in which I worked there was dignity; the patients felt this, too. They often said: 'I was glad when I knew I was coming here'; and 'I asked the ambulance man where he was taking me, and when he said the name of this hospital, I didn't trouble any more. I just went to sleep as contented as a child.' And also 'It's nice and snug here. I always said that, and I always shall — it's like I was back home in my own bug-house.'

The ratepayers felt they had a right to be here, and the atmosphere of charity was absent. Of course I personally know nothing about voluntary hospitals except from endless appeals received by post, and the sight of medical students in ridiculous fancy dress rampaging through the streets and rattling collecting boxes at passers-by.

Not many of the nurses were politically educated or even politically conscious, but I should say that most of the doctors were at least Socialists.

April

We have had one or two air-raid warnings, but so far no raids. At the sound of the sirens the wardens walk about, but the streets otherwise empty very quickly and quietly, though the buses keep on running. I think that when the real air raids start, people will not trouble to take cover so much. At present this careful 'taking cover' is more a sign of goodwill.

There is a wardens' post by the big block of flats in the street opposite. Looking out of the window I saw a practice; it was a strange sight. At a signal there came from each corner of the street these curious, unreal figures walking in a ceremonious way towards each other. They had rattles in their hands and wore tin helmets. But now these modernistic Tweedledums and Tweedledees and the balloons over London, which look beautiful in moonlight, have taken their familiar places in the background of our lives.

Norway and Denmark have been silently, cleverly, and treacherously occupied. Mr Chamberlain's reference to Herr Hitler missing the bus has naturally not been well received.

June

To-night at the first-aid post I heard the following conversation between Red Cross nurses sitting round a gas stove.

1st VAD: 'Are you writing letters?'

2nd VAD (writing in a notebook): 'No, not exactly' (scribble, scribble). 'You see I'm doing my dog's accounts. I always allow my dog tuppence a week pocket money, and then if the little fellow breaks anything he has to pay for it himself — all out of his own allowance.'

3rd VAD (a tall girl, fond of winter sports in peacetime Switzerland): 'That's funny, we used to allow our dogs pocket money too, and the cats as well, but we gave the dogs more than the cats; we thought it only fair because a cat can't bite a postman's trousers the way our dog did — though I must say that little escapade cost Whisky all his cash for some time to come.'

Another inane conversation. A Red Cross nurse, looking through a newspaper: 'The Duke of Luxembourg has had his leg amputated. H'm'm — poor boy.'

Another nurse: 'Good thing he's not like Leopold. Do you know that boy Leopold has disappointed me almost as much as the Duke of Windsor disappointed me.'

The third VAD then said: 'I don't know about you, but I've finished with King Leopold.'

Sometimes the Red Cross nurses talk in a rather hostile way about the women and men ambulance drivers and rescue squads, with whom we share the canteen.

'When I see them I pass the time of day with them if they pass the time of day with me, but of course with Ikey it's different. With Ikey I really had to put a stop to it quick, because he could have got real nasty.' And about the ambulance girl-drivers: 'Some of them think they're a cut above us. I can't think why!'

All this sort of thing is much less apparent than a few months ago. Most of the snobbish distrust has gone out and more friendliness come in to the Civil Defence station, but from time to time class consciousness rears its ugly head. There is a strong belief in security partnered by privilege, and therefore the privileged status is still a thing to be pursued. 'Of course Sister Wiggins surprises me. She does really. She always talks to them all on this outfit.'

'She may talk to them here, my dear, but she wouldn't dream of being seen dead with them outside. I admire her for adapting herself, I do really.'

When these sort of instincts have been talked out, friendships are formed more in interest groups, or age groups, but not in class groups at all. Class consciousness ceases to act as a reflex action.

***

My war work hours are divided between a Civil Defence station, on the other side of the park, and a small out-patients' department in a working-class district near a general hospital. The main room of this out-patients' building is small and dark and, although lighted with electricity, it looks gas-lit. There are benches in the hall where the patients wait, and also in the little surgery and treatment-room on the right. In the main room there is a desk where people can hand in their cards and get particulars taken, and half-way down this room there is a black sideless medical couch. The place has the look of a 'doss house' on the stage while a Russian play is in progress. Time: the evening. The trained nurse in the mauve dress, wearing gold-rimmed spectacles, says: 'There is always one of us trained people on duty, so you must ask us if you want anything.'

There are two woman doctors who stay here, usually for about six months, until they are transferred and others take their place. They are young, their manner with the patients very good. During their off-duty hours they live in rooms upstairs.

When I told the mauve-dress-spectacled nurse that I knew almost nothing about medicine because I was only a Red Cross auxiliary, she seemed very pleased indeed. It was surprising that a confession of ignorance could so delight anyone.

In the ARP duty room there are the full-time ARP workers. The fat worker who looks like a cosy theatre 'dresser', a rather anonymous grinning young boy, and a Jewish girl with her hair 'whooshed' up in front high above her forehead. There are two other women, one with horn-rimmed spectacles and one with pince-nez; two Indian medical students — one fat and smiling, one old and quiet. The people in this room hum, knit, talk, and ask each other questions from a large book of medicine which they have got out of the free library. They also play cards.

The patients wait, sitting on the wooden benches in the dim-lit room. Most of them wear dark shabby suits, and their white bandages show up very clearly. When the nurse calls out: 'You can come in now', the draped statues move and shuffle into the small surgery. The girl with the hair worn high from the forehead moves into the surgery too. Whenever possible the ill people undo their own bandages. There is a kind of pathetic, homely cordiality here. The patients seem to have great confidence in the nurses. They like to get in a little talk about their own lives.

'Funny thing about my arm — can't turn it right over this way. Never been able to! Once I lost a job through it. I tried to twist my body right over to make it seem like my arm was all right. That was a job on the railway what I missed.'

I go out to dinner with the high-haired girl, thinking of the way in which the women at the time of Marie Antoinette used to dress their hair at an immense height. We eat at a local Lyons. High-hair asks questions in a quick nervous way. About France: 'Were they to blame at all?' Fortunately she does not really want any answers to the questions she asks. She is friendly and gay. The other workers like her. 'Ever such a sweet girl, Lydia is!'

***

This evening a Red Cross nurse at the first-aid post told me: 'You know I haven't been to a theatre since Edward VIII left us. You see I always drink now "to the King over the water", and I shan't go to a theatre till he comes back. Some men can change their kings as easily as they change their socks, but not me. Edward the VIII is always Edward VIII as far as I am concerned,' and as an afterthought she added: 'Anyway, I can't afford theatres now.'

To-night I was off duty. The siren went at one-thirty am. Later, the three tenants living in this building came out of their flats and strolled down to the basement at the invitation of a young bearded colonial musician who lives there. He has a large studio room with a grand piano in it, but the electric light and gas had been cut off because it is unpaid. The room was lit with candles. The musician wore a velvet jacket. He had side-whiskers and altogether there was a rather old-fashioned, false du Maurier *Quartier Latin* atmosphere.

The woman music teacher also came down, and the girl who lives in the flat above her. The conversation was about old Vienna and so on, and the musician gave the music teacher a slim volume of bad American poetry. He was given to uttering out terrifically sweeping statements, and seemed to be a kind of frustrated Fascist.

Some German refugees living in the half-basement flat on the right talked and shouted to their children, but there was no gun-fire to be heard, and no sound of bombs. The velvet-smoking-jacketed young man told us that the Fuehrer (Hitler) was a great artist. 'You can see it by his face,' he said. The answer came to me at once: 'Possibly — but you can't see it by his paintings.' But I did not trouble to say this aloud.

The young man was collecting cigarette cards because he thought they would stop being issued in war-time, and so would have a certain documentary interest. I left some for him, a few days later, on the ledge where they put the tenants' letters. He came up and thanked me. Soon afterwards he left the building, and the grand piano stayed on in the empty basement flat as a kind of hostage. I heard that he had volunteered to work on a farm because he was a Conscientious Objector. I do not know if he had always been one. My only interest in him was as an example of one individual pacifist linking up in his point of view with the Fascists.

July

Some Englishwomen here are occupying themselves entertaining and planning for the Free French. I found a few French soldiers evacuated from Dunkirk having tea at D's. None of them knew a single word of English; most had been wounded; a tall, fresh-faced farmer had several fingers of his right hand shot away. They were staying at some big stadium — either the White City or Olympia — and complained continually about the English draughts. They said that the English commandant at the camp was very well liked by all the men. When I asked if this commandant spoke very good French, they told me that he did not know one single word, and after a time the French farmer added: 'But the English sergeant knows a lot of French.'

Two of the Frenchmen were from the Midi. They had a vineyard, and now were troubled and anxious about it. One of them told me that he had fought with his regiment for four days. They were short of supplies, without proper communications, and had very heavy casualties. They had been taken off at Dunkirk, but the ship got blown up, and so he had been in hospital some time, but now was well again. Talking of the war in France, he said: 'What happened? Were we sold by our Generals or what?' And the quiet sad man who had a small wireless shop somewhere in the south, said: 'I should say we were well sold!'

All these men were returning to France. They had been given their choice, and decided to go back. Each had something to say about this. 'You see, I have to look after my vineyard', or else, 'I must look after my grandmother. She is seventy-six', or, 'Now I'm wounded there's nothing much more for me to do. No use to go on living in the London draughts — and, after all, if the English arrive in France, we shall all be there ready to help them.'

Perhaps it is difficult for anyone to take a world view, but it was most difficult of all for these particular Frenchmen. They were simple fellows without much thought or knowledge of anything outside their own particular district in France. They had been given the chance to join General de Gaulle. They had not heard of him before, but their instinct was: 'In future we shall avoid all French generals!'

All these men were wearing English tweed suits, lent by people of the 'hunting, fishing, shooting' classes. It gave the Frenchmen the appearance of actors dressed up as English landlords.

The one who owned the small wireless shop was also a violinist. He was sad and quiet, but in his rather loud-patterned tweed coat and grey flannel trousers he had a touching dignity.

August

We often have daylight warnings now. Some of the people who go to shelters walk more slowly after the siren sounds. They look like people going to church.

From my window one day I saw a man carefully unharnessing his horse and putting the cart in front of it as a protection. On a very clear day when the sky was a cloudless blue, I saw two parachutes come billowing down. They were both escaping airmen from a 'plane that had been hit: although they landed five or six miles from where I was living, I watched them for a long time, surprised that they came down so slowly.

The woman musician in the ground-floor flat was teaching a nine-year-old child the other day. The siren sounded, followed by considerable gun-fire. She asked the child:

'Wouldn't you like to stop your music lesson for a bit?' and got back the answer: 'Don't trouble about me. You see I live at Southampton.'

So far Southampton has had the most severe raids.

Although at the beginning most people had taken shelter at the sound of daylight sirens, yet at night they do not seem to trouble. One evening in the Chelsea Cinema a slap-stick comedy was being run through. Suddenly right across the seat of the trousers of one of the comedians the words 'Air Raid' flashed up. It happened by chance, but was a great success with the audience. Someone said in a bored manner: 'It's that voice again', and someone else answered: 'Oh, you mean "Syreen".'

There is a theory that people living near the docks learnt this pronunciation from hearing Greek sailors talk about their ship's siren.

About an hour later, when the cinema show was over, the audience trooped out, discussing the merits and faults of the film. A man walking in front of me was talking to his companion about the majesty of London seen by searchlight. He thought the black-out showed up the beauty of buildings which electricity had long concealed by too much glare. Two old ladies walked near me. They were of the umbrella'd, long-skirted school whose sayings used to make up about twenty-five per cent of the jokes in *Punch*. A warden told them there was a shelter nearby.

'But we don't need a shelter,' they said, 'we're going home.'

'Well, I shouldn't walk home too slowly if I were you, madam. They've been rather unpleasantly overhead for some time now.'

The wardens, of course, cannot compel anyone to take shelter, but they do their best to keep people off the streets during air raids.

'The Germans over our heads?' answered the old lady, 'then

we won't walk home at all. Come along, Emily, we'll take the bus.'

In this time of death-from-the-air, the streets are more alive than in peace-time. Figures, shadowy yet purposeful, of people going on duty move along side by side, with others returning homewards from Civil Defence work, or from a few hours' leisure in theatre or in cinema.

In the darkness one sees the outlines of peaked caps and civilian duty gas-masks slung over shoulders. The white hats of some of the wardens show up very clearly. When the 'Alert' is on, even the inside lights of the buses are dossed down; the passengers lean back in their seats incredibly nonchalant. The other night a street musician at the mouth of an archway had not troubled to take his upturned hat from the ground. I heard him mutter to himself: 'I'm more likely to get "Pennies from Heaven" than pennies from the populace to-night!' He was listening to the droning of the aeroplanes overhead. 'It's "b",' he said, 'that's the note of them — "b". If I had a piano handy I could play it!' He shook his head more in sorrow than in anger. 'Now it's gone flat!' He hummed the note 'b' again. 'There you are! As flat as old Ribbentrop's champagne! Poor old Jerry can't even keep his "airyplanes" in tune!'

I went on to the Civil Defence post where I was on duty at midnight. I made my way through the waiting ambulances down to the canteen. Some of the nurses were sitting talking, reading, and studying medical books. The ambulance men were still fighting a battle against enforced inactivity.

A last-war hero who had grumbled his way through four years of fighting and twenty years of peace since, said wearily: 'Wot's old Jerry doin' now? Still playin' "Ring-a-ring-o'-roses" round the sky, I s'pose?'

These ambulance drivers, rescue party men, stretcher bearers, and demolition workers have all given long hours to training, and are anxious to get out into the streets during air raids, but they do not get an opportunity of doing so unless their station happens to be in the district of an 'incident', which is the understated official name for a bomb falling in a populated area.

September

We have been having five or six air-raid warnings each day and long night-time raids lasting eight or nine hours from 'Alert' to 'All Clear'. Some of the streets are roped off owing to damage or waiting for the explosion of delayed bombs. Buses and trains move in a slower, more circumscribed way.

I have bought a bicycle, and must travel several miles a day on it, taking so many streets out of my way. Some people are going to work by the river ferry. Some trudge along, but motor cars are never one-man cars now. I saw a small family Austin with its load of people picked up on the way — Home Guards, Red Cross nurses, a member of a stretcher party, an old lady, and a sister returning to hospital duty, were all emanating in and out of this same small car.

The new anti-aircraft barrage is on at night. Although it adds to the noise people seem to find it rather soothing. The idea that a part of the noise is on our side gives a certain confidence. In the early evenings I pass people walking to the shelters carrying their rugs and blankets tied round with string or straps, or else wheeling their family perambulators filled up with coats or anything else that can keep them warm. The sight of this procession of people with their bundles of bedclothes at sundown in the London streets is deeply touching. Although one is struck by the force of misery, at the same time some of these people have a great dignity in misfortune, so that the humiliation is very suddenly shifted from the sufferer to the onlooker.

Once I saw them all begin to run. It had started to rain and, as they ran along, one or two of them started to laugh. 'Wait till we catch old Nazi-boots! — we won't 'arf give 'im rain, we won't 'arf!'

I am on from midnight until eight in the morning shift at the first-aid post. As it is about four or five miles from where I am living, I go there sometimes before midnight to avoid a journey through bombardment. For the moment I am attached to one of the mobile van units. In the event of a certain kind of 'incident' in a particular district, we should go out in a surgical van with doctor, sister, and two or three other Red Cross nurses. The idea is to deal with casualties at the place of the 'incident'. These vans are well packed, and as compact as caravans or ship's cabins.

The demolition men, rescue parties, and stretcher bearers go out more often than we. The first time I saw them do this it was very impressive. They got into their cars with the various things they needed, pick-axes, spades, shovels, first-aid supplies and so on, and drove out up the ramp of the garage, but it did not seem as if they made a series of moves to get to their cars, start them up, and then steer them out — it was so perfectly timed that it seemed to have become only one movement. The numbers were called out, and almost on the words the rescue men were ready — then they drove out into the bombardment. It was an action of great grace. The movements of the car wheels were faster than the beats of my heart.

All through the night rescue parties were going out. It went on happening from the fall of darkness to early morning. When we went off duty it was beginning to be light again, and all London was lit up with the sunrise and the flames in the sky from still-burning buildings.

When the demolition men and stretcher bearers came out of the bombardment and down into the canteen again, their faces were black with dirt. Some had got grit in their eyes, and the lids were inflamed. They fetched cups of coffee from the canteen, took them back to their tables, and settled down to play cards. Joe took off his helmet and put it on the floor beside him. Charlie still wore his at an angle.

'Funny thing, that old girl we got out of that building kept talking about her cat. That's all she seemed to trouble about — her cat! Fancy bothering about a blinking cat in all this! Cor, what a game!'

'How long were you there to-night, Charlie?'

'Dunno. 'Ell of a long time it seemed!'

While we were playing cards, Harry, the man with the waxed moustache, came up to talk to us. When he had gone Charlie said: 'Now he really is a good officer, Harry is!' And Joe answered: 'Yes, that's it. Always there when anything's on, Harry is! Right on the spot at the start, and the last to leave at the finish!'

A week or two after this conversation Harry got killed on duty during a bombardment.

Even during heavy bombardments I have often heard one branch of the Civil Defence complaining about another. 'As to the wardens — they're more trouble than they're worth, the wardens are. Why, there was one the other night, got asking a lot of silly questions. We just wished he'd go off home and not trouble us no more!'

One morning I walked back through the park, and saw the highest branches of a tree draped with bits of marabout, with some sort of silk, with two or three odd stockings and, wrapped round the top of the tree, like a cloak quick-thrown over the shoulder of some high-born hidalgo, some purple damask. Below it, balanced on a twig as if twirled round a finger, was a brand new bowler hat. They had all been blown across the road from the bombed hotel opposite. A surrealist painter whom I know slightly was staring at this, too. He said: 'Of course we were painting this sort of thing years ago, but it has taken some time to get here.'

In the mornings one sees the people coming out of their shelters carrying the same blankets and rugs. An elderly, invalidish man said: 'It's just like the last war when we were out there, and used to go out and get the rations in the morning. This cold light brings it all back to me. Well, it took us some time, but we beat them then. Of course after we finish with these air raids we will have to start digging old Nasty out of all the places he's put his great black ugly feet in!'

On my nights off duty I sit by the balcony. Fire engines from near-by stations rush through the streets. The men seem to be standing to attention on each side of a long ladder. Often when the engines come back there are three or four men missing. During this last week the casualties in the fire-fighting brigade have been heavy. Completely lit up by flames they continually get bombed again.

Every night now the Civil Defence Army is fighting to a fierce accompaniment of incendiaries, dive-bombers, and guns; the sky is lit up in patches, and a hideous melodrama let loose over London. But I think that, in spite of the horror, the majority are rather relieved that the talking is over and we are shooting it out.

October

I got home one morning to find the pub opposite half burned out, and a skeleton of scrap iron — 'the Guvnor's new car' — standing out in the street. Someone had put a placard on it with the words '1940 model'. A large building in the same street, a hideously ugly white brick block of flats, was now smudged a dirty brown, the result of an oil bomb. The vulgarity of the building was slightly lessened by the oil spluttered over it, but of course it was still exceedingly ugly. A great many refugees live in this block of flats, and some simple people of the streets near-by told me a fantastic theory: 'They say it's quite safe in them flats; you see from the air it makes the shape of the swastika, so it won't never be bombed.'

***

On my night off duty last week the door of my room opened so often with the force of the bombardment outside that I accepted the invitation of the music teacher downstairs to visit her flat. Her brother, recently escaped from some damaged near-by building, was sitting there. There was a piano near the window, and opposite it a music stand.

When I had been about five minutes in this room it seemed to me that these objects were suddenly made to move about as in a René Clair film. Almost immediately afterwards the lights went out, the walls broke up and fell inwards. Some of the ceiling came down, and the door freed itself from its hinges and was hurled into the centre of the room. The shutters and window frames went on splintering up for some time. The floor, which was probably unaffected, seemed to be moving most of all. There was an atmosphere of shipwreck at sea by night, and when the sense of storm stopped there continued on in the darkness the intermittent sound of falling glass which made me think of those half-forgotten chandeliers which always get in the way when one walks into a dim antique shop.

The music teacher was no longer there. It was strange that anything as large as a human being could disappear so suddenly and so completely. It was difficult to see in the ruined room. There were no longer any curtains or shutters, but some of the window panes were still there. I broke one of them with my shoe in order to get out by the area railings.

A troop of men, steel-helmeted, dark-overalled, and Wellington-booted ran towards the house, looking like story-book heroes on the cover of a boys' magazine. They ran up into the house. One of them had a shaded torch, and we saw in this half-light a fallen door not quite flat to the floor. A warden very gently lifted it up and found the music teacher. She recovered consciousness quickly; the cut on her forehead was not serious, but this was the first time I had seen a case of this sort of memory lapse. She did not remember anything that had happened two hours before. These events had been completely erased from her mind by the falling of the door. The wardens asked me if there was anyone else in the house, and as I was saying that as far as I knew there was not, a whole group of people came up from the empty basement where they had been taking shelter — mostly German and Austrian refugees. Probably these people had been living here underground by night for several weeks without our knowing anything about it, and now, struggling through their language difficulties, they were troubling about their possessions in rather a shrill way. 'Please I have lost my identification card.' Once out into the street they did not seem to be certain which underground basement had thrown them up.

'Is this number 42, could you tell me?' and 'Where is number 26?' and 'My gas mask — where is he?'

The young meteorologist, an acquaintance living in the same street, came striding along, tweed-coated, like a man out on a country walk. There was no longer anything we could do here, and he suggested I should have a drink at his flat, which, he said, was quite all right. The door to his flat was hanging from a thread like a dangling milk-tooth; glass, badly broken, pointed downwards in jagged icicle edges. The meteorologist's sitting-room, which was high up, was less damaged than the rest of the house, and although the bombardment continued with considerable strength, we had a false sense of security here, and settled down to drink and argue. He was interested in some idea about the speed at which sound travels in relation to bombs. I could not understand his sound-speed story, and so we had to continue each along our own egotistical lines of conversation.

In the street the wardens argued about which buildings had been 'plastered'. As more buildings came down with a run, they continually said: 'Up she goes!'

Later, we strolled round to my flat to get my bicycle. Some wardens on the look-out for looters helped us to wheel it out, one saying: 'Well, I'll be damned! Fancy it working after all this! The street has "copped it" with a parachute mine. We were only told about them yesterday. Just my luck to get one the very next night!'

On this evening I remember hearing a British officer in khaki talking about some people whom he supposed he had seen signalling from the ground to the air. He spoke of flashes of light being Morse-coded to the enemy. It was quite clear that he was back in the Boys'-Own-Paper-adolescent-mood, and as he was middle-aged he was not likely to get out of it now.

The meteorologist said: 'The real Fifth Column is made up of just such jitter material as that damned officer!'

The house of the rich woman opposite looked battered and lop-sided now, and a small row of luxury houses in a cul-de-sac near-by had all become uninhabitable. When we went out to breakfast we saw that already the shopkeepers had started to mend their windows with thin strips of wood. Civilian refugees came out into the street looking for a café where they could get breakfast. They were tired and dirty, and there was that smell of plaster which I had already grown to know well.

At nine o'clock I rode round on my still undamaged bicycle to have breakfast with some friends in Regent's Park. There was a time-bomb somewhere outside Hanover Terrace, and the usual notice displayed. HG Wells, wearing a corded dressing-gown, was walking down the terrace talking to a neighbour of his, an auxiliary policeman. Later in the morning I went to Broadcasting House to give a scheduled talk in the Overseas programme. I only just got there in time, through the policeman letting me go through a roped-off street.

I picked my way between the bits of broken glass like a pony practising *haute école*. A passer-by said: 'She wouldn't 'arf look a fool if the time-bomb went orf now!' But I think this bit of street had only been roped off to protect people from falling glass from high buildings, and I had a steel hat.

HG Wells is letting me stay in a Mews flat at the end of his garden for the time being. He is going on a lecture tour to America for a few weeks. This flat, above a garage, looks out on to a very clean mews, and is as quiet and restful as a very pretty room in the country.

'HG' has asked me to be very careful to observe the black-out.

November

I was at Victoria Station waiting for one of the Green Line coaches to take me to the country for two or three days. The man at the bookstall was speaking about a paper printed in Scotland: 'Funny, ain't it, that paper sells more copies in the North of England that what it does in Scotland, and yet it's a Scotch paper!' On the words there was a crash, followed by a dull rumble. Reassuringly to everyone around him the bookseller went on: 'It's all right. It's only a time-bomb. It's over Eaton Square way. They were expecting it to go off — and now it 'as!' But none of the people showed any signs of fear. Most of them had forgotten that there was an air-raid warning on at all.

The coach set out. In the streets there were little knots of people staring up at the sky. They still do this. Some were pointing upwards, but I could not see anything. One of the coach travellers remarked: 'You know those bits of smoke up there? They say that when they make a figure-of-eight like that they're just about to drop a bomb on the target.' Another traveller answered: 'I don't know about dropping a bomb on the target, but I hope we don't get machine-gunned on this trip down!' A third said in a conversational tone: 'Somehow the buses don't seem to run as regular as they used to.'

There was a great atmosphere of 'not giving a damn' in the Green Line coach. As we went under a bridge someone said: 'Oh, here they come', and a squadron of aeroplanes roared low down over our heads. The man next to me remarked: 'They're ours', and the one opposite to me said: 'Well, I must say I hope so.' This made all the passengers laugh.

The 'All Clear' sounded, and people smiled, looking down on their newspapers, which they had never stopped reading.

As one goes into the country, people getting in at the different stops treat those who are already in the coach who have come directly from London as if they were soldiers returning from the front line. The newcomers ask eager questions about recent bombardments, saying modestly: 'Of course we ain't 'ad nothing like that down our way.'

All the same, they seem to have had a certain amount of bombing in the small country districts. An errand boy sitting near told me how he had watched several 'dog-fights'. He said with great pride: 'Our boys are wonderful, they are really. They take on ever so many more of the enemy than what they are themselves. They never shirk it. I seen some wonderful things our chaps have done. Of course,' he added, 'I look forward to the day when we get air equality — and still more to the time when we get air superiority!'

The coach went through a suburb, past a line of bombed

two-dimensional houses looking like the wooden toy Swiss chalets which used to be sent to us when we were children.

A pretty woman dressed in WVS uniform got into the coach. When we stopped at a pub she asked me to have a drink with her. She had been on duty in the East End during the time of the dockyard fires. For people living in these overcrowded districts the bombardment was very much worse. Many of the rest centres got full up quickly, and some people had to sleep in damp houses at night while spending their days walking from one form-filling government office to another.

During my three days in the country a man I knew, now an officer in the Army, came over to dinner. He said they had very little news of London, and had always supposed the bombardment to be much exaggerated. It was clear from his conversation that he was rather in the dark about events in the capital, although he was stationed only forty miles away from it.

***

There are air raids every night now. They start about seven o'clock. We know all the sounds very well. A very familiar sound is a particular kind of crackling after the fall of incendiary bombs. We go out then and put the fires out with stirrup pumps and sand. This is not difficult, and can usually be quickly done. There were a few fires in the terrace, and the auxiliary fire brigade arrived. Eric Davis, who was shipwrecked on his way to Singapore in the *City of Benares*, and rescued after eighteen hours on a raft, came back to London and was staying in 'HG's' house. Eric Davis told me the *Benares* went down in forty minutes.

Eric, wearing a mackintosh coat, strolls over to the Mews to help when there are these scrambles out into the open to deal with the falling incendiaries. On the first nights of this kind of thing there were confused figures rushing about in the darkness, and rather the atmosphere of an earlier Charlie Chaplin film, in which Charlie is a slap-stick fireman, but after a night or two it became much more efficient.

Enemy aeroplanes attack in waves, which means that there are always lulls. Sometimes there is complete quiet for as much as ten minutes at a time. One looks at the clock and thinks: 'Only another three or four or five hours', or whatever it may be. The 'All Clear' usually sounds between five and six o'clock in the morning.

Some of 'HG's' windows have been broken. The West End Hospital for Nervous Diseases in the park has been damaged in a way that makes it look like a nervous disease itself.

I go to the out-patients' department of the hospital on certain days in the week. One of the Indian medical students is a fully qualified doctor in India. He looks old, is very quiet and gentle, and has a name like 'Chicago' said backwards. He told me of the recent incident when the tube station near-by was bombed, and casualties were brought into the out-patients' department. Almost immediately afterwards a near-by shelter was hit, and more casualties came in. A third hit near the department broke the windows, so that the lights were exposed to the street, and had to be put out. The patients were moved quickly into a reception room and small operating theatre. He said that the bombardment was so severe that it was not possible to follow the usual routine, and send treated patients home with their relatives and friends; and as all the patients brought several people in with them, the small building became very crowded. A seventy-year-old workman was told, after his wounds had been treated, that his own home had been bombed. He answered: 'Well, this is how I look at it — if it's dahn, it's dahn, and 'e can't knock it dahn again, can 'e?'

These men and women of work-town often speak of the

enemy and even of a whole squadron of bombers as 'he'. Sometimes they mean 'Jerry', the collective name for all Germans in war-time, and sometimes they mean Hitler, but, in either case, this personification of the enemy as 'he' is a kind of gigantic debunk of the whole Nazi melodrama of bombs, paratroops, drawling Haw-Haw, screaming Hitler, limping Goebbels, and all the rest of it.

The Indian doctor told me that during the evening of this incident all the lights went out in the small surgery, and oil lamps were put round the room on the floor. A wounded man remarked: 'It's just like being in a blinkin' Japanese garden!'

The friends and relatives helped the hospital workers with the filling of hot-water bottles, making of tea, and so on. The Indian doctor shrugged his shoulders and said in his sallow voice: 'Well, it all went off all right!'

When I went home in the morning I saw a policeman riding a white horse which was rearing, throwing its head about and trying to walk sideways into buses. A couple who had just come up out of one of the shelters seemed to be very much pleased with this sight. The man said: 'E ain't 'arf playin' 'im up!' and the woman answered, rather sadly: 'No, they never throw policemen — that's the worst of horses.'

In the bus I heard a man saying about enemy aeroplanes: 'It's supposed to be all right when they're just overhead', and the man on the next seat answered at once: 'Well, I think different!' Immediately a fierce academic argument started between the two men. It was still going on when I left the bus.

***

Last night when I made my way to the hospital there was a storm. It was dark, but every now and then the whole district was lit up by gun-fire. Each time this happened I saw the outlines of the gutted-out church opposite the bus stop where

I waited.

Because it was cold and I disliked the noise, I leaned against the doorway of the garden of a somewhat prosperous house, although it afforded no protection either from rain, noise, or shell splinter. A man came towards me through the storm reeling and spinning round like a leaf in an east wind. I do not know if he was drunk or frightened, but somehow his balance was upset by this storm and air raid. He said something which I could not hear, and I asked him if he had seen either a bus or a taxi. He shouted back some other sentence and went down the road, still spinning round and round. When he had gone past, and I could no longer see him, I could still hear his stumbling steps. His heels on the stone road played the part of clumsy drumsticks against the blunt orchestra of aeroplane hum.

I began to make my way down the dark and discouraging road, hoping to find a taxi. I tried to stop what I supposed was a bus, but this turned out to be an Army lorry with great headlights which came on suddenly full strength, as immense cat's eyes in the dark. I said: 'Sorry, I thought you were a bus', and the soldier sitting beside the driver said: 'Excuse me, but could you tell me the way to Finchley? We're completely lost.' The lorry driver was going in the opposite direction to his objective. I directed them back as best I could and, walking onwards, bumped into what I supposed was a telephone or post-box, but it was a police box; three policemen rushed out as if from a beehive hit by a stick. I explained my trouble in trying to get a taxi in order to be at my post on time, and one of the policemen said: 'What you really want is a policeman to walk with you. I wish I was going that way myself.'

I set out once more, walking in the centre of the road, my Wellington boots at least a size too large for me, and my steel helmet so uncomfortable that it seemed to be a size too small. Soon a taxi drew up in an accosting manner, and the driver said: 'I met a policeman what sent me along!' At the hospital door the same taxi-driver remarked: 'I hope we've got no Eye-talians bombing us. We can stand anything but that — it's the last word, when we get the old macaronies coming over!'

The light in the hall of the out-patients' building glared in my eyes so that, coming straight from the darkness, I did not at once see the soldier who was having a fit on the floor. He was kicking and throwing himself about, and the woman doctor and a nurse were wiping his mouth with cotton wool. He was a man from a Bomb Disposal Squad who had probably been affected by a few mild drinks on top of a prolonged nervous strain. Soon the soldier became completely unconscious, and was taken by ambulance to another hospital.

In the duty room the doctor of the mobile van was playing bridge with his wife and two trousered girls from the mobile unit. High-haired Lydia played patience, slapping the cards down on an American cloth-topped table like dabs on a fishmonger's slab. A VAD was trying on a jersey she had knitted herself, saying: 'Do you think my one-and-only will admire this? He's very difficult about his likes and dislikes, my one-and-only is.'

Two men — one a very grey-faced, ill rescue man, and the other a St John's stretcher bearer — asked me to play cards with them. They had great difficulty in explaining the game.

'If you get a run — like, say, four, five, six — then all them cards counts together, like. Or if you get a run of four, like, you can have that, too, and it makes somethink better than what you'd have had if you'd have had the other.' The language limped and halted through the explanations, but fortunately I already knew the game.

The surgery was being repainted, and some of us sat there with the old Roman Catholic nurse, who had brought some sandwiches. The elder Indian student, the one with the name like 'Chicago' said backwards, tried to talk about the economic conditions in Germany, on which he was rather well informed, but the Roman Catholic nurse always came into the conversation with violent obviousness.

'That's what it is with the German youth,' she said, 'they're all taught to be hero-worshippers. That's what they're taught to be — hero-worshippers.'

She wore her prejudices like iron-clad stays, and soon started to tell us some astonishing stories about her life in a maternity ward.

'I was delivering a child, and I said to the mother: "Now you must make an effort to bring this child into the world", and the mother answered: "I can't do no more about bringing this child into the world — and anyhow, it never will be born." I said to her: "Why will it never be born, I should like to know?" — and I can remember it as if it was yesterday — she answered me back, this mother did: "Because I took five bobs' worth of the green death." I sat back on my haunches and I said to her: "You what?" I knew it was my duty to give her a fright, so I told her that her baby would never be right. Of course I knew it was as right as rain, really, but I also knew that it was my duty to give her this fright. But the next day a woman who'd taken a lot of illicit medicine came into the ward — and her baby never did get born. She died in great agony, and I remember now how I looked round the ward and said to them all: "Mothers, let this be a lesson to you. You must never take life which God Almighty has started!"'

It was very early in the morning, and the air raid was still on. We could hear the hum of aeroplanes. A girl from the mobile van looked up ceilingwards and said: 'Well, what do you think is chiefly happening overhead now, if it isn't taking life?'

This old Roman Catholic nurse, who was always bringing sandwiches for her colleagues, had, through the cunning of clerics and the prejudice of prelates, been brought to such an abject state of mind that she was able to act with the greatest cruelty while still keeping to herself the inner smirk of self-righteousness.

Another nurse, arriving for the early morning shift, said to the woman doctor: 'On my way here this morning I saw the moon shining down on those two craters in the road. That is all you can see. It was uncanny. I thought to myself: "Now it's a long time since I've had an uncanny walk like this!"'

Somebody said at breakfast: 'Don't make so much noise. Sister's asleep upstairs', but they got back the answer: 'Oh, shut up. Anybody would think you were the blinking matron!'

December

The other night I went to supper in one of the grand hotels. We seemed to have been suddenly flung into the most vulgar and sordid cinema set. 'Metro-Goldwyn, do your worst!' We were surrounded by dancing, smiling, hand-waving, eyebrow-lifting gilded guests, jogging to brute music around a room of pseudo-Gothic expensive squalor. The bitter-sweet smiling swine circled about and not for one second did the band cease to blare in a monotone. At a table on my left a middle-aged man balanced a bottle of champagne on his head. I thought: 'When he meets another man who can balance two bottles of champagne on his head, it will be the end for him!'

I have sometimes enjoyed evenings in luxury restaurants. I do not know why this particular one acted on my nerves in such a shrill and unbearable way.

A rather agreeable man sitting next to me at the supper-party evidently reacted to it in the same manner. He said that if a bomb should drop at this moment and send all these people off the face of the earth, at least this would give us the chance of being able to feel that we had added our quota to the war effort.

***

To-night there was a curiously Londonian group of hospital helpers at the out-patients' department.

A tall Boy Scout with knobby knees, two Indian medical students, the older one so calm that he reminded me of the kind of men who spend their afternoons playing slow games of bridge in Cromwell Road residential hotels, the chemist's assistant who always comes in and gives his one evening off a week to the hospital, and a young girl hairdresser. A leftish clergyman strolled into the duty room. He feels very bitterly about bad housing in St Pancras and Civil Service obstructionism. A few casualties came in, one an African with a bad knife wound in his face. After this had been stitched up and he was leaving, the doctor asked me to tell him that he should rest when he got home. I walked after him to give this message. The coloured man with the wound across his face smiled widely and answered:

'Ah'm sorry, but ah can't do that. I'm a-going out to "get" the man that wounded me.' Wars within wars!

1941

February

I am working on an eight weeks' course in a government training centre. A certain amount of training in technical engineering is given by workshop practice, lectures, and so on. The works superintendent acts in an advisory capacity on behalf of workers leaving the training centre at the end of their course. He tries to tell them something of the factories asking for employees, and the conditions. Women who are finishing their training course often come in and tell us about their interviews with employers and the ridiculously inadequate wages some of these people still dare to offer them. These stories are always received with laughter, because we feel it is the only thing to do. We often hear that even with overtime, war bonus, and so on, it is exceedingly difficult for a woman worker spending seventy hours a week in a factory to earn more than £2 a week, although the cost of living on the 1st of January this year stood at 96 points above the level of July 1914, and has risen one point above the figure of December last year, due again to increases in the prices of coal and clothing. The Purchase Tax also raises the cost of living figure.

The works superintendent himself is a man of goodwill, and would not allow women trained at his centre to work for the sums employers insulted them by offering. The Labour Exchange executives would also try to support any government memoranda sent in on wages questions. But there are a good many women who, either through a nervous fear of officialdom, or a bewildered wish to get work somewhere, would accept the most inadequate wage. It is a discouraging situation. No doubt there will be some serious discussions and reform on this wages-for-women problem, but it is depressing to observe there are still so many employers of blunted sensibility trying their best to get away with it.

Many of the women seem to have a natural talent for mechanics. They seem to be stimulated at the idea of being given a chance to learn a trade. I heard many stories of the pathetic way in which people have been trying to earn their living in peace-time. Girls in the workshop often say: 'This is much better than scrubbing floors all day!' or 'Better than the Land Army, because at least it'll be permanent, and we shan't all be sent home again after three months!'

The technical engineers who have been chosen as instructors are gentle, competent, and patient. The one who is the most brilliant seems to see propaganda everywhere and in everything. I believe it is impossible for a man like this to read a poem, look at a painting or hear music without seriously asking himself: 'What class basis has it?'

I get back to HG Wells's mews most evenings at about half-past six. The sitting-room looks out on the mews side on trees, so that sometimes I have the illusion of being in the country.

In spite of almost nightly bombardment, having to get up early each morning and set out while it is still dark, and occasionally before the 'All Clear', a certain amount of ill-health and emotional obsession in my personal life, and an intense awareness of the ghastliness of everything around, my life has been much more happy in the last few months here than at any other time elsewhere. I suppose that everyone has this strong individual life going on independently of all outside events.

April

The present possibility of covering great distances in telescoped time adds to the sense of isolation instead of decreasing it. When I went to stay at one of the outposts of the BBC in a country town, I felt as if I were living in a remote land. Although the same war was going on here, it seemed to be a different war altogether, and all the people were looking, thinking, and acting in a different way.

We had two very heavy bombardments on London this month. During the first of these I was at home trying to make some notes for something I am writing. The noise outside was considerable, and the plates in the rack above the cooking stove clattered against each other in unending exasperation. After midnight the events outside seemed to have become too exaggerated for even a pretence at indifference, and also, I had to take over my turn for fire watching. There were plenty of fires to watch. 'HG' happened to be away from London on this first night (though he got back for the second big bombardment), so that I was able to go to the top of his house and, looking from a high-up room, I could see that we were surrounded by seven or eight bowls of flame, as if we were in a jungle camp and the fires were there to keep us free from the approach of wild animals. Unfortunately, exactly the contrary was happening, as these fires must have lit up London very clearly for the attacking aeroplanes.

When these bombardments have been continued nightly for a long period, some of the people who at first had to use courage, now use the suppression of imagination so successfully that they are not really able to react any more. The night-shifts work on in their factories, Civil Defence men, nurses, roof-spotters, and so on take up their posts automatically. They say at the sound of the siren: 'Oh, here's old Adolf and his Loofterwaffer again!' or else they don't even refer to it at all.

On one of these evenings I was reading a speech of Ernst Toller in an old literary quarterly which I found in my room. This speech was full of hope, but now Ernst Toller has committed suicide. I believe a great many German refugees have killed themselves after they have succeeded in escaping and getting into safety. L told me that she had some refugees staying with her. They had been got out of a concentration camp. They knew they were completely secure in her house, and all their troubles of that kind were over, but it was just the sense of being able to relax that made it possible for them to react at last against the horrors they had been through, resisted at the time in the only possible way, through suppression of imagination. L told me that every time the bell rang or a postman knocked at the door the refugees all began screaming and crying, although rationally they knew, and admitted, that the English postman could not possibly be a Gestapo agent. I do not think that bombardment from the air, violent and frightening as it can be, compares in any way to the torture inflicted by one individual upon another. It seems that as far as concentration camps are concerned, whether the prisoner ever does get out or not, it must still be the death sentence for him.

One week during this month there were two nights of intensive bombardment which came to be known as the 'Wednesday' and the 'Saturday'. On the Wednesday I remember walking down the mews in the moonlight, a large fire to the right in the direction of Paddington giving a red light behind the trees, and shining through the leaves, which made them look like copper beeches in the country in the early summer. I was working on a night shift in an engineering shop at this time, and this, my night off, had not been restful. I was too tired to sleep, and went out in the early morning to look at the burning goods station. A small group of rather tired people stood in the road watching. Two women and a commissionaire at a block of flats were talking. One woman said: 'We were asleep, you know', and the commissionaire, misunderstanding, answered: 'No, you can't sleep, can you, really, with this going on?' and the other woman answered back: 'We did. We slept almost to the end — and our children were ever so good. Never made no noise at all, our children didn't!'

These two women — one rather thin and hawk-nosed, the other squat and snub-nosed — talking of 'our children' seemed strange, as if they were just discounting two anonymous husbands. In a little while the two amazons walked off home again.

I went down to the country to stay at the centre of BBC activity — the gigantic talk shop in rural surroundings, always spoken of by Gillie Potter the comedian as Hogsnorton. The evening before I had telephoned to tell my host — one of the BBC boys — my time of arrival. It was like telephoning from the centre of a typhoon into limitless cotton wool. At Hogsnorton the slow-voiced country people were almost unable to understand any message, but fortunately the London telephone operator (who told me he was situated just by St Paul's, at that moment of air raids a very hot spot) played the part of interpreter.

In the train leaving London there were a few country people who had come up to London by excursion for the day. The train was very crowded, and there was a reserved carriage a little way down the corridor. A man was waiting there, looking at a stop-watch. He said: 'If they don't come in two minutes I'm a duchess!' I thought that this was an expression like: 'Either this tram's full or I'm a Dutchman!' — but just before the train was due to start a duchess who had reserved the compartment did arrive. Indeed, her name was stuck up all over the carriage. She was surrounded by a rather toothy, rabbit-mouthed family, who had come up to London with her for a day's shopping. She threw back her veil and sat down, and the family busied themselves with putting hat-boxes, overcoats, and such like on the rack, and sorted out armfuls of shiny illustrated weekly papers. I do not think that these sort of 'Aunt Sallies' are really ready for the fair or even worthy of a throw, but there was something so self-conscious and comic about this concentration of false values in a reserved first-class compartment that all the people round began to laugh at the sight of them, although of course in a quite good-natured way.

Again, in the train, there was this atmosphere of having come from the front line. Unfortunately, I had fallen down and hurt my hand running over to 'HG's' house to get a telephone message. This hand was now bandaged, but the country people in the railway carriage supposed it to be some wound directly concerned with the bombardment, and asked me quite naturally: 'Was that the "Wednesday" or the "Saturday"?'

M met me at Hogsnorton, and we set out for the farm. Jim, the farmer's twelve-year-old boy, was in the kitchen when we arrived, also Mrs Wensdale, the farmer's wife. I was to have my meals here and sleep at Miss Leggatt's red-brick farmhouse, which stood square and proud on the hill about two hundred yards away. We walked towards it along a footpath lined with wallflowers, down the centre of an onion field, carrying our suit-cases in our hands and accompanied by square-faced Jim, the farmer's boy.

Miss Leggatt was nearly eighty years old. Her face had the expression of a laughing crab-apple. She was deaf, but smiled and giggled a great deal. M looked at her with his blue 'ary-ary-aryan' eyes, and brushed his fair hair back with slow hands as he talked to her in a very quiet voice. It was through his eyes that he seemed to be doing most of the shouting. Miss Leggatt and M understood each other about every other sentence.

The room was almost bare. It had two beds in it. One looked comfortable, but Mrs Wensdale had already explained that the comfortable bed must not be slept in, because it had already been booked to someone else. Only the uncomfortable camp-bed was available, and this and had been fixed sideways, so that it looked like a ship's bunk in heavy seas.

Miss Leggatt explained as best she could by smile-signing that this was the bunk for me. There were no cupboards, no carpets, no coal or wood on the fire; only a table in the middle of the room and the sea-storm bunk; but the room itself was large and quiet and high-ceilinged. It looked out over woods, trees, and fields.

I thought that here was a room in which to read, rest, and write, but I was not then completely aware of the forceful personality of Mrs Wensdale down at the main farm. Miss Leggatt, the old deaf dear, was cold and ill, unable to do any housework; and Mrs Wensdale, who was making the most of the BBC and letting out camp-beds in rooms in Miss Leggatt's farmhouse, at a profit to herself, would not trouble to cross the onion field and come up. She said that it was not possible to have a fire made up in my room, so I made up my own camp-bed and rested on it, covered with several overcoats against the cold, completely crushed by the forceful personality of Mrs Wensdale — who was at the same time *kulak* and overseer, merry host and miser.

The life of Hogsnorton is very strange, especially for anyone coming from the violent impacts of a London bombardment. There are about two thousand BBC officials scattered round the district, farmed out in farms, billeted in lodgings. Several have to sleep in one room; and then again several more, since they work in different shifts, so that when some are out others can sleep. The farmers only get a guinea a head per person, and have to give a bed, breakfast, and one hot meal. Mrs Wensdale complained a great deal about this, but combated it by trying to let a room to anyone at any moment at which it was not actually occupied. Mrs Wensdale suggested to a girl who came down to stay that she should sleep in the part of 'X's' bed where he had not actually slept the night before. He was a well-known broadcaster who happened to be away at the week-end. 'He always sleeps on one side only, so you wouldn't mind sleeping on the other — and, after all, he won't be back till Monday!'

The girl moved to a hotel in the town, and when she said she was going out in the morning and would not be back till about four, the landlady answered: 'Don't come back before six, because I always let this room to the major between ten and six.'

M and I thought of writing a short story called: 'It Will be All Right when the Blossom Comes Out' — because that is what everyone here says, but from what I have seen I don't believe that it will ever be all right — even if the blossom does come out!

The communal breakfasts at Mrs Wensdale's farm are very funny. There is an ex-schoolmaster-civil servant who seems unhappy, embittered, and 'edgy'. He tries to wish some unwanted homework on to Jim, but Jim answers: 'Oh, ah — I can't seem to understand these fractions at all', pulls on his school cap, gives his longish grey shorts a hitch, and says: 'I'm off to work now.'

Jim works in the fields, but gets easily tired. He talks a great deal, and has dark, primitive superstitions. 'Funny thing,' he told me, 'whenever I stick long at any work I get some illness. When I spent an 'arf day at the bonfire last month I got chicken-pox. Yesterday I worked several hours in the leek-field and got an 'eadache.' He rubs his forehead against the black dog's forehead. 'Give my 'eadache to you, Satan,' he said. He laughs. 'Our dog got the 'eadache now!' And so Jim goes off to work in the fields again.

***

R is also billeted at the farm. When he comes down to breakfast wearing a camel-hair dressing-gown, the frustrated schoolmaster frowns at him, but remembering the boarding-house rule, 'We're all just one big family here', he is never downright insulting, nor does he ever let a remark go by without some acid comment.

A factory worker came down to stay for a few days' rest, and R asked her vaguely: 'What do you think of this holiday resort?' The schoolmaster came in quick with the words: 'I should hardly call it a holiday resort, although some people may use it as such!'

He regards R as a typical, overpaid BBC boy.

There is another civil servant staying at the farm. He is a man of a different alloy — a master man of another age. He is downright and unprejudiced, and looks like a tall Italian puppet. He wears pince-nez, and seems to be superior to all circumstances. Something he said at breakfast impressed me.

'It's in winter-time that you *can* stand cold water. I think nothing of putting my head in a bucket of ice-water in winter', and as he said this he readjusted his pince-nez.

When I walked down the town with M and R I saw everybody riding about on bicycles; there is an undergraduate atmosphere here, also that particular kind of railway station atmosphere produced by a great many refugees. Some are long, fair-haired, girl refugees, others rather rich-looking; these were chiefly the ones that were trying to get work on the land; and a few of the long, flowing cloaks and beards type. Some of the foreigners were on the BBC, but most of them were only trying to get on to it, and this also gave to the town the atmosphere of Hollywood, where everyone is trying to get into pictures. There are many luxurious bars but few baths. The way in which people live in billets is like the old-fashioned propaganda which was used to advise people against living in the Soviet, and the way people are living outside their billets is like another old-fashioned propaganda used to lure visitors to Le Touquet. There is plenty to drink, but very little food. No restaurants of any merit but several rather refined tea-shops always full of BBC boys, undergraduette blue stockings, and refugees talking philosophy or atrocity.

In a bar with R and M I met a Moroccan soldier. He looked doggedly romantic in his khaki uniform and white turban. He was also child-like and conceited. It was his birthday, and he was offering everybody drinks. He kept going up to different tables and asking the people if they would drink with him, and then he came back to the bar, pleased and smiling, to give his order.

'Four double whiskies, three double gins, five double brandies and — a soda!' After a while an uncompromising British orderly also in khaki came up, and tapped him on the shoulder, telling him it was time for his broadcast, and very sadly, like a child being taken off to bed, the Moroccan star sighed, slung his haversack over his shoulder and followed the orderly out.

Besides this life of bars and broadcast stars there are the pubs, where it is possible to get very good cider. The characters here are like Toulouse-Lautrec drawings. Some old farmers wearing bowler hats, and others with fearsome beards and musty long coats. They talk in a gentle, unhurried way on a low note. 'The weather's agin us!' Once when M and R and I rode back to the farm on our bicycles, we crossed a field and saw a pony coming out from a hedge. This pony seemed to be completely dressed in brambles, and we felt as if we had arrived in some strange hinterland and should have to wait for a long time before civilisation could overtake us again. The pony looked at us in a bewildered way from its robe of brambles, as if the last thing it expected to see were BBC officials on bicycles.

The case of Mrs Wensdale is very strange. She is by inclination a complete capitalist. She talks about money all the time. She seems to like money very much.

'How much would you give me for this? … And how much would you pay me for that?'

R said: 'If Mrs Wensdale was a woman in a Russian story she would keep on repeating: "My love of money imprisons me — I am in chains!"'

So much for 'Hogsnorton'.

June

Clothes rationing came in. It set the whole town talk-twittering. I think that it will have, if not an equalising, at least a toning-down effect, although probably not much at first. The rich people will still be able to have better quality clothes and new clothes more often, and they will also benefit by the stocks of clothes they already have; there may be a few clothes boot-leggers or, at any rate, certain dressmakers ready and willing to fix up a few well-off and worth-while clients. But at least this legislation will mean that no one will like to swank about swathed in furs or anything of this kind. In class problems clothes have often been the basis for a kind of cruelty. There was a time when employers would not have allowed their maidservants to go out in a pretty hat or dress, and even within the working class itself those who have been able to get hold of slightly better clothes go up several grades right away. On the better stockings, the cheap fur, and the good serge dress they can blitzkrieg from working class to petty bourgeois.

***

On my way out to get my rations I stopped at one or two tobacco shops. 'No cigarettes.' Several people came in. They all took it well.

'I suppose you haven't got any cigarettes, have you?' or, 'Do you think you are likely to get any cigarettes at all?' and the shop people answered: 'Well, we don't know really. We keep on hoping.'

It was easy to be superior to these small difficulties, because it was a fine day. I bought some neat tobacco and some cigarette papers. I stopped in the park and rolled cigarettes. On a high building some workmen were mending the roof that had been destroyed by bombs. The workmen were in good spirits, and kept calling out to each other. Two Civil Defence men in blue uniforms were sculling slowly over the canal. Behind them a bank of flowers in bloom. In front, the people on the path stood as still as statuary, waiting to feed the birds, who skilfully avoided the boats as they swam their way to the water's edge. Two soldiers passed, talking in complete agreement; both wore British battle-dress, both smoked cigarettes; they spoke to each other in Spanish.

At the beginning of the bombardment there lived near me in K Street three men known to all the small shop-keepers around as Olaf the Swede, Jacques the Frenchman, and Belgian Louis. Sometimes these three fellows used to run out of their shops saying: 'The big guns go "boom, boom, boom"!' and looking heavenwards they put their fists one before the other in front of their mouths and puffed out their cheeks like angels blowing trumpets. On this day of sunshine in Regent's Park I wondered suddenly what became of Olaf,

Jacques, and Louis. Although I know very well what has become of K Street.

I had to go down to Chelsea and try on a dress that was being altered. The little dressmaker's legs, in black stockings, were very thin; she wore sad little stumpy black boots like liquorice stuck on match-sticks. The room was full of photographs of people in white blouses and hair done on high, and at one end of the room there was a large reproduction of two little girls, very well dressed, sitting in the open air at a picnic with their smiling well-dressed mother. One of them was handing some bread to a ragged boy and girl. The picture was labelled 'A Little Lady Bountiful'.

August

To-day I went to see an employer at an optical lens factory. I went up from the Labour Exchange with the formal green card. This dingy Dickensian character almost stunned me with his stupidity. He seemed to be unaware of any social changes at all, and his proposed wages for all women workers in his factory are thirty shillings a week. When I pointed out that this was not a living wage he answered, apparently quite sincerely, that he thought it was a very good wage indeed for an unskilled worker, and that after all everybody's standard of living had to come down. When I said that, on the contrary, the cost of living had gone up, he was utterly unable to grasp this. He told me that the workers in an optical lens factory were able to learn a very good trade, which would make them certain of a job after the war.

There are apparently thirty-five different operations and, as far as I could figure it out, at the rate at which he arranged for his employees to be taught, it would take seven years for them to perfect even twenty-five of these operations, and the workers would then still be only semi-skilled. If, however, they persisted a few years more, they might reach the skilled status, and by this time would be well on the way to be earning almost three pounds per week.

Small factory owners such as this must employ so few workers that they do not come into any serious scheduled class. With their lack of all liberal education, social consciousness, or goodwill, they are some of the most dangerous *saboteurs*.

When I told an official at the Labour Exchange about this interview, she checked up on it, and decided not to send this employer any more workers or give him a second chance of wasting anyone's time with his idiotic talk.

When I walked home through Regent's Park there was a mist. A squad of Home Guard went past. One middle-aged man wore pince-nez; he was playing a mouth organ, the others were singing quietly; two of them looked very young. Seen in a half-light the small group of volunteers of all ages and all classes on the march had something so hopeful about it that I supposed the whole thing might be a mirage.

Notes

BY KRISTIN BLUEMEL AND KATE MACDONALD

Night Shift

Monday

Government overall: Government-issued work clothes symbolised increasing government control over private industry, with private factories like Braille's requisitioned for essential war production. In March 1941, when Minister of Labour Ernest Bevin's Essential Work Order (EWO) became law, the government gained authority to assign workers to jobs considered essential war work and prevent employers from sacking workers without permission of the Ministry of Labour.

Home Guard: Affectionately called 'Dad's Army', this was the civilian militia composed of 1.5 million male volunteers who were otherwise ineligible for military service.

Tottenham: north London borough.

Kilburn: north-west London borough, known for its Irish immigrant population.

high school: a class-based comment, indicating that her daughter attends a school known for its academic focus with the expectation of pupils going on to further education.

two trousered girls: prior to going into industry, these two 'mannish' characters were, presumably, Land Girls, women who served in the Women's Land Army, a civilian wartime organisation that filled vital gaps in the agriculture labour force opened up by men's departures for military service.

Government training centres: Government-run centres, intended during peacetime to bring unemployed workers and employers together, prepared workers for new jobs in industries considered essential to the war effort. Ernest Bevin, Minister of Labour, expanded their capacities in 1940 to include registration and reassignment of skilled engineers who were working in trades considered non-essential.

air raids: German bombing raids usually took place at night. Starting on 7 September 1940 there were seventy-six nights of continuous bombing in London, with only one night of reprieve due to fog. Industrial workers on night shift were exposed to some of the most dangerous conditions of civilian life during the Blitz, as these workers did not shelter during raids and most of the bombers got through defences.

concentration camp: The Nazi concentration camps (1933–1939) were set up to isolate and torture Jews, political rivals, homosexuals, Jehovah's Witnesses, and other persons considered threats to the Nazi state. British popular knowledge of Nazi extermination camps was limited until January 1942, when the British press reported that over 1,000,000 Jews had been mass murdered since the beginning of the war.

bubble and squeak: a standard 'leftovers' meal of fried potato, cabbage and onion.

three 'a'pence: three and a half pence.

a red handkerchief round his neck: a sign of the lower working-class, or poverty, in that he can't afford to buy or keep clean the detachable white collars worn by the clerkly pay grade.

North-country: the area north of Birmingham to the Scottish border, whose inhabitants have distinctive regional accents.

Stella's Star or Maggie's Mag: pulp story magazines for women that provided a largely working-class readership with most of their print entertainment during the early twentieth century.

fire watchers: civilian volunteers who waited with stirrup pumps on rooftops or in streets in order to extinguish fires set by small thermite incendiary bombs dropped in clusters of about 70 per 'breadbasket' by German bombers. Government response to the threat of fire was slow and the organisation of neighbourhood watches was often spontaneous. Only after 1941 did fire watching become compulsory.

All Clear: the steady two-minute blast on the siren, usually sounding around dawn, that announced the end of the night's air raid. The first sounds of an air raid were the wailing sirens that Churchill described as 'banshee howlings'. The bombers, the anti-aircraft or 'ack-ack' guns, the bombs' impact, the fire engines: all composed part of the outdoor cacophony that Holden's workers hear faintly beyond the indoor factory noise.

Tuesday

Bovril: the salty beef tea extract associated since 1870 with war-time feeding of troops and civilians. Food rationing began in January 1940 with limits on bacon, butter and sugar. Almost all foods were rationed by 1942.

pay as you go gramophone: public broadcasting did not yet routinely play dance tunes and popular jazz, swing and big band melodies, so the public continued to rely on gramophones where there was no live music.

Labour Exchange: State-funded unemployment centres, which in wartime controlled the registration and categorisation of war workers and where they would be sent.

not union members: trade unions were wary of women's unionisation but even so, unions grew in members and strength during the war in large part due to Bevin's commitments to workers.

Before becoming Minister of Labour, he had been general secretary of the Transport and General Workers Union.

Swan-pen writers: Swan pens were a prestige fountain pen imported from the US, and suggest here a well-to-do or middle-class owner.

Wednesday

white weddings: changing attitudes towards love and marriage during the exigencies of war meant that traditional marriages were increasingly replaced by whirlwind wartime romances, rash marriages, unfaithful spouses and increasing numbers of babies born out of wedlock.

Woolworth heiress: Depression-era American heiress of the American Woolworth stores fortune, Barbara Hutton, was the 'Poor Little Rich Girl' of international fame and tabloid reporting.

Thursday

Oxo: beef stock marketed in dehydrated cubes, to be made into beef tea or used in soups and gravies.

Civil Defence: the civilian volunteer organisation established by the Home Office that until 1941 was called Air Raid Precautions (ARP). It coordinated with the Women's Voluntary Service (WVS) to manage ARP wardens, the Auxiliary Fire Service (AFS), medical services, fire guards, rescue parties, and welfare, among other groups.

Youth Hostels: what would become the present-day Hostelling International movement began in 1912 with the establishment of a voluntary hostel for young travellers in Germany. Between the wars the network of hostels expanded and was used widely by travellers of all nationalities.

fight in Spain: the Spanish Civil War (1936-1939) attracted the service of many English leftists and Communists who sought to defy fascism and advance international socialism by serving in the Army of the Spanish Republic against General Franco's nationalist forces. George Orwell fought in Spain as an affiliated member of the anti-Stalinist communist POUM, narrowly escaping death by a sniper's shot through his throat.

Walt Disney friendliness: Disney cartoons were distributed from 1928, and many of their films helped to create the Golden Age of Animation in the 1930s. The character of Pluto the dog was created in 1930.

Friday

petty packets of money: sex discrimination was institutionalised in British war industries, with women workers receiving on average 53% of men's wages for similar work. Trade unions actively worked against equal pay policies out of fear that male workers in the military would suffer reduced wages upon their return to civilian life.

them damn bombers: The Germans used a range of bombers in the Blitz, including the Stuka or Junkers Ju 87, a terrifying dive bomber; the Dornier Do 17, the slow 'Flying Pencil' used in about 25% of the German Blitz attacks; and the Heinkel He 111, also slow but with a bomb capacity twice as large as that of the Dornier.

to meet those fellows: the Royal Air Force defended Britain against invasion after the crushing defeat of the British and Allied forces in Norway and at Dunkirk. The Battle of Britain, the only exclusively air battle of the war, is officially recognised as lasting from July 1940 to 31 October 1940, overlapping with the beginning of the Blitz.

the East End: The Blitz began in earnest on 7 September 1940 with a massive bombing raid against the docks of East London. German bombers and their fighter escorts attacked an area underneath more than 800 square miles of sky, resulting in what became legendary fires that raged for days in the docklands.

Saturday

'the Saturday': 19 April 1941, the night of the notorious air raid that followed 'the Wednesday' of 16 April 1942. Each raid dropped over 1000 tons of high explosives on London, the most devastating attack up to that point.

machine-gun fire: the sound of the anti-aircraft guns or 'ack-ack' that attempted with relatively little effect to defend the city against German bombers. On average, over 2,000 shells were fired for every plane brought down.

barrage balloons: large silver balloons attached by cables to heavy lorries. There were over 400 moored above London in an effort to force German dive-bombers upwards into the range of anti-aircraft fire, and were seen by Londoners as comforting companions; increasingly, teams of women took over their management.

It Was Different At The Time

1938

April

Bohemian thanklessness: In her twenties, Holden was twice painted by Augustus John, a time when he was considered England's best portrait painter. His parties and promiscuity were as notorious as his paintings were celebrated.

Felicity: based on Holden's intimate friend, the novelist and poet Stevie Smith, born Florence Margaret Smith. Smith lived in Palmer's Green in north London and worked for Frank Newnes' publishing companies throughout the 1930s and 1940s.

Eddie Cantor: American stage, film and radio star famed for his energy and inexhaustible humour.

Sally: Perhaps based on Stevie Smith's older sister Molly (Ethel Mary Frances), who earned her degree from Birmingham University, and loved acting and recitation.

Norfolk jacket: man's belted tweed jacket for country wear, with large pockets for carrying game. By being worn in the city it suggests that the wearer has little interest in conventional social codes.

September

radio: the British Broadcasting Corporation won monopoly control over public radio broadcasting in a royal charter granted in January 1927.

regular news bulletins: reporting on the Munich crisis and Prime Minister Neville Chamberlain's efforts to avert war glued the British to their radios. On 30 September, Chamberlain brought home news that he had capitulated to Hitler's demands, sacrificing the Sudetenland of Czechoslovakia in return for a shameful 'peace in our time'.

ARP: the Air Raid Precautions Act came into effect on 1 January 1938, requiring local councils to set up all ARP services in their areas.

quarter-days: the aunt receives her income from investments, which is paid to her four times a year on the traditional rent-days deriving from the feudal system.

October

Victor: possibly Humphrey Slater (1906-1958), an English Communist who served with the International Brigades in Spain. Holden had a troubled romantic attachment to Slater that lasted for years.

Basque children: up to 20,000 Basque children were evacuated from Catalonia and granted asylum in the UK, USSR, and other countries.

Daladier: Edouard Daladier was Prime Minister of France at the outbreak of the Second World War.

November

November: Kristallnacht, the Nazi pogrom against Jews in Germany, took place on the night of 9-10 November 1938. It was widely reported in the British and international press.

December

Mosley's meeting: Sir Oswald Mosley (1896-1980) was the leader of the British Union of Fascists, founded 1932. The activities of his paramilitary forces, the Blackshirts, led in October 1936 to the Public Order Act of 1936, which banned uniforms and quasi-military style organisations. He was monitored by the British government until being interned in May 1940.

1939

April

International Brigade: on 1 April 1939 General Franco and the Spanish nationalists controlled all of Spain. The International Brigade had disbanded by October 1938.

Shirley temples: Shirley Temple was a hugely popular child film star, with trademark blonde ringlets.

Popular Front: an unofficial coalition between diverse political parties opposed to fascism, including the Labour Party, the Independent Labour Party, the Communist Party of Great Britain, the Liberal Party, and anti-appeasers among the Conservative Party.

September

September: war with Germany was declared on 3 September 1939. Neville Chamberlain announced the declaration of war at 11.15 am on BBC radio.

December

Sitzkrieg: the Sitting or Phoney War from 3 September 1939 to May 1940 during which time virtually no military engagement between the Axis and Allied forces took place.

Ramsay MacDonald: MacDonald had been Prime Minister after the First World War, and had been one the most well-known interwar British politicians, with a prominently large white moustache. He had died in 1937.

cold black night: blackout regulations came into effect on 1 September 1939, requiring all civilians to cover up any source of light at night that could guide German bombers. With road fatalities mounting, within a couple of weeks trains and buses were allowed to mask but not completely obscure their headlamps, making travel on public transport slightly less dangerous.

1940

January

LCC hospital: a London County Council hospital was a state institution, run by local government, that oversaw numerous aspects of public health, including disease prevention, school medical services, the ambulance service, maternity services, care for the mentally ill, residential tuberculosis centres, and inspection of nursing homes.

April

Norway and Denmark: Norway and Denmark had declared themselves neutral countries upon the outbreak of war but on 9 April 1940 Germany invaded and occupied both countries. The British army and navy suffered a humiliating defeat in Norway when Winston Churchill was First Lord of the Admiralty and Chamberlain was still (barely) Prime Minister. Chamberlain resigned on 10 May 1940.

June

VAD: a Voluntary Aid Detachment nurse was a volunteer civilian nursing assistant working in military and state hospitals as needed.

Leopold & the Duke of Windsor: Leopold III of the Belgians surrendered the Belgian army to the invading German army on 27 May 1940, and was widely denounced for treachery. The Duke of Windsor, as Edward VIII, had abdicated the British throne on 11 December 1936 rather than give up the divorced woman he wished to marry.

Lyons: Lyons Cafés were a chain of cheap but respectable restaurants.

du Maurier *Quartier Latin* atmosphere: George Du Maurier's 1894 novel *Trilby* had made Parisian bohemian living in the artists' *Quartier Latin* notorious and alluring.

July

French soldiers evacuated from Dunkirk: the British snatched psychological victory out of military defeat at Dunkirk by organising a mass civilian evacuation of British and French troops by an impromptu 'armada' of public and private vessels of all sizes, rescuing the soldiers trapped on the beaches of Dunkirk between 26 May and 10 June 1940. Most French did not choose to join the Free French, were repatriated, and became German prisoners of war.

General de Gaulle: Charles de Gaulle had been a brigadier-general in the French Army and Under-Secretary of the State for National Defence and War in the government of Prime Minister Paul Reynaud immediately before Reynaud resigned and his successor Philippe Pétain signed an armistice agreement with Germany. De Gaulle narrowly escaped to London in June 1940, from whence he led the Free French.

Southampton has had the most severe raids: worse raids were to come to Southampton in November – December 1940 in what came to be called the Southampton Blitz.

September

long night-time raids lasting eight or nine hours: the London Blitz began in earnest in mid-September 1940.

HG Wells: Holden was a tenant of Wells's mews flat overlooking Regents Park from 1940 to 1941. This scene reappears in different forms in her private diary and *Night Shift*.

November

WVS: the Women's Voluntary Service was founded in 1938 by Stella Isaacs, Marchioness of Reading, to assist ARP services. Members put themselves in real danger by supporting ARP wardens and firemen during bombing raids and attending to the injured and displaced afterwards, helping tens of thousands of civilians.

Haw-Haw: Lord Haw-Haw was the radio name for Irish-American William Joyce, a senior member of the British Union of Fascists, who escaped to Germany to avoid British internment. He broadcast demoralising Nazi-propaganda talks to the English (though he was widely regarded as a traitor and a figure of derision) before being captured by the British in northern Germany at the end of the war. He was hung for treason in 1946.

1941

April

two very heavy bombardments: 'the Saturday' and 'the Wednesday'. See *Night Shift*, 'Saturday' chapter for Holden's fictionalised version of this experience.

Hogsnorton: a farcical name for the BBC centre for evacuated staff located at Wood Norton Hall, Evesham, in Worcestershire.

Aunt Sallies: fairground game in which you try to knock down a large wooden figure by throwing a ball or a bean bag in its wide open mouth to win a prize.

June

clothes rationing came in: each person was allocated a number of points to spend on clothes and other rationed goods. These were distributed in the form of coupons; each item of clothing had a value of a certain number of coupons, e.g. a woman's coat was worth 18 coupons, a pair of underwear worth 2. In 1941, each person got 66 clothing coupons a year.